The Price Model

A Mitch McKay Story

Steve Flaig

Hamilton Publishing—Dallas, TX
ISBN: 978-0-692-12967-8
Libraryof Congress Control Number: (Pending)
Title: The Price Model | Steve Flaig
Digital distribution | Paperback Edition, 2018

Dedication

To Janet and Mrs. Pitt...wherever you are

Chapter 1

I tossed my gym bag onto the backseat of my car. Before I shut the door, I double checked to make sure I'd zipped it closed. It has something called "Fresh Flow" technology that's supposed to keep it and its contents odor free. That sounded good when I read the list of features on the tag when I bought it, but mine must be defective since when I open it, I'm still overwhelmed by the rank smell of T-shirts, shorts, a jock, and socks that have been fermenting in an enclosed space for 12 hours or so. Of course, this is still a reasonable trade-off since leaving it open in my car for the day generates a smell so toxic that it brings even the most robust air freshener to its knees.

After ensuring my automotive air quality didn't exceed EPA-recommended guidelines, I opened the driver's side door and let the electronic memory seat place me in my desired driving position. In terms of automotive innovation, I vacillate between whether this or heated seats are the most ergonomically satisfying. Not having to grapple with that bar thing underneath your seat to return it to its proper configuration is certainly more convenient and less aggravating than shifting back and forth until you locate the perfect spot—particularly when a previous driver is much shorter than my 6'2" frame—but the warm embrace of my leather-covered driver's seat on a December night is one of life's most underrated pleasures. So maybe it's a seasonal thing.

I drive a black 2011 Infiniti G37. I spent more than I was

planning to when I bought it, but I spend a lot of time in my car, so I justified it as a work-related expense. Along with the heated seats, it has a CD player, satellite radio, and a USB port in the console that I can plug my iPod into. It also allows me to open my garage door and make and receive cell phone calls, but figuring out how to set them up required looking in the owner's manual so I decided I could live without having those capabilities at my fingertips. Most importantly, it blends in. People tend to notice if you follow them in a Ferrari or a Range Rover, and in my business, that is not a desired result, so blending in was an essential component of my vehicle purchase checklist. However, blending in does not mean having to sacrifice some measure of style and comfort and an Infiniti is nice without being conspicuously nice so even if someone is asked to describe my car, the best they could probably do is say it was black.

I started up the car and made a left onto Woodward and followed that down to 13 Mile, made another left, and headed to Main Street. Main bisects the city of Royal Oak and over the last few years has become very popular with the hipster crowd who frequent its boutique shops—someone needs to sell those goofy little hats and skinny jeans— and bars. I took Main for another two miles and pulled in to the parking garage beneath my office building. After outmaneuvering the accountant with the office on the second floor for a parking spot near the elevator, I gave my gym bag one last check to make sure it hadn't figured out a way to open itself on the drive; it hadn't, so I locked the car and took the garage elevator up to my office on the third floor.

As offices go, mine does a good job of helping project the image of integrity and competence I want to instill in my clients. I'm a private investigator and, to most people, that conjures up either images of Phillip Marlowe and guys wearing hats with "heaters" under their jackets or some overweight, balding, middle-aged loser in an ill-fitting polyester sport coat sitting in the bushes with a long-lens Nikon trying to catch a straying wife sweating up the sheets with the pool boy. I'm neither, and since by the time most people work up the courage to Google "Private Investigators," they've already reached a point of hopelessness or desperation that not that long ago seemed to only happen to someone else I want them to feel as relaxed as possible.

My job is to help them feel they have an ally who will treat them with dignity and respect. The office of McKay Investigations has an entrance area that I painted with, what I hope is, a soothing Hunter Green and furnished with a cherry wood coffee table and two comfortable cordovan-colored leather chairs. I keep the magazines current—*Sports Illustrated, Good Housekeeping, Vogue,* and *GQ*—since no one likes having to read a two-year-old copy of *Time* while they're waiting to tell you about perhaps the most intimate portion of their lives, and I've hung a couple nice prints of pleasant landscapes on the walls to complete the experience. Unfortunately, that air of tranquility is immediately violated when they walk through the door.

Nikki Hunt, my receptionist, office manager, and accountant, was previously well known in the adult film business as Nikki Blue, with the surname matching the color of her hair. We'd met two years ago when I helped her extricate herself from a dispute between the producer of her movies and the new Mexican partners he had taken on to help finance his growing empire. Apparently, the cartel was interested in diversifying their business interests. He wound up headless, and the Mexicans are now serving life terms in the federal penitentiary in Marion, so to spare Nikki the uncertainties of unemployment, I'd offered her a job. I've never seen one of her movies, and I promised her that I never will, but if her skills in her previous profession matched those she's displayed in the time we've worked together, it's not hard to see how she'd become a "star." Within the first six months, she'd cleared all my outstanding receivables, implemented a new accounting system, and renegotiated our office lease. She's currently taking night classes toward a degree in finance. Her fashion sense, however, still leans more towards "adult actress" than "administrative assistant."

"I've never seen that one before," I said as I walked in the lobby. "Just what exactly is that color?"

"It's called Ravishing Raspberry. What do you think?" Nikki had long since given up on blue and now regularly found new colors, that would never appear in even the biggest box of Crayolas, to accentuate her shoulder-length coiffure.

"I like it. They really did a good job on the bangs."

"You should see the back," she said as she stood up and turned around.

I had to admit that it did do a nice job of highlighting her sleeveless black-latex dress, which in turn was accentuated by matching knee-high black-leather gladiator sandals with stiletto heels.

"Looks great, Nick, but isn't that dress just a little uncomfortable. It seems like it would be kind of restrictive."

"Oh, no. That's the beauty of latex. It really gives with you."

I'd have to make a note of that.

We probably could have talked fashion for another hour or so, but business is business, so I inquired what we had scheduled for the day.

"Oh, yeah, you've got a walk-in. She was waiting outside when I got here. She wouldn't give me her name, but she said she knew you so I got her set up in your office."

4

"You just let someone in because they said they knew me? They could be anybody. They could be in there looking through my confidential files."

"Really? Like they'd find anything. We keep the important stuff in the safe and that's under *my* desk. And I'm the only one around here who can remember the combination."

Fair point.

Electing to take the risk that the woman in my office wasn't armed or a crazed maniac, I opened the door and began to say hello. I stopped mid-sentence when I saw Olivia Price sitting in one of the green upholstered chairs in front of my desk. It had been ten years since I had last seen her. She looked the same—ivory skin, deep-green eyes, and a head of copper-colored curls that framed her face like a halo. A quick check of her red-nailed left hand told me she either hadn't been—or no longer was—married. She was wearing a silk peach-colored blouse and gray slacks and black low-heeled shoes. She'd hung her Burberry raincoat over the back of her chair. I was dressed a little more casually in an old pair of Levis, brown lace-up shoes, and a faded blue polo shirt.

After recovering my ability to speak, I elected to go with mischievous yet charming. I said, "Hello, Olivia." I can be a smooth talker when I need to be.

She stood up and hugged me, and I was immediately back in a place I hadn't known for a very long time. She smelled faintly of Chanel No. 5. Like her, subtle and classic.

"Hello, Mitch," she said as we uncoupled and she folded with feline grace back into her chair.

I sat down behind my desk. There were a million things I wanted to know. I settled on "What can I do for you?"

She was as beautiful as I remembered, and she was twirling her hair the way she always did when she was nervous as she began, "I know it's been a long time, but I didn't know who

5

else could help me."

That was as far as she got before the weight of whatever brought her here caved in upon her and the tears began. If meeting with a private investigator is the last thing most people think they will ever do, breaking down in front of them must be second. I suppose priests and counselors hear a lot worse than I have from some of my clients, but sometimes I wonder. I got up and grabbed the tissue box I keep on my desk and handed it to her.

"I'm sorry", she said as she took a tissue from the box and dabbed at her eyes. "All the way down here, I kept telling myself that I wouldn't cry. Tim is dead."

Tim was Olivia's younger brother and a genius. I'd known him when he was fifteen years old, just completing his senior year of high school. She had told me once that they thought he had Asperger's Syndrome, a lower level type of autism that retarded his ability to do things like pick up on social cues.

When I'd visited at her family's house, he was typically busy doing something relaxing, like working out calculus problems. He'd stop when I popped into his room so we could watch some new episode of a science show he had recorded with the express purpose of him explaining why the theory being discussed had serious flaws. All these memories came back to me as I attempted to absorb what she'd just told me.

"What...how did it happen ?"

Her tears had stopped but her eyes were rimmed with red as she began. "He was killed during that protest on Saturday in the school library. Some eco group that's demanding the university divest all fossil-fuel companies from its endowment fund tried to take over the building. Fights broke out and the police had to come break things up. A lot of people were arrested."

"I saw something about it on the news, but they said they

were not going to release the name of the victim until the family could be notified. Wasn't a professor killed that same night? I didn't keep track of it after that," I responded.

As I listened to her, I noted the dark circles under her eyes and how her shoulders bowed under the weight of weariness and grief. Perhaps noticing the change in her own demeanor, she shifted in her seat to straighten herself against the back of the chair and brushed a stray curl from her eye and continued.

"They said that as things took place on the ground floor, all the book shelves on the third floor were tipped over and smashed. Tim was studying on the fourth floor and the police think that whoever did it must have continued up there and done the same thing. He was killed when the shelves fell on him. His skull was fractured and his chest was crushed. They said he was probably killed instantly. A geology professor was also killed that night. His name was Walker. The police think they might be connected, but since he was killed in his office in the Nat Sci building they're not sure".

After a few minutes, Olivia got up and walked toward the window in my office. It doesn't offer much of a view, unless you like to watch traffic or catch people in the building across the street looking out their windows *at you*. It was one of those days where it was about to rain and, although it was only 62 degrees, even the shortest walk leaves you feeling that you'd taken a stroll through a Turkish bath. She stared out the window for a moment and then turned back to me.

"I need you to find out what happened to him, Mitch."

"Olivia, it sounds like you know what happened, and the police appear to be doing the same things I'd do. Are there any suspects?"

"They say they think it's probably some of the Planet Action people—that's the name of the group that was protesting. But I think they're wrong, at least when it comes to Tim."

A lot of my clients want me to prove something couldn't have happened the way they've been told that it had. I tell them to save their money, that it happened the way they were told. Most accept that as validation and thank me for my time. Some don't. They insist that something has been missed or that the person they knew would never do something like that. I've never had one that I could tell what they wanted to hear in all that time. My experience as a private investigator, and the five years before that as a Detroit police officer, led me to agree with the East Lansing PD.

The mood in the room seemed to change. The weariness in her voice was gone and her speech seemed detached, almost analytical as she faced me and posed her question, "Every shelf in that row on the third floor fell like they were dominoes. Only three stacks fell on Tim. They did nothing to the rest of the row. Why is that?"

Although it did seem odd, it was far from the smoking gun she was seeking. "Maybe that's all they had time to do, or maybe those were the shelves closest to the elevator or the stairs," I answered. "I'm sure the police have thought about that. Assessing crime scenes is in their job description. You don't think someone did this deliberately?"

She walked back to the chair and sat down. "I know it doesn't make sense. You knew Tim. Who would want to hurt him? Something about this isn't right. That's why I need your help."

"I'm not sure what you want me to do. The police seem to have things covered, and like you said, 'Who would want to kill your brother?'"

I then shifted into the conciliatory mode I use to explain to a devastated client that some good could come out of finding out something like their spouse was cheating on them. They could go to counseling, or even if the marriage dissolved, it was their chance to start over. I don't think it ever works, but you've got to try. "I won't even try to tell you that I know how you feel, but this sounds like a horrible, horrible accident. I understand wanting to find a reason for why it happened, but it won't bring him back."

Her manicured hands balled into fists and she slammed them on my desk. For a moment, a tense silence prevailed. It was obvious she was demonstrating exceptional self-control to avoid using a popular two-word response to my attempt at grief counseling. Firmly and evenly, she said, "Don't be condescending to me. You don't know how hard it was to come here, but I need your help. I need you to do this—for me."

I need to drop conciliatory from my repertoire.

In a blur of latex and Ravishing Raspberry, Nikki burst through the door and volunteered, "Do you need me to take this bitch out?" I told her that that wouldn't be necessary and that everything was fine. Hesitatingly, she began to close the door but not before assuring both of us that "I'll do it. Just let me know."

Oddly, Nikki's intervention helped alleviate the tension in the room.

"Your secretary is very protective."

"Most of the time she's harmless. But I will tell you that if you use the word 'secretary' around her. I can't be responsible for her actions."

After Olivia's cheeks quickly retreated from an angry red to a muted pink, she said, "I'll apologize to her when I leave. Please come up and talk to the police and the people who were there. If you agree with their conclusions, I'll let it go."

I had not been back to Michigan State since I'd left ten years ago. There was no reason to; I'd never wanted to be one of *those guys* who needed to replenish the adulation that becomes fainter over the years and have people tell me "things haven't been the same since you left." And based on the circumstances of my leaving, I couldn't count on that type of reception even if I was. That part of my life exists only in some old scrapbooks buried in my parents' basement.

I knew I couldn't say no, but sometimes the worst part of a job is having to validate a client's concerns or fears. When someone tells you they just want to know the truth, they really don't.

"Cops don't like people looking over their shoulders, Olivia, especially private investigators. It's not like they consider us to be part of the team. I can't promise I'd be able to find anything they haven't already told you, and based on what you've said, it sounds like they're all over this. I'll come up and talk to them and look at things myself. But I've got to ask you: 'Are you sure this is what you want?' Like I said, even if I did find something, it's not going to bring your brother back, and it could even make things worse."

She answered without hesitation—"I have to know Mitch." Then she reached into her tan Coach purse and pulled out a checkbook. "How much do you need to start?"

I got up and walked around to the front of my desk and facing her, leaned back on its edge. Spread around my office was a chronology of my life since we had last been together. Photos of me and my parents at my graduation from Wayne State, as a rookie in my blue uniform with the Detroit police, and others populated the glass-paneled legal bookcase I'd bought when I had first opened the office. My college diploma and my investigator's license hung in frames on the wall behind her.

"Put it away," I said. "I can be there tomorrow. Let's say 9:00."

She pulled out a card and wrote her address and phone

number on the back and handed it to me. "I'll see you at my place at 9:00. Thank you, Mitch."

She stood up and for an awkward moment we stood there, neither of us knowing exactly what to do next. At last, she stuck out her hand. We shook and then she was gone, taking ten years with her as she walked out the door.

Chapter 2

After answering Nikki's immediate question with "Yes, we'd had a 'thing' but that was a long time ago," I asked her to put together everything she could find about Tim, the accident, and anything else that went on that night. I'm sure she wanted to know a lot more, but I told her I needed the information as fast as she could get it because I had to go to East Lansing in the morning.

Within an hour, she laid a thick folder on my desk. "That's all I could find. How long do you think you'll be gone?"

"Honestly, I don't think more than a day. I need to talk to the cops working the case, but there just doesn't seem to be anything *nefarious* behind this, just a tragic accident."

As I said before, Nikki runs the office so logically her next question was, "Are we getting paid for this?"

The look on my face gave her my initial answer.

"Okay, so this is a freebie. Since we don't normally give 100% discounts, what's so special about this one? I've known you for two years and you haven't been in a relationship, and I use the term loosely, that lasted more than maybe a week. I keep things in my refrigerator longer than that."

A life that included an alcoholic mother, an absent father, a long line of "uncles" (two of whom abused her), a first arrest for possession of methamphetamine at 12, and becoming a porn starlet at 18 does not spawn sentimentality, so I tried to explain my time with Olivia in the most unvarnished manner possible. Even then, she'd probably call me a wimp. Maybe I should have put on my gun to "butch up" the explanation.

"Like I told you, we were together in college. It didn't last very long, but it was very intense and it didn't end well. I just left. It wasn't right, although I thought it was the best thing to do at the time. This is the first time I've seen or talked to her since. She just lost her brother and is trying to make some sense out of it. I think this is the least that I can do."

She sat down on one of my chairs. The latex squeaked a little as she did. "Okay, I get it. You were a piece of shit and now you're trying to make up for it."
Yeah, that pretty much sums it up. "Are there any more of these 'intense relationships' that I should be factoring into revenue projections?"

I assured her Olivia was the only female I owed restitution to, and after summarizing her thoughts on the matter with a final "Good," she left my office and went back to her desk with her latex frock giving with her all the way.

I walked over to the little refrigerator my parents had bought me my freshman year and now resides in my office, and grabbed a Diet Vernors before I sat down to look over the information Nikki had found. The file was about a half an inch thick and, although I had only expected newspaper write-ups, I was still impressed with what she'd been able to assemble in such a short time. I grabbed a pad from the drawer in my desk that holds the usual office supplies and my gun, a Beretta 9 millimeter populated with CCI +P124 Gold Dot hollow points for stopping those who need to be stopped, popped the top on the can, and opened the folder.

I started by quickly reviewing the contents. On top were the media write-ups I had expected. The incident had gotten coverage from both the Detroit papers, the *News* and the *Free Press*, as well as the Lansing area daily, the *State Journal* and the *State News*, the university's student paper. Each had written lengthy articles covering the incident itself, the aftermath to date, and a smattering of human-interest articles about its impact on the participants, the school, and what each characterized as a "traumatized" student body.

Further down the stack, however, were copies of the reports from the campus and East Lansing police forces and Tim's autopsy reports. Nikki had taken the liberty of testing the security structures for the appropriate city and state databases and finding them wanting, had obtained information she thought might be relevant to the case. This is illegal of course, but appreciated nonetheless. I asked her once how a woman of her "unique professional background" had acquired her hacker abilities. She'd responded with "C'mon, I ran my own online website and sometimes, you've got to neutralize the competition."

God bless free enterprise.

I read through everything twice to be sure I didn't miss anything, but they all added up to just a more-detailed account of what Olivia had told me. Planet Action was a campus-based environmental protest group that had been conducting a variety of actions. None were terribly original. They included the usual sit-ins and defacing of public property spiced up by a couple of their more-zealous members chaining themselves to the front door of the president's house and demanding that the school divest all fossil fuel-related companies from its endowment holdings. Their efforts appeared to be paying off since every story mentioned that the board of regents were going to vote on the issue this coming Saturday. As might be expected, sentiment regarding the vote's outcome appeared to be evenly split between those who found things like cars, electricity, and home heating to be amenities they couldn't live without and an equally vociferous number saying they could.

Neither police report indicated a preference for the outcome of the impending divestiture vote. Since the incident had resulted in a homicide, maybe two since a geology professor had been killed in his own office the same night neither department was speculating that they were related. The East Lansing police had primary jurisdiction on the case.

The autopsy report also confirmed what Olivia had told me, albeit with photos of the victim I could have lived without. Cause of death was due to massive head trauma, meaning he died before the combined weight of the book shelves and their contents left his chest cavity crushed and broken, and the position of his body and the fact that the earphones from his iPhone were still in place indicated he probably never heard the wave of books and wood shelving as it hurtled towards him.

Nothing I read gave me cause to think that Tim's death was anything other than the tragic result of literally being in the wrong place at the wrong time. Even though I had no desire to make the trip, I was sure it wasn't going to be an extended visit.

I chugged down the last of the Vernors, unplugged my Mac and stuffed it, a charger, and the file into the black canvas briefcase I keep next to my desk and got ready to leave. Reaching into my desk drawer, I grabbed my gun, shrugged on the leather shoulder holster I carry it in, grabbed the black sport coat I keep in the office to cover the holster, or for special events, sometimes both, and walked out and told Nikki I was leaving and that I'd call tomorrow to let her know what I'd found.

Chapter 3

It was a cold, clear February night. In the still silence, you could hear a boot crunching in the snow from far down the street. Although it was only 2°F outside, an unusual number of the male residents of Oaklawn Drive were performing a variety of tasks that probably could have been completed at a more opportune time. Messrs. Smith and Wilson both stood stamping one foot and then the other to keep warm while their dogs strained against their leashes, apparently attempting to express in a mode of canine communication that it was time to get moving or go home.

Mr. Walzyk across the street was putting the fine touches to his already-shoveled driveway, and a few houses down, the titular heads of the Jones, Johnson, and Salva households stood swaddled in camouflage hunting suits in front of the latter's Buick Regal debating the merits of Firestone versus Goodyear snow tires. Unsurprisingly, these fits of home improvement, auto maintenance, and pet exercise tended to coincide with the visit of yet another head coach, normally seen only on television to the McKay family home. It had been this way since late October, as coaches from as far away as California and Texas and as close as Ann Arbor made the pilgrimage to the three-bedroom, one- and-a half bath red-brick home in Sterling Heights to convince Mr. and Mrs. John McKay to bestow upon them, and their fine university, the honor of spending the next four years molding their eldest son Mitchell into a man they could all be proud of, in exchange for his quarterbacking their team to victory on fall Saturday afternoons, of course.

Completing 69 percent of your passes for 3,641 yards and 36 touchdowns tends to put you on coaches' radar and when you're 6'2" and weigh 195 pounds as well, you move from "interesting prospect" to "must-have recruit" with amazing alacrity. Every day brought a mailbox stuffed with catalogues from schools where the sun always shone and well-groomed, white-toothed, extraordinarily good-looking students apparently spent all their free time in front of the student union, handwritten letters from coaches congratulating him on his latest game, and notes from more than a few eager coeds who couldn't wait to "show him around campus" — Mitch always got rid of those before his mom saw them. The phone rang incessantly, to the point that his dad had their number changed three times but within a day of the change, the calls started again. And more than one overzealous recruiter had been physically removed from the Sterling Heights High campus, including the guy from Penn State who snuck into his English class.

Each day when he pulled into the school parking lot in his black 1970 Chevelle SS, he became the orb that the rest of the school revolved around. Sterling Heights High was a good school where middle-class kids came and learned their math, science, and English before venturing on to a state university or entering the workforce. It was like thousands of its interchangeable peers across the country, until it had the top recruit in the nation as the quarterback of its football team. Suddenly, Mitch was the vicarious fulfillment of not just the hopes and ambitions of the school's students, but of the faculty as well. On more than one occasion, a teacher or principal had attempted to establish a degree of comradery by informing him that, "You know, I played ball in high school," an assertion typically followed by an awkward silence and "Good luck this week." Naturally, there was no lack of female attention, but more interesting to him was that even the various groups of students, from the motorcycle jacketed burnouts to the most gothic thespians, all of whom were decidedly "anti-jock," seemed to look at him with at worst benign indifference, rather than outright disdain. And for *them, that was saying something.*

Although the enthusiasm of his neighbors hadn't waned, for Mitch and his parents, visits from THE head coaches had become routine. It didn't matter if it was Tennessee, Alabama, or Ohio State, they all followed a common script. The coach would always arrive alone, the flock of assistants who had obsequiously professed their interest and concern for his college years were by now fulfilling this same role with the "gotta-have" guys of next year's class, driving expensive rental cars—one guy had even shown up in a Range Rover. They had no need to appear understated since in most cases they were the highest-paid employees on their states' payrolls. Unlike the assistants, the coach would eschew school-labeled clothing and walk to the door in a suit and tie that cost as much as a semester's tuition. His role in the process was to close the deal and this required a formality that inspired trust in the kid whose name would be regularly prefaced by an expletive by the start of fall practice, and his parents—particularly the real influencer in the decision-making process—mom.

Upon entering the house, his pursuers always came up with some variation of "What a beautiful home you have here." Mitch always wondered what they would've said if they had lived in a double-wide on blocks. Then they would sit in the nicest room of the house, although some coaches preferred the dinner table, and begin their well-rehearsed sales pitch. Since the living room contained the couches that no one could sit on—"those are for company"—that's where Mitch and his parents chose to entertain the parade of suitors for his services. As everyone sat down, some snacks and coffee would be offered and the coach would pronounce them "delicious," even, as in this case, they'd been made by placing little prepackaged dough squares onto a cookie sheet and popping them in the oven for 15 minutes at 350°, and the pitch would begin. Closing the deal meant closing the parents, so after the coach had proclaimed Mitch to be a fine young man, his portion of the evening was pretty much over.

From there would come the earnest presentation of the school's superior academic record, and his own personal dedication to seeing that each of his players' graduate—even though most of those who did wound up with degrees that had a low level of marketability. The erstwhile suitor would proclaim his sincere concern and empathy regarding the important dilemma they faced in deciding with whom to entrust their boy, followed by the pledge to watch over him like "he was my own son." Of course, this same paragon of virtue and benevolence would be calling their progeny a "grab-ass snotball,"and worse come the fall but for now, he was Pat O'Brien speaking with the same earnestness that propelled the celluloid heroes of Notre Dame to "Win one for the Gipper." By now, Mitch had heard enough of these heartfelt entreaties that he marveled at their ability to project the sincerity needed to breach the walls of even the most adversarial parent. A couple of them seemed to have given the same spiel for so long he thought they might even believe it.

Tonight's visit would be the last. They had heard from all the schools that Mitch was most interested in, and after this evening's visit from Michigan State, they would sit together to evaluate each school and make their decision. Unlike the powers of the SEC, ACC, and each of the other three major conferences that had come calling, Michigan State had been almost an afterthought. Although they had had some decent teams over the years, the first thing that came to mind when you looked at their record was what a good basketball school they were. Their last season had been a 3-and-9 disaster that prompted the hiring of a new head coach. Unlike the Spartans' in-state rival, the University of Michigan, the head coaching position at MSU didn't offer the cachet that induced the big-name coaches across the country to break their unbreakable commitments to the schools "they would never leave," so they had settled on an unknown who'd spent the last three seasons as the offensive coordinator at Bowling Green.

Despite their distinct lack of a football pedigree, MSU had continually been on the right side of the cutline each time he revised his list of prospective schools. Mitch had met their coach twice already and he liked his enthusiasm for playing the role of David in a conference of Goliaths. He told Mitch he was looking for players who wanted to help build something. "Going to a school like Alabama is great. They've got a terrific program and you'll compete for the national championship every year" he'd said. "But isn't the chance to do something that no one thinks can be done more exciting than becoming the new cog in an old machine?"

It was 8:00 when Jim Tolliver's red 2005 Tahoe pulled up and parked in front of Mitch's house. Even for winter in suburban Detroit, where cars were washed sporadically at best, his looked like it was long overdue for a meeting with water and a sponge. Gray grime streaked along its exterior like the wake of a boat, and the salt buildup around each tire had been there long enough to contain fossilized remains. He wore a black knit cap and a plain black overcoat that he held shut against the cold with his left hand. Compared to the entrances of some of the other coaches, Notre Dame's had brought a priest with him, Jim Tolliver looked like he could have been any General Motors middle manager coming home from the office. As he walked toward the house, Mitch wondered if his neighbors were wishing they'd just stayed in, watched ESPN, and made the kid walk the dog.

As Tolliver walked up the drive, Mr. and Mrs. McKay put on their smiles while Mitch brought in a Dansk tray with three coffee mugs and a plate of oatmeal cookies and set it on the coffee table where it was within reaching distance of all the evening's major participants. As he shook his parent's hands, Mitch was struck with how ordinary he looked. His blue suit looked closer to a Marshall Field's than to an Armani, and was coupled with a tie and crisp white shirt that he'd probably bought at JC Penney's and he carried a small soft leather briefcase with him. He looked like someone about to explain to the McKay's the benefits of whole life versus term insurance.

His face was still pink from the cold and he wiped the last of the frost-initiated tears from his eyes as he sat down on one of the room's tan couches. Thanks to the steady stream of Mitch's suitors, the couches had seen more use in a couple of months than they had in 15 years. After he took a sip of his coffee and passed on the cookies, Tolliver looked at the three McKay's sitting together on the opposing couch and said, "Mr. and Mrs. McKay, I know I'm not the first coach to sit here and you probably have a list of questions and things you'd like to know about Michigan State and how we would use Mitch, and I'm more than happy to answer them, but first I'd like to talk with Mitch for a moment."

His parents looked at each other and then at Mitch and nodded their agreement.

"Mitch other than to play football, what's important to you about the school that you choose?"

The question caught Mitch by surprise. The process had enabled him to create a reservoir of stock responses such as "I'd like to play in a wide-open offense," and "Because I want to play for the best," but that wasn't what Tolliver had asked.

After some stammering, he blurted out, "That they provide me with the best possible education." Boy, there was something he'd probably never heard, but none of the other coaches who'd sat in that same spot had even bothered to ask. Tolliver shook his head ever so slightly and looked directly at him and asked him, "All the schools you've spoken with can provide you with a quality education. I'll be honest with you. I've sat across from hundreds of kids over the years, and I've found that they fall into two categories. The first are the ones that have no plan for their futures other than to play in the NFL, and I've coached a few of them. Most of them don't make it, and far too many have left school with either a worthless degree or no degree at all. The other group is made up guys who have a plan for their future and understand the value of the opportunity that is

21

being presented to them. Sure, they want to play in the pros, but they understand that the odds are against them and they need to be sure they are prepared for life after football. What I want to know, Mitch, is which group are you in?"

He felt like the arrested guy in an episode of "Law and Order" and he didn't have the option of asking for a lawyer. This wasn't how it was supposed to go, Tolliver should have been effusive in his praise, telling his parents that kids who can throw the football like their son are precious and rare. This guy wasn't talking to him as a future quarterback but as a prospective student.

"I've thought a lot about eventually joining the FBI. They look mainly for accountants and lawyers. I'm not interested in being an accountant. I've done some research and my plan is to major in criminal justice, wherever I go, and then to law school."

While his parents looked as if he'd just correctly answered the question on "Final Jeopardy," Tolliver reached into the briefcase and pulled out a new MSU student handbook and a course catalogue. For the next two hours, they discussed all the courses he would need to take and how many credits he'd need per semester to graduate in four years.

At 10:15, Jim Tolliver said his good-byes and thanked Mitch for considering Michigan State. By 10:20, he'd made his decision.

Chapter 4

My house is a little smoky red brick bungalow with wood siding that I painted a muted yellow, Sherwin Williams calls it Ivory Castle, on N. Blair Avenue. It's a quiet street with lots of young families and every other yard seems to have incorporated some number of bikes, and one of those yellow-and-red plastic cars, into their landscaping. Most of the houses were built in the late 40s and early 50s to house GI's who'd returned from the war and made the transition to middle management at General Motors, Ford, or Chrysler. The spindly maple and oak trees they'd planted all those years ago are now about 40 feet tall and their leaves cover the street like a canopy with different shades of green in the spring and summer and a panoply of reds, oranges, and yellows in the fall.

A hard-fought street hockey game was taking place in front of my house as I pulled up so I had to wait for two of the participants, one in a home Wings jersey while the other was clad in Blackhawks garb—must have gotten it from an-out of-town relative—to temporarily move the net nearest to my driveway out of harm's way.

I pulled into the driveway and noticed that the hosta I'd planted last year on either side of my porch steps were all coming back and, combined with the evenly spaced junipers planted by the previous owners, gave the place a welcoming façade. I'd added the hosta because they were cheap, and the guy at the nursery told me that they were perennials that didn't require much attention. I haven't inherited my parents' enthusiasm for gardening—their backyard looks like it was pulled from the pages of *Better Homes and Gardens*, so cheap and low maintenance are integral to my landscaping vision. After opening the chain link gate that bisects my driveway to prevent intruders from entering my backyard sanctuary, I pulled the car into the garage, closed the gate, and walked through the side door into Casa de McKay.

In its 65 years, my house has had only three owners, with me being the third. It still has its original hardwood floors, arched doorways, solid-wood doors with glass door knobs, two bedrooms downstairs, one of which I use for an office, and my upstairs bedroom runs the length of the house. Even though its only about 1,000 square feet, it's perfect for me. From the side-door landing where I was standing, you can turn right to go down the stairs to the basement or walk straight into my well-appointed kitchen. I think it was last updated about 40 years ago, except for the tile floor I'd installed to replace the original linoleum. The yellow painted cabinets and white appliances are kind of cool in a retro sort of way, but linoleum is aesthetically offensive no matter what the era.

Like all good investigative professionals, my house is protected by a home security system which, in my case, is a fourteen-pound pug named Fang. I got her—Fang is a unisex name—from an old client, Jane Darwell, who'd gotten sideways with a competing breeder, and needed me to prove that he was forging American Kennel Club registration papers to sell mixed-breed dogs as purebreds. You can't make this stuff up. Fang was part of a new litter and made my selection process easier when she shoved one of her siblings out of the way to come lick my hand. Aside from her prowess as a guard dog, any burglar seeking to unlawfully enter the premises does so at the risk of being licked to death, she is always happy to see me, shares all my political views, and never asks questions during the most important part of a movie. As I came through the door, I could hear her running down the stairs, accelerate through the living room, lose traction on the slick kitchen floor, and finally slide to a stop at my feet.

While I had no reason to doubt Fang's excitement at my arrival, I decided to take her out just in case and she confirmed my suspicions under the big scotch pine that dominates a large portion of my backyard. The mugginess had passed, leaving behind a cool evening that left me comfortable in my jacket. I sat down on one of the rocking chairs from my recently uncovered set of patio furniture and watched Fang patrol the yard from my deck. She follows a set pattern that begins at the row of holly planted along my back fence and gradually moves toward the rear of the house, keeping her nose to the ground in a vigilant effort to determine if the premises have been violated by any unwanted intruders. Occasionally, the unwary rabbit or squirrel will venture into her domain, unleashing a fury of violent barking and a futile chasing of the miscreant from the yard. She's never caught one but judging from her enthusiasm, the capture of a small mammal remains on her bucket list.

As I watched Fang, I found myself thinking about Olivia and what she had told me about Tim. I never considered myself a "romantic," and the length of my relationships is best measured in days, not weeks. But even if I had been, my time on the Detroit police force and as a private investigator had exacerbated my fatalistic beliefs regarding the potential endurance of any loving relationship to the pathological. In both occupations, I had seen first-hand the level of cruelty that one human being can inflict on another. When a betrayed spouse sat across from me relating the circumstances that had caused the synchronicity of what was to be a lifetime together to metastasize into bitter recriminations and soul-crushing despair, I'd find myself wondering at what point had one or the other decided to rekindle those early feelings of excitement and infatuation elsewhere, leaving their partner alone and craving what their spouse no longer had to give. Olivia, of course, had been before all this.

I had met her in a used bookstore in March of my sophomore year on one of those cold, rainy days where everyone you pass on the street walks with single-minded focus and the stock of smiles and friendly gestures is in short supply. I was there to see if they'd been able to add to their inventory of Robert Ludlum books, or "Bob" as my roommates and I liked to refer to him. We'd been working our way through his catalogue and considered ourselves to be true aficionados who preferred his lesser-known titles like *The Scarletti Inheritance* and *The Rhineman Exchange,* as opposed to those dilatants who spent their time wondering if Jason Bourne would ever catch Carlos the Jackal. Poseurs. After being pleasantly surprised to find a copy of *The Gemini Contenders,* I made my way over to the classics section. I was in the process of broadening the scope of my literary knowledge and had undertaken my own "personal development" program where I read one of the more well-regarded works from the western canon for each "fun-fiction" book I devoured. I'd liked *The Return of the Native* and was thinking I'd see if they had *Tess of the D'Urbervilles* when I saw her.

She was wearing a blue raincoat, jeans, and red wellingtons and was holding a well-worn copy of *Wuthering Heights* in her hand. She must have felt me looking at her because she looked up and smiled softly and then continued to leaf through the book. My M.O. for meeting women at the time was to pick them up in one of the many bars that serviced the MSU student body, and since she obviously wasn't intoxicated, and reading a book because she *wanted* to, meeting her required a skill set I didn't possess. I did a poor job of feigning interest in the titles between 'H' for Hardy and 'B' for Bronte, but she either didn't notice or didn't care enough to comment, and when I was close enough, I chose to impress her with my extensive knowledge of English literature: "Charlotte was always my favorite Bronte sister. I've always found Emily to be overly morose. Would it have been so bad to have Heathcliff wind up with Catherine?"

"Morose", she responded, "Compared to a woman who falls in love with a man who keeps his crazy wife locked up and then goes blind when she burns down his house?"

There's that.

"But Rochester and Jane get married and have a baby at the end. So, wouldn't you say that Charlotte is the more upbeat of the two?"

"Maybe, but I wouldn't characterize either of them as optimists."

We stood there and talked for a half hour, and, after I asked her if I could buy her a drink, talked for another three.

She told me she was a computer science major with her long-term plan being to obtain her doctorate, and about her family and their legacy with the university. Her parents had met there and both sets of grandparents were alumni as well, and her brother who in her words was a "genius" was sure to go there as well. I told her I was an only child who'd unfortunately missed out on the genius gene, and I was working on a degree in criminal justice. Fortunately for me, her interest in subjects like the criminal mind, the American system of justice, and investigation techniques made up for my lack of knowledge about all things computer related, except for the fact that I owned one. She was cute and serious and I fell in love with her right there at that corner table in the back of P.T. O'Malley's.

Being the quarterback for a major college football team is obviously a unique experience. The rush of adrenalin you get when you take your place behind center in front of 80,000 people can't be duplicated. Everywhere you go people know you, and even those who don't certainly do after the professor points you out on the first day of class. Guys are either in awe of you or want to punch you in the face, especially the drunk ones, and any number of girls are willing to show you things they didn't learn at their mother's knee.

I'd be lying if I said that I didn't find it intoxicating, but I also found myself becoming increasingly skeptical of people's motives. You don't want anyone to think you're paranoid, so let's just say you become deeply suspicious. Not to sound ungrateful, but I was becoming tired of people's feelings towards me being dependent on what dangled from my right shoulder, and with Olivia I didn't have to worry. Until the night her roommate answered my knock on their dorm-room door, she didn't even know I played football for the first month we were together. She was my refuge, and even though I never said anything about it, she instinctively understood that my time with her was something that I didn't want intruded upon because of what I did for 12 Saturdays every fall. This even extended to her family. Driving back to school after I met them for the first time, she said she'd told her dad that asking me about football was off-limits, because "Mitch gets tired of talking about it."

The sun had hidden itself, like it did every evening, behind my garage and Fang was giving me her "I think it's about time you fed me" look, so I opened the doorwall and prompted her to come inside by asking her if she wanted to eat. I've read that some scientists believe that dogs can understand what is being said to them in a rudimentary way, of course. I'm not sure of the full breadth of Fang's vocabulary but she's clearly mastered the terms "eat" and its more enticing companion, "treat." I closed the door behind me as she raced to take her customary position in front of her bowls with her tail vibrating at hummingbird-like speed, and, after tossing my jacket onto the kitchen table, I filled one with water and the other with her food and ended her anticipatory frenzy by setting them down in front of her.

While she quickly satiated her gustatory desires by wolfing down her small dog-sized high-protein salmon and vegetable bits, I checked the messages on my answering machine. One was from my mom inquiring about whether she was ever going to see me again—the woman wields guilt like a club—and quickly browsed through my mail, where a piece from Publisher's Clearing House informed me that I may have already won $10 million. While that's exciting, it still wound up in the discard pile. I have a friend who believes that his chances of winning are increased by the more magazines he elects to subscribe to. His house resembles a doctor's waiting room, and I believe he is the only subscriber to "Alaska Magazine" in the state of Michigan. So far, his strategy hasn't paid off, but he insists it's just a matter of time. His wife thinks he's an idiot. I say if you take away a man's hope, what does he have?

Finding nothing that required my urgent attention had been delivered by phone or post, I set about finding something to satisfy my own epicurean desires. I surveyed the refrigerator for something that hadn't expired yet, and saw three bottles of pop, some milk, an open can of black olives, and a half a bag of radishes. Fortunately, I found an old Stouffer's Mac and Cheese hiding behind a box of popsicles in the freezer. I popped it into the microwave. I doubled the cook time to account for the fact that it appeared to be encased in a block of ice. Upon the sound of the ding I took my entree, the can of olives, and a bottle of Faygo Rock N' Rye into the living room and flipped on the TV in time for the beginning of the Red Wings game.

Fang is an avid Wings fan, so she settled in next to my feet as I ate my dinner and we both watched them snatch defeat from the jaws of victory by letting the Bruins score two goals in the last five minutes. It was now after ten. I got up and gathered the remnants of my dinner and carried them into the kitchen and tossed them into the trashcan I keep under the sink. As a firm believer in utility and since I hate to wash dishes, my meals either come in their own containers or are eaten off a paper plate with plastic utensils that I buy in bulk from Costco. As they say on TV, it makes cleanup a "breeze."

My briefcase was still lying by the side door where I'd left it. I grabbed it and went back to the couch to look through the file again and add anything I might have missed to my notes. Nothing new emerged as I worked my way through the file. Harley and Ward, the detectives in charge of the case, were following the same path as I would've taken. Someone and potentially more than one were going to prison for manslaughter at least. Everything they'd found pointed to members of Planet Action, and it was only a matter of time before they had suspects in hand. The only reason the investigation, had probably taken this long was to ensure that the case was airtight due to its visibility. I'm not overly political and I think that you should stand up for what you believe in but in this case, Tim had died and the lives of some fellow students would be devastated.

One set of parents that had looked forward to attending their son's graduation would now be attending his funeral, while those of the perpetrators would only see their sons or daughters on prison visiting days. All the hopes and dreams packed into twenty or so years erased because of the composition of a university's investment portfolio. Tragic and senseless, but I still couldn't see the underlying causes that Olivia desperately hoped for me to find. By the time I'd finished up, the news was over and it was after 11:30. Fang was asleep and snoring, and that struck me as a good idea, so I turned off the television and went to bed.

Chapter 5

Wisps of snow snaked across the black asphalt parking lot as Mitch McKay and his father pulled into the parking lot. Christmas break had purged the university of a large helping of its students and what limited activity they'd seen on campus on their way to the Hannah Administration Building resembled a resort in the off-season. Mr. McKay maneuvered his red LeSabre into a parking space and turned off the engine. Mitch fumbled a moment with his seat belt and sat quietly staring out the window. Neither father or son spoke at first, and the uncomfortable silence was finally broken when his father turned to him and offered up his best attempt at advising his son for what was soon to be the worst day of his young life, "I'm sorry that this is happening to you, son. I think you should be ready for the worst. You and I both know that what you did was wrong—very wrong, but I think this whole thing has been blown way out of proportion and what they're doing isn't right. Your mother and I are proud of the way you've dealt with the situation. We all have to live with the consequences of our actions, but—"

As his father's voice trailed off, he looked down at the dirty gray carpet at his feet, appreciating what his dad was trying to do. Life wasn't like an episode of "Leave it to Beaver" where Ward always knew exactly what to say, and, no matter how big, Beaver's and Wally's problems were solved in 22 minutes. Without him saying it directly, he knew that he was telling him was that whatever the outcome, this was a problem of his own making and he was expecting him to accept his punishment without complaint or excuses. He turned back to face the window and said softly but firmly, "I know, Dad. I did it. I got caught. There's no one else to blame."

There was nothing more for either of them to say. Silently the duo got out the car, closed their doors, and walked toward the tinted-glass double doors of the building to learn his fate.

As they neared the building, Mitch replayed the events that had led up to this point in his head. It was the week of the Michigan game. The Spartans had begun the season ranked number 12 in the country. They won their first game, with Kent State playing the sacrificial lamb 56–7, followed by one-point win at Notre Dame on a last second field goal. After winning their next four games, they were 6 and 0 and ranked number 8. The Wolverines were undefeated, and beating them would give the Spartans the inside track for the Big 10 championship and a trip to Pasadena for the Rose Bowl.

A single elective class had started everything. Balancing school and football had been difficult at times during his two and half years at the university. His days were consumed with practices, conditioning, and film sessions, the related activities dictated by his status as the "face" of the team, including speaking to local students and civic organizations, and fulfilling what seemed like an endless stream of media requests.

Most nights found him in his room in the house he shared with three other guys from the team studying until one or two in the morning. It wasn't uncommon for him hear his housemates leave to partake in one or more of the many "nonscholastic" activities available to the more socially oriented undergraduate and still be working when they returned from the evening's revelry. Despite the rigors of his schedule and gaping holes in his social calendar, he carried a 3.7 GPA and unlike most of his teammates and fellow bachelor's degree-seeking students was on schedule to graduate in the prescribed four-year period.

The demands on his time had only increased this season when the Athletic Department launched its Heisman campaign on his behalf.

Based on its claim to annually identify the best player in college football, the Heisman Trophy is the sport's most-prestigious award. If you've played football at least once in your life, you've imagined what it would be like to sit in the front row at the New York Athletic Club and hear your name called. As Mitch quickly learned, 'campaign' was the operative word in seeking to join an extremely select fraternity that only added one new member each year. You could throw for 50 touchdowns or run for 2,500 yards but if your school didn't unleash its own supporting media assault, you were a guy with nice stats who could watch the awards ceremony on TV along with a few million others.

Months before the first fan walked into Spartan Stadium, the school's Sports Information Department had compiled a list of all award voters, identified key analysts and media personalities and the story ideas that they would pitch to each of them, and assembled everything into a multifaceted plan that rivaled the Allies' strategy for the Normandy landings in ambitiousness and complexity.

He wasn't the quarterback or team captain, he was the "product," and they would market him with the same intensity as a new car or deodorant. Votes were just another measure of market share and their job was to ensure that this year he held the dominant position. He had his own website—where you could purchase your own "McKay for the Heisman"-branded apparel and merchandise, Twitter, and MySpace accounts. Each week his stats and a link to his selected You Tube-available highlights were sent to a predefined list of recipients and no interview opportunity was too small to pass up. Of course, he had a role in this process as well. Achieving the level of performance on the field that would place him within the realm of contenders was a given but it was his participation in the off-the-field activities that was essential.

Although both Tolliver and the Sports Information staff had advised him to take fewer classes for the fall term to accommodate the increased time demands, saying, "You can go back to a full load next

34

semester," he'd disregarded their advice and taken three of his major classes and what was supposed to be a blow-off political science class as an elective.

The volume of work required for the first three had been about what he'd expected, but Poli Sci had turned into anything but a blow-off. Four required books to be read on the syllabus, a couple of papers plus the mid-term and final, all taught by a professor who made no secret of his contempt for so-called "student athletes" equated to 2–3 hours a night on that class alone. He'd been able to maintain the delicate balance between his increasingly conflicting responsibilities to that point but three mid-terms and a 10-page paper that he hadn't even started on "The Impact of the Cuban Missile Crisis on U.S./Soviet Relations" resulted in him making the decision that had things collapsing down around him in a matter of weeks. Being prepared for the mid-terms would require even more hours of study than usual, but he couldn't do that while researching and writing a paper at the same time. One of the team managers knew a guy who wrote papers for $50 and guaranteed an 'A.' He'd delivered and $50 and three days later, he slid the paper into the envelope hanging from the professor's office door and went to practice. Two weeks later, he got the paper back with a terse, "See Me" written in red on the cover page.

In the minds of many students, and a sizeable number of the faculty, at colleges across the country no phrase is as polarizing as "student-athlete," especially if the term is being applied to a football or basketball player. Very few major college athletic departments make money, but their football and basketball programs generate most of the revenue they bring in and fund the remainder of the school's teams from gymnastics to swimming. From the standpoint of the university itself, they provide nationwide exposure that manifests itself in an increasing number of applications from prospective tuition-paying students, and a winning team helps spark the desire on the part of many alumni to add an extra zero on their *contribution checks.*

As the popularity (read money) of collegiate sports has grown, so has an on-campus caste system that fosters estrangement between the athlete and the remainder of the student body. At Michigan State as well as at most of its counterparts, this means providing athletes with not only full scholarships but clothing, meals, and facilities like the school's Duffy Daugherty Football Building and Skandalaris Football Center that are unavailable to non-athletes. For those on the outside looking in, this degree of perceived privilege and athletic apartheid calls into question the college's central mission of serving as a center of higher education. The tension between elements of the school's faculty, students, and its athletes is like two geological plates along a fault line. It's always there and the pressure builds up over time until some event or events occur to cause a disruption.

Recent incidents of academic fraud involving athletes receiving credit for nonexistent courses and submitting papers that had been either written for them or completely plagiarized had occurred at multiple schools recognized as major football "powers," thereby creating heightened demands that both the National Collegiate Athletic Association (NCAA) and its member universities institute more specific and severe policies to rectify these situations. The movement had gained momentum when a letter signed by over 100 college presidents had been published in the New York Times *demanding the immediate implementation of more stringent academic guidelines by the organization to maintain "the integrity of collegiate athletics." The irony of the fact that many of these same academic leaders allowed their athletic departments to act as autonomous fiefdoms apart from the school itself was apparently lost amongst all the righteous indignation. Mitch's paper brought the issue to Michigan State.*

There wasn't a single thing that he could say in his own defense

36

when Professor Littman confronted him regarding the paper when they met in his office. His initial thought had been to wonder how his academic duplicity had been discovered. How could they have known that he hadn't written the paper himself? While he didn't ask, Dr. Littman was quick to explain that his transgression was plagiarism. Apparently his "ghostwriter" must have been overbooked, because the paper he sold Mitch had been written two terms ago by a student who had taken the same course. The university's standard punishment for misrepresenting someone else's work as your own is a failing grade for the class. Standards weren't going to apply in this case.

The process proceeded swiftly and inexorably. Littman informed him he was going to request a disciplinary hearing. When Mitch asked him what that meant, he was informed that the hearing would be held to determine his fate at the university. The hearing took place during the following week. Tolliver spoke on his behalf before a panel comprised of the deans of the College of Social Sciences, Graduate Studies, and Undergraduate Studies. He pointed to Mitch's performance to date as a student, his community relations activities and, finally, he expressed his belief that his removal from the football team and the corresponding publicity would constitute a degree of punishment far above what a normal student would receive in a similar circumstance.

His entreaties were met with solemn silence. It was obvious that in their eyes Mitch was the unredeemable perpetrator and Tolliver, a willing accomplice. They asked him if he had anything to say on his own behalf. He knew that he'd be asked and he'd thought about potential responses, but there is no eloquent way to explain away the fact that you'd cheated. He said, "No." They told him they would review their findings with the university's president and that he would be advised of their decision. With that, they were dismissed. It had taken only 30 minutes.

At five o'clock that afternoon, he received the call telling him to be in the president's office the next morning. He called his dad and told him about the meeting. They talked for an hour. When they were done, he hung up the phone and cried.

A secretary led them into the wood-paneled office. President Susan Wilkerson, Tolliver, Chris Simon—the school's athletic director, and a woman Mitch didn't recognize sat around a small wooden conference table. They all stood up when he and his father entered the room.

Tolliver looked like he was carrying a grand piano on his back. Lines of tension creased his forehead, his shoulders were hunched, and his blue suit looked like he had just pulled it out of a mailbox. He was the only one of the four who reached to shake both their hands; he told each of them, "I'm sorry." This display of decency drew an icy stare from President Wilkerson. Simon and the woman, who was introduced as Julie Adams, the director of public relations, glanced quickly at them and then found something interesting to look at on the polished table top. Wilkerson's face on the other hand gave no indication of her sentiments one way or the other as she brusquely indicated that they were to take the two seats at the opposite end of the table.

Wilkerson pulled her chair closer to the table, took a drink from the bottle of water she had in front of her—Mitch noticed he and his father were the only ones without some type of drink in front of them. Apparently, they weren't expected to be there long enough to work up a thirst. Wilkerson sat up straight, adjusted her suit, and began to speak. "We all know why we are here, so let's precede with the matter at hand. Mr. Tolliver and Mr. Sullivan are representing the Athletic Department, and I've asked Ms. Adams to attend as the university will naturally have to release a statement regarding the final disposition of this inquiry."

Julie Adams looked like she was going to be sick. As she took another sip from the bottle, and fastidiously screwed its white cap back into place, Mitch looked over at his father. He sat still, his *hands folded in front of him on the table, and looked directly at President Wilkerson. Mitch shifted forward in his chair and put his hands in his lap so that no one would notice the slight tremor that had become increasingly more pronounced since they'd sat down. Looking out the window to his right, he saw the phalanx of news vans from the major Lansing and Detroit stations, each with their roof-mounted satellite antennas to ensure their viewers would be the first to hear the rendered verdict. Off to one side, he saw that ESPN had arrived to broadcast his humiliation to its nationwide audience. Already that morning, he'd been contacted by multiple print and broadcast reporters offering him the opportunity to "tell his side of the story". He said no to each.*

Freshly hydrated, Wilkerson continued. "You are a well-known representative of the university, and fairly or unfairly more is expected from you. Actions such as yours reflect negatively on the school and our primary mission as an educational institution. Although others in this room may disagree with this decision," she said and gave a sideways glance toward Tolliver, "after a thorough review of your actions, in accordance with the documented procedures of Michigan State University, it is our decision that your status as an active student be immediately and permanently terminated. Do you have any questions?"

Silence cloaked the room. He felt as if all his blood had rushed to his head. He thought he might be sick. He put his hand on the table to steady himself. They weren't suspending him and kicking him off the team—they were expelling him. President Wilkerson's pronouncement reverberated in his head as he fought to form a response. The sound of his father's voice punched through his confusion. "My son made a terrible mistake, and he deserves to be punished, but don't you think that this is excessive? A suspension of some type and dismissal from the team would be understandable, but I find it hard to believe that expulsion is the normal course of action for offenses like this. You've obviously chosen to make an example out of him."

Although he spoke in an even tone, only Mitch knew that he only talked this way when he was seriously pissed off. He also realized that no matter how severe being kicked out of school seemed, his father had no leverage for any attempt to change the verdict.

President Wilkerson leaned back a little in her upholstered chair, took a moment to collect herself, put her hands together, and steepled her unadorned fingers. Only the slight flush in her cheeks betrayed her annoyance at having to explain her decision. "Mr. McKay, I can assure you that your son's position as an athlete at this school was not a factor in our decision. He has committed a severe breach of the most elemental covenant of academics and ethics. In this matter, his punishment is within the parameters of the university's written guidelines."

Regardless of what she said, everyone in the room knew that this was about more than a paper. Expelling him enabled Michigan State to uphold an image of academic integrity to both the public at large and its own faculty by demonstrating that its athletes were not above the rules. His actions allowed the school to use him as the sacrificial offering to satiate a growing perception that the connection between the university and its Athletic Department was tenuous at best. The trap, as it were, had always been waiting and he had walked right into it.

His father pushed forward in his chair to speak, but Mitch stopped him by placing his hand on his arm and saying, "It's okay, Dad." Then, turning to face the others seated around the table he said, "I'm sorry" and to his father, "Let's go."

Chapter 6

It was still dark when I woke up. The accumulated effect of countless early-morning workouts I guess. I rolled over to check the clock on the nightstand by my bed and, just like every day, it told me that it was 5:00 a.m. Fang was scratching the side of the bed to let me know that she was ready to get a start on the day, so I pulled on a pair of shorts and we both went downstairs. I opened the doorwall and we went outside. Whatever sleepiness that had been hanging on met its demise when I stepped onto the deck and into a 50°F morning. Fortunately, the length of Fang's morning ritual was in direct proportion to the thermometer and we were both enjoying the warmth of the kitchen about two minutes later.

Fang had taken up her position in front of her food and water bowls and as soon I filled them was face down in one of them in a state of food-induced bliss. I flipped on the radio to listen to one of those political call-in shows where everyone is either a "fascist" or a "liberal pinhead", while I grabbed a banana, some strawberries, and yogurt from the refrigerator and a couple of ice cubes and plopped them into the blender. I added the recommended amount of protein power and a few pulses later was enjoying a delicious and healthy breakfast smoothie. Normally, I have a bowl of Cap'n Crunch or Apple Jacks, but I hadn't been to the store to pick up the dietary essentials lately. After I finished, I rinsed the blender out with steaming hot water. I figured anything I miss will at least be sterile, and headed upstairs to pack.

I pulled down a leather valise-style duffel bag and tossed in enough clothes for a couple of days. I still didn't see where this was going to take even a day, but it's always good to be on the safe side. Since I usually showered at the gym after my workout, I grabbed what I needed for the day and put it in the odor-defying duffle. I checked my drawer for a clean pair of sweats. Finding none, I gave the smell test to the couple of sets in my dirty clothes hamper and put on the one lowest on the pungent scale. As a further precaution against being guilty of poor gym etiquette, I "Fabreezed" myself with the bottle I keep in the bathroom. After splashing cold water on my face and brushing my teeth, I grabbed my jacket, keys, and gun, turned off the radio, gave Fang a good-bye rub behind her ears and headed out.

My gym is never too crowded at 5:30. I waved to a few of the regulars, including a few cops I know as I walked through the place to stash my stuff in my locker. The facility itself is pretty spartan. There are no ferns or juice bars, it doesn't offer spin classes, and no one is wearing any fabrics that *breathe*, but it's perfect for me. I stopped lifting a long time ago and now my workouts alternate between boxing drills and yoga with heavy cardio thrown in for good measure. Today, I skipped rope for thirty minutes, hit the speed bag for another fifteen, and finished up by simulating ten rounds through a devastating pummeling of the heavy bag. After I showered, I ran by the office to check with Nikki who was adorned in a form-fitting pink T-shirt with "Don't Annoy Me" bedazzled on the front, black leather pants, and leopard skin pumps—about another case that we were working. An auto parts manufacturer thought his CFO might be supplementing his salary — he was, and by eight, I was on the road to East Lansing.

I took Main to 11 Mile, made a left, and veered onto I-96 and headed north. Spring in Michigan is always an iffy proposition. If you start out thinking the day will be overcast and a little chilly or muggy, you won't be disappointed, but when you have one like today with the sun taking over the sky and a warm breeze, you're pleasantly surprised. I was so taken aback that I opened the sun roof. The only time that I'd used it up to now was when a half-gallon of ice cream I'd bought escaped from its bag and rolled out of sight behind my golf clubs. It took me a day or two to get it into the dealer to be steam cleaned, so the retractable roof aided in keeping the air breathable by helping create my own personal wind tunnel. I've put my groceries in the back seat ever since. It took me 45 minutes to get to the Hagadorn Road exit. I exited and took Hagadorn to Grand River Avenue and made a left.

You'll find a Grand River Avenue in virtually every college town in the country. Small independent businesses catering to every possible student need from textbooks and all manner of apparel, to over-the-counter birth control (for both sexes) and beer are purchasable via a short walk from anywhere on campus. Students craving sustenance can partake in the variety of offerings available from the multiple restaurants and take- out places that punctuate the thoroughfare at strategic intervals. When I'd been a student, the food cartel was made up of strictly locally owned businesses, including the Peanut Barrel—a date with a Rodeo Burger was on my itinerary, but I noticed that a few national chains like Five Guys were attempting to establish a foothold.

I hadn't stepped foot on the campus in over ten years but it was as I remembered it. Oaks and maples provided shade for the students heading to and from the buildings that made up the oldest portion of the campus. Looking to my left, I could see the dun-colored façade and vaulted archways of Berkey Hall standing guard over red-bricked Morrill Hall with the

Student Union Building in the distance and the Gothic finials of Beaumont Tower standing as sentinels above them all. Before I completely lost myself in reminiscences, I reached the light at Collingwood Drive and turned right. Olivia lived a few blocks down the street. As I headed toward her house, I noticed that one of the unwritten laws of East Lansing real estate still applied: aesthetics improved the farther you lived from campus. Most student-occupied dwellings are found in the first two to three blocks of the multiple streets running perpendicular to Grand River, and simple cost-benefit analysis on the part of their landlords has long since led to the extinction of any type of landscaping or exterior adornment. Unfortunately, actual homeowners also live within these "student ghettos" and even a "yard of the month" is a lonely oasis in a neighborhood populated by vehicles with negative blue book values that offers the opportunity for someone to throw up in your shrubs every weekend.

Olivia lived in a white, wood-sided one story with two large windows, each framed by black shutters, and a red door in the front. The house sat on a small lot featuring two large maple trees and a lawn so lush it looked like a carpet. I made a mental note to switch lawn services. Since her yard also featured recently planted flowers, she had obviously cultivated an interest in landscape design that eclipsed my own since the last time we'd seen each other. I parked in the driveway. She must have seen me coming, because she opened the door before I could knock.

Chapter 7

She was dressed in jeans and knee-high brown riding boots along with a soft green sweater that matched her eyes. I don't think Olivia has ever understood how beautiful she is. When we were together, I'd catch guys sneaking a look at her, while others just dropped all pretense and stared. At first, it was a bit of an ego boost that the object of their attraction was with me. However, it didn't take long for me to stop flattering myself and realize that to spurn them meant she had to even be aware of them. Her focus was always on what was in front of her; whatever was on the periphery didn't matter. With her, I felt the same way.

After an awkward hug, she invited me inside. I followed her into the living room. Like her yard, the interior of the house was a bit more "developed" than mine. While my chosen décor is based on a "multiple components-for-one low price" model, she'd focused on creating a comfortable space by building the room around a few nice pieces, complemented with some eclectic accents, like the old steamer trunk she was using for a coffee table, and two vibrantly colored Persian-style rugs to highlight the polished hardwood floor. She asked if I wanted something to drink but the bottle of Rock N Rye I'd had on the way up had vanquished my thirst for the time being.

I sat across from her as I gave her an overview of where I thought things stood. "I had Nikki pull up everything she could find on Tim's death. She was even able to get the autopsy and police reports."

"Is that legal?" she asked.

"Technically no, but Nikki can be quite resourceful when the situation calls for it."

She looked a little unsure about that but why quibble about methodology?

"I read through everything a few times and all of the accounts, public or otherwise, are consistent. There are no witnesses, but the police are sure that the same people who knocked over the shelves on the third floor are the ones responsible. I'm actually surprised that they haven't made any arrests yet, but it looks like the Planet Action people have circled the wagons and the cops haven't been able to get someone to roll over on whoever did it."

She already knew this of course, but maybe the consistency between each of the accounts would make her reconsider her belief that the police were on the wrong track. Naturally, I was wrong. She immediately dismissed what I thought was a preponderance of evidence by asking, "Okay, where do we start?"

Resigned to my fate and being a good detective, I laid out my backup plan which pretty much began and ended with talking to the police.

"We start by talking to the detectives handling the case, Harley and Ward, and finding out if they've learned anything new that might indicate that what happened to Tim was more than a case of being in the wrong place at the wrong time. Our next step, if there is one, will be based on what they tell us."

Fortunately, this plan of action was satisfactory to her. It was coming from a trained professional after all.

"Should we call them first to let them that we're coming?" she asked.

"Cops don't really like explaining themselves to outsiders, particularly private detectives. No one likes someone second guessing their judgment or wanting to look over their shoulder, especially a guy who has been hired to do just that. They don't look at investigations as a collaborative exercise. So, no. We'll just pop in. It's harder to say "get lost" when the sister of the victim and her hired gun are standing in front of them."

Then, I sealed the deal with "I'll drive" and we left to see what the East Lansing PD had to say.

I personally believe that all municipal buildings begin from a standard design plan that is easily modified to suit its intended purpose. Make it bigger, add some bars, and you've got a prison, remove the bars, it's a high school, and so on, and the home of the East Lansing Police Department did nothing to make me alter my theory. It was a boxy one-story brick building whose exterior color scheme ran the gamut from light brown to slightly lighter brown. The station was only five minutes from Olivia's house, but that had given us enough time to plan our strategy. She would ask to speak to the detectives and I would take the lead in the inquisition part. I'm a firm believer in planning no matter how self-evident the situation. You want to make sure everyone is on the same page.

The main desk was being manned by a fresh-faced, ponytailed officer, whose enthusiasm indicated she hadn't been on the job for longer than a couple months. She happily informed us that "Yes, both Detectives Harley and Ward are in" and she'd call back to tell them they had visitors. In the spirit of one good deed deserves another, I showed her my license and politely informed her that I was carrying a permitted weapon. This prompted the appearance of another officer who was happy to relieve me of my gun, while also indicating his approval, "A Beretta. Nice." Since we were being so familiar, he took the opportunity to give me a quick pat-down, just in case.

Shortly after my up close-and-personal encounter with their fellow officer, two men who I presumed to be Harley and Ward, emerged from a door behind the main desk. Maybe I just give off a vibe but immediately upon seeing me with Olivia, the looks on both of their faces changed from congenial public servants to "who put the turd in the punch bowl?" I guess I just have that effect on some people.

Recovering their sense of decorum, they said hello to Olivia and then the older of the two men introduced himself as Detective Kevin Harley. He didn't bother to shake my hand. Detective Brian Ward, who didn't seem to share his partner's concern that I might be carrying a communicable disease, shook my hand and directed us toward a glass-walled conference room. Being perceptive is part of my job, but it didn't take an expert to see that the relationship between them was a little "strained."

Harley struck me as ex-military, probably the Army or Marines, and was the only man I'd ever met who could stand at attention while walking. He appeared to be in his mid- to late forties and at 6' and around 200 pounds; you wouldn't be going out on a limb to guess that he had a gym membership. A crew-cut sat atop a broad face with a jaw so square you could have mistaken his head for a cinder block. His body was contoured like a house safe with tree trunk-like arms sticking out of it; all of it was perched on the two cement columns he used for legs. Today, he'd elected to package all of this in a gray suit whose seams must have been screaming for mercy. Ward, for some reason, looked familiar to me. He was younger than Harley, late 20s or so, 6'5" with an athletic build and wearing a blue pinstriped suit and a silver Tag Haeur watch on his wrist.

Any meeting, whether it's for business or trying to determine who killed your brother, always begins with a little idle chitchat, a little banter to demonstrate that "Hey, we're all friends here" before the unfriendly part starts, and this sit-down was no different.

Harley was the one who broke the ice with a personal question. "Mitch McKay. Aren't you the one who got kicked off the team right before the Rose Bowl for cheating on a test or something? Man, you blew it. You could have been in the NFL. Now you're a PI. Do you know how many guys would have killed to be you?"

Nice to meet you too, detective. I could feel Olivia put her hand on my arm, and Ward took a step away from his partner and rolled his eyes. Apparently, based on his experience, he didn't think that Harley was a shoo-in for the department's congeniality award.

Despite what he might have thought, this wasn't the first time I'd elicited this response upon meeting somebody over the years. Repetition has helped me craft a succinct response. "That was me. I did something stupid ten years ago. I've put that behind me," a nicer way of saying, "Yeah, I screwed up big time. I wished it had never happened, but I like what I do, and if you ask me anymore about it, I'll beat the crap out of you." It's all in the delivery.

"Hey, I didn't mean anything by it—", Harley apologetically began before Olivia cut him off with "I've asked Mr. McKay to help me explore the circumstances behind my brother's death. This is no reflection on the work that you are doing, but Mr. McKay is a close family friend whose opinion on the case is important to me. We don't wish to take up a great deal of your time, so can we please get started?"

Harley moved to speak, but Ward quickly cut him off.

"Why don't I take you through what we've got so far, and then we'll answer any questions you may have."

Olivia and I nodded our assent and he continued, "We know that the incident happened around 7:30 p.m. as multiple witnesses reported hearing the shelves being pushed over. I say *around* 7:30 since no one mentioned hearing the shelves on the 4th floor fall over. Our theory is that whoever pushed over the shelves on the third floor immediately continued on up to the 4th and pushed over the shelves on that floor, too".I thought about asking him about why only the last three stacks that had killed Tim were overturned, but I decided to wait to hear everything he l had to say first.

"We got the call here at 7:45 and got to the library around 8:00. The campus police had done a good job of cordoning off the scene and keeping everyone contained until we got there. Detective Harley and I went up to four first to examine the body," before he quickly caught himself and backtracked to "I'm sorry Ms. Price, I meant your brother."

Olivia responded with a quiet "Thank you" and asked Ward to go on.

"We found him in a study carrel along the rear wall of the building. The cause of death, and the ME confirmed this, was massive head trauma. Death was instantaneous. There were no other wounds or marks on the body to indicate any type of physical altercation. Blood analysis didn't show any DNA other than your brother's'. We fingerprinted the scene and the shelves, but it's a library so there is no telling how many people are in there every day. The librarian told us that floor isn't heavily trafficked, as it contains mainly books on things like physics and chemistry, stuff that most students would tend to avoid, but even so, it's not like they do a lot of dusting up there so some of the prints we did find could be months or even years old. I'm sure you know about the protest that took place that night, so between the Planet Action protesters, who were all wearing the same black hoodies, and the students who were in there, there were 213 on the lobby level and another 100 on the other floors of the building. We brought in every extra man we had and took statements from all of them, but no one claims to have seen anything. Most of them probably didn't. It doesn't appear that anyone was on your brother's floor, and it looked like a brawl had taken place by the time we got there so someone—or multiple suspects—could have slipped into the stairwell, pushed over the shelves on both floors, and come back down and been absorbed into the melee. Since Planet Action seems to have been intent on causing some type of provocation, we suspect that it was members of their group that did it. There also may be a link between what happened in the library and a professor who was murdered in his office in the Natural Science Building, but we haven't found anything definitive on that yet."

So far, what Ward had told us was consistent with what I'd read. Based on what he'd said, their theory about what had happened on the third and fourth floors made sense, but it seemed like they'd hit a wall.

"So you've definitively ruled out that Tim wasn't the focus of what happened?" I asked.

Again, Ward beat Harley to the draw: "We've talked to everyone we could find who knew him here, including his graduate advisor Dr. Knowles, all of the geoscience graduate students, and the students who have been in his classes for the past three semesters. As Ms. Price can tell you, we also spoke to her."

"And you didn't find anything?"

"Nothing", he said as reached for a can of Diet Coke. "It seems like he kept mainly to himself, but everyone we spoke with had nothing but good things to say about him. He was like a rock star in his department. Knowles was pretty broken up when we talked to him. He said your brother was 'the most brilliant student' he'd ever had, and the other students in the department seemed to share the sentiment. The ones in his class all said that he was a little odd but enthusiastic and very patient and genuinely concerned that they understood the material. Not even an inkling of a harbored grudge or a pissed- off student looking to get back at him for a bad grade."

I could almost feel Olivia's eyes boring into the side of my head willing me to ask the question she felt the police were overlooking so I obliged her, saying, "One thing that strikes me as odd is why did they push over all the shelves in that row on the third floor but only the three that killed Tim on the fourth?"

Up until now, Harley had been sitting across from me doing his best imitation of a human fist, but apparently he either thought that he and Ward had fulfilled their duty to the family or maybe his suit was constricting blood flow to every part of his body, but in either case he stood up, put his hands on the table, and leaned so close to me I could see the hairs in his nose, and in a voice a drill instructor would envy, let me know that as far as he was concerned, the Q&A portion of our session was over.

"We've told you where things stand in the investigation. We don't need some ex-jock PI coming in here and second-guessing us. You might have been a big deal back in the day McKay, but that doesn't mean we owe you any favors. We're done here." And without another word, he left the room and walked back to the door that led to the rear of the building and disappeared behind it.

Was it something I said?

The room was quiet for a moment and then I said, "I don't know about you, but I miss him already." Ward stifled a laugh, and began to apologize for his partner's abrupt exit—"I'm sorry about that. You guys know things like this don't usually happen here and, on top of that, it happened at the school, so there's a lot of pressure coming down. And we are nowhere on the other murder. And—." He interrupted his mea culpa and leaned back in his chair before saying, "Yeah, there's a lot of pressure to close this one, but Harley, how do I put this? Harley's a prick. He was some big-time detective in Chicago, but there were more than a few accusations of abuse that the higher-ups looked the other way on, but then he arrested the son of an alderman—drugs or something, and worked him over pretty good. They couldn't overlook that, but the alderman wasn't wild about the press finding out about his kid's extracurricular activities, so they agreed that it was best for all of them for Harley to resign. No one would hire him, but the chief had worked patrol with him when they were both starting out, so he goes from all the action in the Windy City to the mean streets of East Lansing. Let's just say he hasn't adjusted too well."

I'd known cops like Harley when I was on the force in Detroit. Although some of them were bad from the start and used the uniform to mask their own insecurities and prejudices, most started out believing that they were the "good guys" whose job it was to protect the community and make it a safe place for everyone. Unfortunately, life, particularly in a big city, isn't always so black and white. Even "good" people do bad things, and over time, all the lines begin to blur and everyone becomes culpable in one way or another. The mother whose son was just shot down in the street should have known he was in a gang, the crack addict is just as guilty in his own way as the person who sold it to him, and the young girl hit by a stray bullet is simply collateral damage in an ongoing, unwinnable war. For guys like Harley, the only distinction between cop and criminal was that one wore a badge.

Since we were all in agreement that Harley probably wasn't the person you'd want soliciting donations for the Policemen's Memorial Fund, I turned back to the question of the disparity between what happened on the third and fourth floors. "I've looked at the layout of the library. The stairwell doors are located on the eastern side of the building, so whoever did this came out of the third-floor stairwell and pushed on the shelves at that end, but I don't understand why they'd get to the fourth floor and run to the opposite end to tip over the last three shelves in the row."

While Harley didn't seem to find this unusual, it was obvious Ward wasn't so sure. "We've been working to answer that. Harley is convinced that the same people are responsible for what happened on both floors. The campus police had the building on lockdown in less than 10 minutes. We've checked ourselves and it's virtually impossible for someone to run back to the door on the fourth floor and down the stairs and out the main doors in that time. And based on everyone we've talked with, your brother didn't have any enemies. I have to admit that everything continues to point back to a protest that went very wrong."

"I guess what I'm not seeing is why are you so sure that it was the protestors that did this?" I asked, "Like you said, there were over 300 students in there as well."

Ward took a drink from his can of Diet Coke, and looked a little sheepish as he responded, "My fault. I've been going over this so many times I forgot to tell you we *do* have multiple witnesses that say they saw three or four people dressed in the protestors' black hoodies running toward the ground floor stairwell door."

"But no one has been able to identify them?" Olivia

interjected.

"All the witness accounts are consistent. They only saw them from behind, and we've haven't been able to get anything from any of the Planet Action people so far. Our best shot is to get one of them to roll on the others, but right now, all we can really charge them with is trespassing and vandalism which doesn't give us a real hammer to threaten them with."

"What about their leaders?" I asked. "Can't you charge them with inciting a riot?"

"We still might, but they're claiming it was a peaceful protest until some of the kids in the library started to get physical. It's a difficult case to make and the DA refuses to go there unless we can find something more conclusive, and I doubt we're going to find anyone who's going to tell us that someone told them, 'Let's go to the library and kick some ass' even though it's obvious they went there hoping something would happen. You've got a right to protest and express your opinion, but if you think that violence is the best way to get your point across, maybe the problem is you."

It was obvious that, at least at this point, Ward and Harley were stonewalled. "So what is your plan going forward?"

"It's tough since Planet Action has circled the wagons. Right now, we're talking to the university about working with us to lean on them by threatening all of them with suspension or expulsion. A legal slap on the wrist is one thing, but the thought of the kid coming back home to live might cause mommy and daddy to do a little arm twisting, but so far the school isn't willing to go that far, especially with this divestment vote scheduled for Saturday."

"Why would that make any difference?"

"Your guess is as good as mine. But then again, I don't understand why anybody would pay attention to a bunch of folks who think the world is a great place except for the people. Let them drive their Priuses and leave the rest of us alone."

"You must be a real popular guy living in a college town."

"Hey, I call them like I see them."

All three of us laughed, and then I asked him about the murdered professor. Both happening on the same night couldn't be a coincidence. "You said you were nowhere on the other murder. It seems like they must be linked somehow."

Ward shook his head and divulged, "That's the way we see it, but the building was empty at the time. His body wasn't found until the next evening. Cleaning woman. Being part of the library protest makes sense. He didn't exactly hide the fact that he thought the whole climate-change thing was bullshit. We dusted the whole office but as you might expect, as a professor he had students going in and out, and there were no prints on the body. His computer didn't show anything unusual. It looks like he was working on an exam for one of his classes when the killer surprised him. We do have the killer's blood. Found it on this square paperweight thing that was used to bash in Walker's head. That will be great when we have a suspect. There's almost 50,000 students here and God knows how many faculty and staff, and that's even if he was killed by someone with a connection to campus. You could say that the suspect pool is pretty large."

Some cases are like that. He and Harley would continue to work it but with no witnesses and no one with a clear motive, their only real hope is that someone who did know what happened might come forward, or place an anonymous call. Eventually, people lose interest in even the highest-profile cases, and the press moves on except for maybe a periodic retrospective on the case, including a few theories by self-declared "forensic experts" but even those would taper off with time. Ultimately, the Walker murder would wind up on a cold-case shelf in the East Lansing PD's basement.

I was about to tell Ward I knew where he was coming from when it hit me.

"Wait a minute. It just came to me. You're Brian Ward, the point guard. I knew I'd seen you before. I saw you play as a freshman. You were good, but something happened."

He smiled. "That's me. I went to high school here, saw you play a few times, and playing for the Spartans was my dream, but then I blew out my knee at Purdue and that was it. I tried to come back, but I wasn't the same. Quickness and speed were gone. Coach Izzo was great. Let me keep my scholarship. Got my degree in criminal justice and joined the force. I guess some people would say I'm not very ambitious, but I like it here. Gotta a house, a wife—she's a doctor, and a 5-year-old boy."

"He gonna play ball?"

"Let's put it this way. I started taking him to games before he could talk. The other day my mom asked him what he wanted to be when he grew up. Most kids you know, they say they want to be a policeman or a firefighter, but he didn't hesitate. Told her, 'I'm going to be a Spartan and play for coach Izzo.' I'm good with that. How about you? How'd you wind up as a PI?"

"Well, after my 'departure,' I finished up my degree at Wayne State. After that, I spent five years with the Detroit PD. Finally figured out that I like working alone, so I got my investigator's license and here I am."

"Look man," I continued, "we've taken up enough of your time. I think I'll talk to that grad advisor Knowles just to get a feel for what Tim was working on and see if he knows why he was in the library that night. At least try to make a little more sense of the thing. I'll keep you guys in the loop on the off chance I find anything. If you'd do the same, I'd appreciate it."

"Not a problem. I'll just have to hide in a closet so Harley doesn't see. He is one tightly wound dude."

Chapter 8

The spring flowering plants in the Beal Botanical Gardens were in full bloom, producing a colorful mosaic. Deep wine-colored Japanese maples intermingled with the multiple shades of green offered by a variety of conifers were complemented by the vibrant accents of yellow daffodils, purple irises, red and pink azaleas, and a rainbow of tulips. This was her favorite time of year. Every season brought its own unique beauty to the Michigan State campus, but even a crisp blanket of snow or the brilliant reds, yellows, and oranges that fall brought to the trees along the Red Cedar River were no match for the palette of colors that was reborn every spring.

University President Margaret Sanborn stood staring out of her office window looking at the gardens. She did this a few times a day to relax and refocus, but the events of the day had already negated their calming effect. In the two years since she'd come to MSU from the University of Miami, she'd been able to forge a strong relationship with the school's board of regents. They'd backed her decision to fire both the hockey coach and athletic director three months after her arrival and to undertake a $500 million building initiative to upgrade the on-campus cyclotron and replace the Natural Science Building to complement an aggressive high school-recruitment effort targeted at bringing more National Merit Scholars to the campus. Better facilities and an influx of students in STEM (science, technology, engineering, and mathematics) fields would provide fertile ground for new research initiatives, and that meant more federal and private grant money, the real measuring stick for a school to move up in the academic pecking order. When she'd presented the proposal to the board, she'd made clear that her long-term goal was to make the university one of the top ten research institutions in the country, bypassing the University of Michigan in the process. They'd bought into her vision, and if they surpassed the school down the road in Ann Arbor, so much the better. But now, the foundation she'd built was crumbling beneath her.

The calls for the university to divest its holdings of all fossil fuel-related businesses had started out as a few words on signs at some small on-campus protests. "When exactly did the passion and idealism finally give way to more cynical, pragmatic perspectives?" she wondered. She smiled softly to herself and sat down upon one of the upholstered wingback chairs that guarded the antique Chippendale breakfront she'd bought upon her arrival.

Somehow the "divest" demand galvanized the school's multiple environmental groups and suddenly the random ten-to twenty-person protest had become organized into 200–300 person demonstrations that included more and more of the faculty, with attendant media coverage. All the state's major papers had taken sides on the issue, talk radio had made it a staple of discussion and even the *New York Times* had weighed in with an editorial stating that Michigan State had become the first "true university battleground" in the war against climate change. Open civil war had broken out within the board and by a 5–3 vote, a date for a final vote on the issue had been scheduled.

Sanborn didn't have a strong opinion on climate change one way or the other. It's not that she doubted that the earth might be warming, but since it had been hotter and colder at different points in history, fluctuations in solar activity made more sense to her than CO_2 emissions. Apocalyptic predictions of what might happen in 100 years also struck her as senseless demagoguery. People have adapted to the changes in the climate for centuries, and she didn't see why it would be any different now. One hundred years is a long time to prepare for events that may—or may not—happen.

Divesting the university's fossil fuel-related endowments would impact the school's $2.5 billion endowment fund by up to $500 million. That alone would have a dramatic impact on finances, but the fallout within the ranks of the alumni donors was incalculable. Ken Wheeler, a graduate who'd made his fortune by building an international oil rig services company, routinely donated a million or more a year. That would be gone, and who knows how many others he might take with him.

Those donors advocating for divestment were important, but no single one of them matched Wheeler's level of contribution, and an analysis she'd had run by the Alumni and Fund Raising Office indicated that the impact of a decision not to divest would be considerably less than the alternative. Dealing with the fallout from multiple "green" organizations would be unpleasant, but losing $500 million and a substantial number of major donors would be devastating. To head off a potential schism, she had lobbied the board for a more diversified, balanced portfolio strategy that would dilute the total fossil fuel-related holdings, but hardliners from both sides had rejected it. The friction between them had also been exacerbated by the two murders that had taken place, particularly the one of Tim Price. The divestment faction had adopted him as a martyr to their cause, even though the police suspected that one or more Planet Action demonstrators had toppled the shelves that killed him. Their opponents also were trying to capitalize on the tragedy by railing against them with charges of extremism, and the word 'terrorists' had invaded more than one conversation she'd had with a regent or outraged alumnus.

She checked her watch. It was ten minutes until her meeting with Grayson Tyler. She'd never met him, but in her time as a college president, she'd met plenty like him. Preening sons and daughters from well-to-do families who after a life of spent in homes the size of a shopping center, expensive private schools, and weekends at the country club rebelled against all the "injustices and exploitation" their parents stood for by vocally supporting the right causes before joining dad's firm or taking a Wall Street job. 'Arrogant' and 'clueless' was how she described them. She'd been unsuccessful up to now in steering the board toward a "no" vote on divestment, or even a tie where she could cast the deciding vote. Being "green" may be a nice way to demonstrate you care about the planet, but the color has a much different context at a major university, and she thought Grayson Tyler might be able to help her in getting the board to recognize that distinction.

Her thoughts were interrupted by the intercom on her desk that her assistant used to inform her that "Mr. Tyler was here." Sanborn told her to give her just a minute and then show him in. In that time she walked over to her large—pool tables were smaller—hand-carved wooden desk, sat down in the overstuffed leather chair that stood behind it, and prepared to meet young Mr. Tyler.

As her assistant ushered Grayson Tyler into the room, Sanborn couldn't help but think that he was a walking cliché. Expensively cut sandy-blond hair stood atop his lean 5'10" frame. His face was all precise angles that suggested the perpetual smugness of one who'd never served, suffered, or sacrificed but had no problem demanding everyone else do so. He was dressed in a long-sleeved blue-striped Polo button-down shirt, Rag & Bone khakis, and suede Burberry loafers. She didn't stand to greet him as he was led to one of the chairs across from her desk but before he sat, she leaned forward to shake his hand, forcing him to all but lunge across its broad expanse. After evaluating her options, Sanborn concluded that a successful resolution to the vote depended on changing the nature of public opinion. On a factual level, the benefits of fossil fuel usage were not only indisputable economically, but the correlation between their usage and the growth and development of emerging nations was also well documented. The issue of climate change had driven all interested parties to the extremes. Whether climate change was largely a function of human activity or not, the belief in the need for radical changes in the sources of energy production had reached a level bordering on religious zealotry and the purveyors of oil, gasoline, and natural gas were regularly under siege.

In Sanborn's experience, emotional appeals were always preferable to intellectual debate and those who shouted the loudest usually won out in the end. The tragic events of the previous Saturday night had certainly cast a level of suspicion on the tactics of the supporters of the divest movement, but although the police suspected Planet Action protestors for the death of Tim Price, they had been unable to identify and arrest any suspects. An arrest or arrests of Planet Action protestors would call into question the motives of members of the divest movement, including positioning them as violent extremists to some of those currently occupying a middle ground, and this change in public perception might dissuade some regents from voting to divest. This was her strongest course of action. She had little doubt that Grayson Tyler knew who the perpetrators were, and she had some tools of persuasion that weren't available to the police.

Tyler sat down and crossed one khaki-covered leg over the other. If he was nervous about being summoned to a meeting with the president of the school with no reason given, he didn't show it. He gave off an air of casual arrogance. Sanborn gave him a thin smile and opened the file that lay before her.

"Let's see. Grayson Tyler, Brother Rice High School, political science major, 3.2 GPA. Looks like you've just got a couple summer classes to go before you graduate."

Tyler sat up a little straighter, and a subtle smile grew across his face. Sanborn looked at him over the top of her steel-rimmed reading glasses. This kid has been told how great he is his entire life. "Just another one of the 'everyone's-special' drones that school systems seemed to spew out in increasing numbers each year," she thought to herself. She glanced back down at the file and continued, "You're one of the leaders of Planet Action, and I see you are going to work for Congressmen Perkins when you graduate."

A brief look of surprise appeared in his eyes — he hadn't told anyone about the job in Washington. It had been hard to keep it to himself. He hadn't even told his parents. Working as an aide focused on environmental issues to the congressman was just the first step in the career he envisioned. He'd calculatingly been working toward this during his four years as an undergraduate. Every class taken, the selection of his academic advisor, and the organizations he joined had been part of the process. It had been during his junior year that he decided that climate change was the issue that presented the fastest path for advancement in Democratic politics. For him, it was a means to an end, and he'd ride the wave as far as it would take him. It wasn't that he didn't care about the global impact of rising temperatures on the planet, but a couple of degrees over 100 years didn't particularly strike him as any reason to cut back on the air conditioning or start driving an electric car.

It was only for a moment, but Sanborn detected the look of disbelief in his eyes. She'd surprised him. She had known that she would. "Oh, was that a secret?" she queried, laying the knife to skin. "I have a few friends in Washington; one of them must have mentioned it."

He didn't know exactly why, but Tyler realized that what was about to be said in the next few minutes could undo everything he'd spent the last four years working towards. His heart began to beat faster in his chest, and he could feel heat rise on the back of his neck. Something seized in his stomach and every muscle in his back felt like a knotted rope. Through conscious effort, he kept control of his breathing while he uncrossed his legs and leaned back a little in the chair to relieve some of the tension. He didn't know where President Sanborn was about to go with this conversation, but he knew he had to keep calm if he was going to be able to navigate his way through it.

"It's not a big deal. I thought I'd keep it a secret so I could surprise my parents by telling them in person," he said with feigned indifference.

"I'm sure they'd be very proud if the job was still available to you. As I'm sure you know, Grayson, Washington is a city that runs on secrets, but everyone pretends to be above reproach and no one invites controversy into their office."

His face fell like a shade. "You see, your little group's actions have attracted a good deal of attention to you and this university. A young man and a member of our faculty died, Grayson, and the police have no suspects. This puts both of us in an untenable situation."

She spoke slow and methodically, continually pushing her metaphoric knife deeper and deeper. Were his eyes starting to get moist and glassy? She wasn't sure.

He couldn't feel his legs or his arms and his heart was racing. He was an animal caught in a trap, and Sanborn was closing in on her prey. Too quickly he blurted out--did his voice just crack?—"I've told the police everything I know. No one wanted that to happen, but—"

She quickly interrupted him. "No one ever wants something like this to happen," she said evenly, "but it did. I've got a problem here, Grayson, and I see you as the solution. I can make a formal recommendation to the Scholastic Committee that you be expelled for inciting a violent incident on campus, not to mention the damage that was done. Everyone wants to see the guilt in this situation personified. Doesn't matter if you did it or not, you'll still be guilty. Making you the 'face' of this tragedy doesn't totally make my problem go away, but it will buy me the time I need."

He was crying now and had to gulp for air between every few words. "I didn't do it," he wailed. "You've got no right to do this to me" was issued and followed up by a futile attempt at what, intimidation? "I'll call my dad—"

"I've got a phone right here, Grayson, but you see a decision to expel you is up to the school alone. Oh, he can attend the deliberations, and even speak on your behalf, but in the end, you'll be asked to leave and that decision will be irrevocable. And shortly after that, you'll receive a nice note from the congressman saying that they don't have an opening after all, but wishing you the best of luck in your future endeavors."

At that moment, she let her face soften, and she looked at him with empathy in her eyes and leaned toward him as she continued, "But, I think you know who is responsible for this don't you?"

Tears mingled with snot on his face. He tried his best to wipe them away with his sleeve. He did know, but they'd agreed to remain united. There would be charges for vandalism and trespassing and possibly even inciting a riot. Those could get knocked down to misdemeanors, and maybe some of them dismissed outright, but the police wouldn't be able to prove anything regarding Tim Price's unfortunate demise if they didn't talk.

He didn't think twice.

Two hours later, the East Lansing police received an anonymous tip.

Chapter 9

Sometimes it's what you don't see or hear that makes you think that things aren't exactly as they appear. It's human nature to try and make things fit the narrative, and even though every investigator you'll ever meet says they "follow wherever the facts lead them," it's a skill few of them truly master. We see things as they are. It's simpler that way. We believe people are inherently good, and can't conceive that the old guy on the corner who keeps his yard immaculate could be a child molester, or that the woman in front of us at the grocery store would shoot her husband while he's sleeping. But sometimes they are, and they do.

A good investigator let's himself go to places others won't and asks questions any "nice" person would never ask to determine what happened. Yeah, they also tend to have pretty fucked-up personal lives, an occupational hazard you might say. I think I'm good at my job, but I'm also a homeowner, small business operator, regular voter, and I pay my taxes on time, so even though my longest relationship is with my dog, I think I'm doing a pretty good job of maintaining my work/life balance.

However, after listening to Harley and Ward, I had becoming increasingly convinced that while blaming Planet Action for Tim's death made sense on a superficial level, they—or at least Ward—had doubts regarding the veracity of the theory.

I was glad Olivia decided not to exercise her right to tell me

"I told you so." As we sat in my car in the police parking lot, I verbally ran through what Ward had told us to enable Olivia to verify what we'd heard.

"Everything about their theory of the case makes sense. Even that Professor Walker's murder is tied in some way to the events in the library. But there are gaps that aren't supported by any actual evidence. No one saw what happened on the fourth floor, and why did they bypass all the rows between the stairwell door until they would have been close enough to see, or at least hear, Tim working in the carrel? They certainly wanted to cause some damage but killing someone, no way. And the Walker murder doesn't fit. What does breaking into a single professor's office in a completely different building have to do with a protest?"

As she endured my hypothesis, Olivia was content to not interrupt and let me ramble.

"But, even if Tim's death wasn't the result of the protest, why would anyone want to kill him?"

We both let my question hang in the air for a few seconds until she broke the silence with the question first, "So what now?" I wasn't sure. It was followed up with a practical suggestion of "You must be starving. Why don't we go to lunch and figure it out there?"

I was, and I couldn't come up with a better idea.

The Peanut Barrel is a burger-and-beer joint that features a pail of peanuts on each table and has been a student staple forever. Since the average college student is very adaptable, eating a grease-laden burger—the best kind—along with a basket of fries that would feed a small third-world country is acceptable fare at any time of day, so the place was already packed when we arrived. As I've gotten older, I've found that when it comes to food, I will sacrifice quality for brevity every time and I was just about to suggest that we leave when I heard someone call out, "Hey, Mitch!"

A couple of people turned at the sound—I guess Mitch is a more common name than I would have thought—but when I saw Billy Addington striding toward me, I aptly deduced that I was the party in question. Billy was one of the nicest people I've ever known but when he strapped on a helmet and shoulder pads, his behavior bordered on the psychopathic. He was 6'5" and when he'd played he'd weighed 250 pounds, which from the looks of him was about 20 or 30 pounds ago, and when he hit someone, they looked like they'd stepped on a landmine. He had an apron tied around his waist and got from behind the bar to the doorway and proceeded to where we were standing in about two steps, at which point he embraced me in a spine-adjusting bear hug that most people pay a chiropractor a couple of hundred bucks for.

"Man, I can't believe you're here!" Olivia received much the same greeting but with less spinal fusion.

Billy was one of those guys that even if you haven't seen them for 20 years, it was like you were still in the middle of the last conversation you had. As Olivia and I checked ourselves to make sure no lasting damage had been done, he said, "You guys here for lunch? Let me grab you a table" and with that, he walked over to a two-top and gave its occupants the "It's time to pay the check and leave" look and two minutes later, we were sitting at our freshly bused table. Billy pulled up a chair from a nearby table and sat down.

In rapid-fire fashion, he attempted to close the gap from when we'd last seen each other. "What are you guys doing here? Are you still a cop? Seen any of the games this year? Are you guys together? Married? Kids?" Olivia smiled as Billy paused to take a breath and I did my best to respond. "No, I'm a private investigator now, and Olivia asked me if I would look at her brother's death. Caught a couple and I'm optimistic about this season, and no, we aren't together, although we are both still single and I have no offspring that I know of, but I can't speak for Olivia."

She offered, "I remain childless" as clarification.

Raising his voice so he could be heard over the lunchtime din, Billy said, "I didn't know that was your brother. I'm so sorry. I hope you don't mind me asking, but I thought the police said it was some of those 'green' wackos."

For various reasons, I didn't want to get into a detailed explanation about the actual purpose of my visit, or that I was beginning to agree with Olivia's suspicions, so I said, "Nothing like that. For insurance purposes, it helps to have a second verifying opinion." Then I immediately changed the subject: "So what about you? Do you manage this place? Last I remember, you were with the Browns."

"Well", Billy began, "one kind of led to the other. I *was* playing for the Browns, and in the off-season, I was coming back to finish my degree. I finished it up two years ago, and about that time, the guy who owned this place decided to sell it. I figured it would be a good investment. I mean look around. I figure if MSU doesn't move, this place will never go out of business. Anyway, that season I blew out my knee. The doctors took one look and said that was it. So, I decided I was going to be a "hands-on" owner. So far it's been great."

He pulled out his wallet and opened it to show us pictures of his wife and daughter as he finished. Olivia declared they were both adorable and appeared to get a little misty when she looked at the one of Billy and his daughter walking, her tiny hand engulfed in his. Just then, a loud crash emanated from the kitchen, and after entering my number in his phone, Billy left to resolve one of the many issues that I'm sure "hands-on" owners deal with every day.

An extremely up-beat waitress named Cheri came and took our order: Rodeo Burger, fries, and a Diet Coke for me and a pear salad and iced tea for Olivia. As we ate, we discussed the best way to proceed. If someone meant to kill Tim, there was no apparent motive. Except for the occasional unfortunate accident, most people who kill someone tend to be *highly motivated*. To determine if his death had been purposeful, we needed to get a better understanding of who he was, what he was working on, and his recent interactions with friends and contemporaries. In other words, we needed to try and determine who disliked him so much that they thought dropping a thousand pounds or so of books on top of him was a good idea.

"Did Tim have any friends or neighbors that he was close to?" I asked.

Olivia shook her head. "You knew him. He was high functioning, but he didn't have any friends per se, or at least not any that he ever told me about. He might have talked about someone in his graduate program from time to time, but I don't remember anyone specific. He did share an office with someone, but I can't remember his name right now."

"Okay, so he had no close friends. He did have neighbors though, and we need to talk to them. You never know what might set someone off. Back when I was working in Detroit, we had a case where a guy killed his neighbor because the color of his garbage cans didn't match. We also need to talk with that professor Ward mentioned, Knowles. He was his advisor and head of his dissertation committee. They must have spent a lot of time together. Did he ever mention him to you?"

"Only in passing. I know he liked him. He was the main reason Tim chose to come here. His father was one of the original scientists who identified the impact of increased levels of CO_2 on the climate, and Knowles has become one of the major voices of the climate-change movement. They've helped make MSU one of the leaders in climate research. Tim was really excited about working with him."

"Have you ever met him, like at one of those faculty party type of things?"

She looked at me like I had a third eyeball and said, "No, Mitch. We're not even in the same department, and I think you've seen one too many movies. Faculty life isn't a perpetual round of cocktail parties where everyone stands around putting knives in the backs of people they're competing with for tenure."

"Okay, good to know. Let's go talk to Knowles. Is it possible to see what his schedule is online?"

Olivia opened up her laptop and began to type. "His schedule and office hours will be on his web page, but that doesn't guarantee he'll be there if he has open time. He had one class today at 10:20 and no scheduled office hours. Let me call and see if he's in."

With that, she grabbed her phone from her bag and dialed Knowles' office. "No answer, just voice mail. Should I leave a message?"

"Let's try the admin first."

She dialed a second number and got a live body. She introduced herself and explained that she was the professor in the Computer Science Department whose brother, and Dr. Knowles' student, had died in the library incident and would like to meet with him for a few minutes—for closure. The woman must have been obliging because the next thing I heard was, "Oh, I'd appreciate that," and she made a gesture for me to write something down. "Okay, I'm ready. 6248 Heathfield Drive. Great. Thank you very much."

The lunch crowd was beginning to thin out as she stashed

her phone away, so we could use our "inside voices" to carry on our conversation.

"She told me he's been working from home for the past few days when he doesn't have class, and she knows he's home because he just called her. His house isn't too far from here — fifteen minutes or so at most."

"Sounds like we should pay him a visit", I said. I motioned to Cheri for the check, and after a quick good-bye and a promise to "stay in touch" to Billy, we were back in the car and on our way to the home of Professor Arthur Knowles.

We were about halfway to Knowles' house when my phone rang. Brian Ward was on the other end. "Hey," he said, "I thought I'd let you know before you heard it on the news or something. We arrested three of the Planet Action protesters about fifteen minutes ago for Doctor Price's brother's murder."

If this were a movie, I'd have done a double take, but I couldn't see a reason for comedic effect, so instead I mouthed to Olivia that they'd made the arrests and asked, "Where did this come from? Two hours ago, you had a theory and no suspects and now you have three people under arrest. What happened? Have they said anything?"

Judging by his response, I think Ward was only slightly less surprised at this recent turn of good fortune. "We got an anonymous call on the tip line giving us the names of the three people responsible. They're all students, two males that both live in the same apartment and the third, a girl, in one of the dorms. Each of them broke down as soon as we arrived. Admitted that they pushed the shelves over on the third floor but had nothing to do with what happened on the fourth. The only conflict in their stories is who came up with the idea in the first place. We grabbed everything we could out of each of their rooms, including the hoodies they all wore. No signs of blood on any of them," he said.

It was hard to keep my eyes on the road, listen to Ward, and try to decipher the questions Olivia was pantomiming to me, so I pulled into an apartment complex and parked before I asked, "Did any of them have a connection to Tim?"

"I don't think so. None said they knew him and we've had a chance to cross-check their class schedules. They're all underclassman and they weren't in any of the same classes, and none of them were in any classes that Tim taught or TA'd for."

"That's not a whole lot. Do you believe them?"

The fact that Ward didn't hesitate before responding underlined my belief that he was shooting straight with me.

He replied, "I'm not sure. It just doesn't feel right to me. Their stories are consistent, and I know most people don't look like they could kill someone, but these three, no way. One looks like a band geek, the other's an ex-high school jock, and the girl was a cheerleader and all of them look scared out of their minds."

"So, what are you going to charge them with?"

"For now, murder two."

"Not manslaughter?" I interrupted.

"No. As of now, they still are the only suspects we have for your friend's brother's death, and Harley's convinced that they did it and is itching to get another crack at them before their attorneys' get here. Says he's let them sweat long enough. Maybe he thinks this is his ticket out of here. Back to Chicago as the conquering hero, that type of thing."

"What about the DA? Does she feel the same way that Harley does, or is she just looking to make a name for herself?"

"Nah, I don't think so," Ward replied. "I think she and the school would just like this to be put to rest as quickly and quietly as possible. I don't think they see any clear winners here. I'm sure she'll offer them a plea."

"So, what happens next? Are you guys going to take another run at them to see if they might know anything about who killed Tim?"

"Like I said, Harley's going to try. I don't think that's going to get us much. Their stories are completely in sync. A couple more minutes with Harley might take care of that. They'll be taking them over to be arraigned in a little while. I'm sure they'll get bail. Don't know anything about their backgrounds or how much money their families may have, but you know those parents are going to do everything: mortgage the house, sell the portfolio, to make sure their kid doesn't spend a night in jail. Can't blame them. These kids aren't exactly prison material, if you know what I mean."

"Most prisoners aren't in there due to their outstanding social skills," I said, "but even though someone dropped a dime on them, it seems like it might be a heavy lift to get a jury to convict."

"It might but we've got a dead body and three kids whose actions match the method used to kill him. I've seen cases made with less and I've got no real credible alternative theory."

I asked Olivia if she had any more questions. She shook her head no.

"Okay, I guess that's all I have to ask right now. Good luck with Harley. We're on our way to see Knowles, Tim's committee head. I'll let you know if that turns up anything. Keep me in the loop on your end if you can."

Ward said he would and ten minutes later, Olivia and I arrived at the residence of Professor Arthur Knowles.

Chapter 10

Knowles lived in one of those areas where you have neighbors but don't have to see them if you don't want to. Each home sat on at least an acre of land and was surrounded by enough trees to qualify as a forest. Although it was only three in the afternoon, the shadows cast by the array of maples, oaks, cedars, and pines were already doing their best imitation of an eclipse, and solar-powered lights illuminated the porches of the houses we passed.

Knowles lived in the last house on the dead-end street. It was built on a rise facing back down the length of the street, giving it the appearance of the home of a feudal lord looking down upon the inferior accommodations of his vassals. The house itself was one of those concrete-and-glass abominations that resemble the answer to a geometry problem gone horribly wrong, and fit in with its surroundings like a cold sore on the Mona Lisa.

After navigating a path that would have satisfied half the daily-step requirement of a FitBit, we arrived at a metal front door whose last place of employment must have been an industrial warehouse. To avoid breaking my hand, I chose to ring the doorbell and shortly thereafter, the door opened to reveal a well-dressed young woman who couldn't have been older than either Olivia or me. She smiled and said, "Hello. May I help you?"

She was petite, maybe 5'3", and wore a rose-colored top with gray slacks and a diamond bracelet and wedding ring that together were worth the equivalent of the GDP of an island nation. Her blonde hair was fashioned in what used to be called a "pixie cut" that accentuated her small nose, blue eyes, and full lips.

I figured she must have been Knowles' daughter, so I asked if either Mr. or Mrs. Knowles were in.

"I'm Mrs. Knowles. I was just on my way out. My ride should be here in a moment."

Having clarified the family-pecking order, Olivia and I introduced ourselves and explained that if it was convenient, we'd like to speak with her husband regarding Tim's research and perhaps find out why he had been in the library that evening.

"Oh, my God. Arthur told me all about it. I am so sorry for your loss. As a matter of fact, he's in his study right now. I'm sure he'd be happy to speak with you. Please come in."

She stepped aside and we entered the foyer. "He's taken your brother's death very hard. He says it a senseless tragedy like the accident that killed his roommate in graduate school," she said.

"What happened to his roommate?" I asked.

"He was killed in a car accident. His name was Kevin Adams. Arthur says he's the real reason he decided to make climate change the focus of his research. His dad was already one of the foremost experts in the field, but he didn't want to be compared to his father. Kevin was very interested in it. You could say he was Arthur's father's protégé. It was only after he died that he shifted his research emphasis."

If it was possible, the house seemed even bigger on the inside. From our vantage point, we could see a living room that was about the size of a mall parking lot and a dining room that could easily have been rented out to host weddings and bar mitzvahs. Both rooms were furnished in a minimalist style that people who live in "modern" houses seem to prefer.

Everything was a mélange of white leather and chrome, with each piece of furniture carefully selected from what I could only assume was the Marque de Sade collection. The floors were gray-stained concrete accented by strategically placed—what else—white rugs. Taken all together, the place offered all the warmth and charm of an airplane hangar. Before I could offer up something lame like "I like what you've done with place," Olivia without a hint of false sincerity said, "You have a lovely home."

As she began leading us down a long hallway that seemed to divide the house, she responded to the compliment: "Oh, thank you, but I've been wanting to redecorate this place forever. Arthur's ex-wife did all of this, and I think it's as cold as she was, or at least as cold as he says she was. It's not very inviting."

I had to agree. Most hospital rooms have more of a 'Come in, put your feet up' feel than the humble abode of the Knowles family.

Perhaps feeling there wasn't much more to say about interior design, Olivia asked her, "How long have you two been married, Mrs. Knowles?"

"Sara, please. A little over a year. It all happened quite quickly. I always figured I'd get married, but I thought it would be after I finished my master's at least."

"Oh, were you a student here?"

"I was in geosciences. I was halfway to getting my master's when Arthur asked me to be his TA. Everything else just kind of happened from there. Arthur got his divorce and we were married fourteen months ago."

I guess Dr. Knowles liked to get close to his students.

Before either of us could follow up on the Knowles' matrimonial history, Mrs. Knowles opened a door to her right and led us into the study. It shared the same basic design theme as the rest of the house, with its most striking feature being an exterior wall made up of floor-to-ceiling windows. An older man was sitting in a white leather chair next to a large fireplace, while Knowles sat at a glass-topped desk that looked out of the window wall at the myriad trees lining the side of the house. Sara Knowles announced our arrival and explained to him who we were and that we had come to speak with him about Tim.

Arthur Knowles turned his chair and rose to greet us. He was built like a runner with his 6'4" frame composed of long, lean muscle topped with a face that resembled the bust of a Roman emperor. His gray-flecked black hair brushed backed from his face accentuated his gray-blue eyes and aquiline nose, and his skin bore a faint olive hue. Dressed in a cream sweater and mocha-colored pants, neither of which were available in any store you might find at the local mall, he radiated an air of condescension so heavy that I thought he might pat me on my head rather than shake my hand. After he looked over Olivia like a connoisseur reviewing a wine list, he shook her hand as well and invited us to sit down on one of those couches that was as comfortable as a park bench. Before he sat, he introduced the man sitting in the chair as his father, Dr. Patrick Knowles, professor emeritus of the Geoscience Department. His father didn't acknowledge us or the introduction but rather sat staring down at his shirt, which prompted Knowles to explain, "Please excuse my father. Early on-set Alzheimer's. He has his good days and bad. Today, unfortunately, is not one of his better ones. Sara, do you think you could take dad to his room? He looks tired" and with that, Mrs. Knowles gently helped Patrick Knowles from his chair and guided him out of the room.

"Mitch McKay, why does the name seem so familiar?" His face was a study in concentration, and just as I was about to explain that I was a private investigator, he said, "I remember now. You were that football player who was expelled in some type of cheating incident. As I recall, it caused quite a scandal at the time."

"Yes, sir", I offered. "That was a long time ago. I'm a private investigator who is helping Ms. Price tie up some loose ends regarding her brother's death."

"What loose ends would require a private detective?" he asked while looking at me like I was something that he'd just found on the bottom of his shoe.

"I'm a friend of the family. We just have a few questions and from what we gather, you might have been the person closest to Tim" to which Olivia added, "My brother, as you know, was not overly talkative and he rarely spoke about his research. I guess I'm just trying to make sense of what happened."

"I'll tell you what I can," he said as he sat down in the chair vacated by his father. ""Let me begin by saying that I think your brother's death was the tragic result of the actions of an overzealous mob. We may tangentially share a concern for the impact of human activity on the planet and the dangers of its effects, but their passions come from a place of fear and an overdeveloped need to belong to a cause. My concerns are not based on raw emotions whipped into a frenzy by a group of leaders brandishing the rhetoric of a carnival barker. Lenin referred to these types of advocates as 'useful idiots'; I believe that description to be an accurate summation. Your brother had one of the most brilliant minds I have ever had the pleasure of mentoring. I think the politics surrounding the issues we are continually seeking to better understand does violence to the fact that people like myself, my father and your brother are, were scientists. Theories cannot simply be made up. Our findings are the result of objective, empirical research.

That's what makes your brother's death even more tragic. I can only speculate on the breakthroughs that he might have made throughout his career."

Olivia interrupted his soliloquy by asking, "What exactly was Tim working on, professor? The last time I spoke with him he seemed excited about the progress he was making on his dissertation. He didn't explain it to me, but he did say that he thought his findings could be very helpful in understanding—what did he call it, climate cycles or the cycle of climate, something like that."

Knowles got up and began to pace back and forth across from where Olivia and I were sitting. As he began speaking, I couldn't help but think he was addressing us in the same way that he'd talk to a class.

"Thanks to the work of scientists like my father, and those of us who have followed, climate change is a scientifically proven theory," he lectured.

I wanted to ask him why he thought there were scientists who disagreed with his assertion, but he was on a roll, so I couldn't see any reason to interrupt him.

He continued, "The overarching goal now is to understand the interaction of all elements with greater precision, so that we may speak more confidently of the sequence of corresponding impacts and their severity and develop empirically based solutions to arrest them. Let me provide you with a little background that will help you understand what your brother was working on."

His pacing had brought him back to his desk, where he absent-mindedly arranged some papers and while staring out the full-length window, he continued, "You see there are many elements that must be factored into the development of a climate model. Although we continue to improve our understanding of the interrelationship between the variables that effect longer-term climate trends, in this case warming, their predictive accuracy is an area that is continually being refined. This is not to say that we don't understand what the long-term impact will be, that is an area that the most zealous of our opponents continue to use to arouse the passions of those who do not understand the complexity of the issues involved and refuse to believe that we will suffer severe consequences, if we continue to not to take corrective action. Perhaps the variable that we least understand is the impact of cloud formations. We know they have a 'prophylactic effect' by shielding the sun, but we are far from understanding their formation patterns and their interactions with things like our oceans and their rate of evaporation. Your brother's efforts were focused on developing a true predictive model of cloud formation and corresponding impact that could be used in our climate models to provide a higher level of predictive accuracy, as well as aid us in understanding our historical climate temperature patterns."

"I assume he must have had some success", offered Olivia. "Like I said, he seemed excited about it. He said that he'd already completed over a third of his dissertation."

Knowles returned to his chair, shook his head slowly, and said, "I'm afraid your brother came to feel that he'd hit a wall in his work, that it was, in fact, a dead end. He and I had been talking about how he might move forward."

I couldn't speak for Olivia but due to the unyielding "cushioning" of the couch we were seated on, I was losing all feeling in my legs so I stood up and began pacing myself.

I was regaining feeling in my feet when Olivia asked, "What type of dead end? It seems like it must have been very unexpected since so little time lay between the last time I spoke with him and his death."

"He never said. He just came to me one day and said he was

wrong, and that there was no point in pursuing it any longer. He said he'd wasted enough time already."

"And you never asked him to explain why he felt there was no point in continuing. No offense, professor, but that doesn't make sense," I said.

My question seemed to annoy him a bit as his body stiffened and then just as quickly relaxed before he replied, "Tim, your brother, was the most outstanding student I've ever had, and I think that was due in part to his unique ability to, er, focus. I think his disability, for lack of a better term, enabled him to quickly understand and find solutions to complex problems. He wouldn't stop until he found the solution. I've personally seen him work for days to locate the source of a single anomaly in an algorithm. When he said there was no point in proceeding, I had no reason to doubt he'd exhausted every possible alternative, and to review the situation with him would have been pointless."

"How was my brother dealing with it? It seems like he was back to square one and would have had to go through the entire process of getting a new topic approved."

"Naturally, he was initially upset, but when I last spoke with him and he seemed to have already identified some new lines of inquiry. As I said, your brother had an excellent mind and would have been a powerful asset to the department and its reputation. The Geoscience Department here at Michigan State is generally recognized as one of the top locations for climate-change research. As you may know, Dean Mallory has been confirmed to be the new secretary of the EPA. I don't mean to trivialize the impact of his death on your family, but it is also a huge loss for the climate-science community."

Olivia was about to ask him another question when Knowles looked at his watch, and pronounced, "I'm terribly sorry, but I'm afraid I have another engagement I need to prepare for. I wish I had more to offer you. I'm sure you can show yourselves out."

And with that, we had been summarily dismissed.

Chapter 11

"Something's off about what he's telling us," said Olivia as we began the pilgrimage from Knowles' house back to the car. "If the focus of my dissertation had been wrong, I would have been devastated. Based on what Tim did tell me, hitting a dead end would have wiped out two years of research. Even *he* would have been upset about that."

As we got back into the car, I told her I agreed that something didn't seem quite right. "But, nothing we've seen or been told so far points to anything other than an accident. Do you have a key to his apartment? Maybe there's something there that can point us in the right direction, or at least verify what Knowles and the police have said."

Olivia pulled her key ring from her bag and said, "I've still got one. I haven't been to his apartment since before this happened so nothing's been touched, but what are we looking for?"

That was a good question, but sometimes you don't know until you find it. Even I think it's amazing that I get paid for insights like this. "I have no idea," I answered.

Although the reason for our visit to Tim's apartment was somewhat open ended, it did occur to me that my stay was going to be extended, so I called Nikki to ask her if she'd take care of Fang for the next day or two. She quickly agreed. Nikki doesn't see the care and feeding of Fang as a stop by-once-a day type of thing. Whenever I'm out of town, she moves into my house until I return. I think it's a mutually beneficial relationship. She loves my dog and I think finds the attention of a fourteen-pound canine whose most fervent desires are to be fed and have her stomach rubbed a refreshing alternative to the leering stares of a multigenerational cross-section of mouth breathers. As for Fang, she loves the fact that Nikki carries her around everywhere, let's her sit on any piece of furniture she likes, and is so liberal with her distribution of dog treats that it takes me a week to deprogram her after Nikki leaves. I also asked her to get whatever she could find on Planet Action and Professor Arthur Knowles and email it to Olivia.

Tim lived in a second-floor one-bedroom apartment just off Hagadorn Rd. The complex itself was one of the many that had sprouted up over the years near the campus catering to the student community by offering amenities like fitness centers, free internet, satellite TV, and pools surrounded by beautiful landscaping. It was a safe guess that he had never availed himself of any of them, except for maybe the internet.

As we walked toward his apartment, we saw that a large portion of the complex's residents appeared to be congregated by the pool. Although the temperature was only in the low 70s, I guess it's never too early to work on that tan or severe burn, as evidenced by the smell of coconut-scented suntan lotion emanating from a host of bikini-clad young women and three bare-chested guys passed out on chaise lounges.

I don't know what I expected to see when we walked into Tim's apartment, but it certainly wasn't what I saw. The apartment was small; it consisted of a living area, a tiny kitchen, a bedroom, and a bathroom, all immaculate. A red-covered futon dominated the living room accompanied by a small wood coffee table that must have doubled as the primary dining area. There was no television and the walls were bare, the kitchen counters were devoid of any refuse, and the sink was dish free. As we walked toward the back of the apartment, a quick look at the bathroom determined that no toothpaste residue lay on the sink or flecked on the mirror and the tub was hotel-room clean. Tim's bed was made and an open closet door displayed a systematic organization of color-coded clothing. However, the apartment's ordered aesthetic gave way to chaos upon reaching the room's far wall. WWII London during the blitz must have looked less devastated than the area around Tim's desk. Stacks of books on physics, statistics, and geology stood guard over a series of shelves groaning under the accumulated weight of papers and periodicals. A filthy whiteboard stood in the corner covered with a variety of mathematical calculations that proved that yes, some people do use algebra—and more—in their daily lives. The entire area was outlined by a masking-taped border stuck to the carpet.

"I told the maid that nothing in this area was ever to be disturbed," offered Olivia, who apparently felt an explanation was in order. "She came in once a week. It took me a while to get him to agree to it. He was petrified she'd lose or misplace something. It may look like a mess but it had an order to him. He finally relented when we agreed to demark his work area as a no-cleaning zone."

"Makes sense to me", I said. "You remember that house I shared with those guys when we were together? We could have used a little cleaning assistance."

A shudder went through her body as she remembered the place I shared with three other guys on the team on Milford Street.

"That entire place was a no cleaning zone. It always smelled like beer and cigarettes."

"So, what's your point?" I responded while she rolled her

eyes and sighed in feigned exasperation.

The task of finding something when you have no idea of what you're looking for becomes astronomically more difficult when you are looking through piles of documentation, calculations, printouts, and computer files whose only common thread is that you don't understand a word of what they're talking about.

Since Olivia is a computer science professor, she assumed the task of reviewing the contents of Tim's laptop and due to my ability to read, I attempted to make sense out of everything else. Nothing works better than the old divide-and-conquer approach.

After two hours of pouring through the assemblage of written material that blanketed the no-cleaning zone, I had succeeded in organizing the material into three piles: articles, documents produced by Tim, and who knows. It was beginning to look like this might take longer than one might have expected when Olivia clicked on a file labeled "Geothermal Patterns of Tropospheric Cloud Formation and Temperature Variations: Climate Variability and Physical Manifestations" and discovered a draft of what appeared to be the first three chapters of his dissertation. Why she hadn't gone there first is a mystery to me. She scrolled through about 100 pages of text and graphics and said, "This is too long and in-depth to read here. I'll take the laptop and we can print it out at my place. Have you found anything?"

"Nothing that narrows anything down. We could take it all with us, but I don't think it would make any difference."

She interrupted me in mid-excuse, "Wait—there's a bibliography here. Tim must have been updating it as he went along. Let's see if anything he references is in one of these stacks. That could help us get a better picture of what he was working on."

Although spending hours reading selections from scientific periodicals didn't redline my enthusiasm meter, the idea made sense and we spent another hour culling 25 articles from my piles before deciding we had enough to help us understand what Tim had been working on.

It was too late by the time we left Tim's apartment to attempt to speak with anyone else, even if I wasn't sure who that might be. I was hoping something in Tim's dissertation might help provide us with some direction. Right now, three Planet Action members were in jail awaiting arraignment for Tim's murder, the disparity between the actions taken on the third and fourth floors didn't seem consistent with even an unfortunate accident, and if it wasn't an accident, why would someone want to kill him?

His mentor said Tim's research had hit a wall, but Olivia said he'd been very excited about what he was working on. Not the type of behavior you'd expect from someone who'd just found that he'd wasted the last two years pursuing a dead end. A professor in a related department who was an outspoken dissenter regarding the theory of human activity being the driving force behind changes in the climate had been killed that same night, and the police had no suspects to question regarding their belief that the two killings may be related.

I don't believe in coincidences, but Tim's research was focused on building more-accurate predictive models of climate activity, while Walker thought the whole thing was a crock, so what was the relationship? Summing everything up, I had one death with a plausible explanation that looked increasingly implausible that may—or may not be— related to another death that was obviously far from accidental. Color me perplexed.

The MSU fight song, my ring tone—yeah, they gave me the boot but that doesn't mean I don't still root for them—snapped me back from my state of futile contemplation. I answered only to hear Nikki talking to Fang in that same tone people reserve for pets and infants. "Yes, you're a good girl aren't you, Fang? Who's your favorite babysitter?"

"Uh, Nikki, as much as I appreciate you and Fang's mutual admiration, is there a reason you called me?" OK, I'm a killjoy.

"Oh, yeah. I forwarded everything I could find on those Planet Action people. I'm sorry, I care about the planet and all that, but these guys are in serious need of a life. Let's all skip our morning class and go march around with signs telling people they're devil spawn because they drive a car. If you ask me, I think people have way too much time on their hands."

There you have it. Nikki Hunt, ex-porn star is a die-hard conservative, and yes, she votes straight ticket Republican.

"I appreciate the editorial, Nick, but what did you find out about them and Knowles?"

"I'm just saying. I checked out their website. The usual apocalyptic rhetoric. Been around for about a year or so, as best I can tell. Their 'leader' is some kid named Greyson Tyler. With a name like that, you know what his life must have been like on the playground. Sounds like a brand of tea or something—anyway, I checked on him. He's due to graduate with a degree in political science. Dad's some big attorney in Detroit and Mom's a regular on the Junior League circuit. Looks harmless. Couple of arrests for trespassing. The last one was for chaining himself to a tree that was going to be taken down as part of a new subdivision development. What a doofus. His second in command appears to be another student named Randy Stewart. Same kind of background as Tyler but with a better name. One arrest for disorderly conduct at an East Lansing city council meeting. They were discussing plans for a strip mall that was going to be built on some land he felt should be a protected wetland. I checked—they're building it anyway.

"Knowles is another story. He's big in this whole climate-change thing. Been a professor there for 15 years. His dad is regarded as one of the founders of the movement, so it looks like junior stuck with the family business. He's been quoted everywhere from the *New York Times* to *The Economist*. I've included samples of some of them. Looking at his speaking schedule, I don't see how he has time to get anywhere near a classroom. He even spoke at Davos a couple of months ago. Been married three times, runs marathons, and appears to have made a lot of money from the climate business, investing in companies that sell carbon offsets. Other than that, he seems to be a straight-up guy. I sent everything to that email address you gave me."

"Thanks, Nick. I'm not sure where that takes us."

I could hear Fang whimper in the background and Nikki responding by asking her if she wanted a treat.

"Nikki, don't give her a treat when she does that. Then she expects me to do it, and the next thing you know, I've got a fifty-pound pug. Where are you anyway?"

"In your room. On the bed with Fang."

I began to remind her that Fang isn't allowed on the bed, but decided to thank her for getting the information and watching Fang on short notice instead. I think the deprogramming period is going to be a little longer than usual this time.

I told Olivia about what Nikki had found as we walked up to her house. It was after eight, and unlike the houses a few blocks down, her neighbors all appeared to be in for the night. I set the stack of articles and Tim's partial dissertation on the trunk coffee table, and we both retired to our earlier positions, me in a chair and her on the couch. Neither of us said anything for a couple of minutes. It was a comfortable silence.

I let my eyes wander around the room. If you take the time, you can learn a lot about a person by looking at what they feel comfortable putting on display. Some people can tell you everything you need to know about them by the content of a few shelves or the pictures and curios that line a mantle. Olivia's living room demonstrated the closeness of her family. Pictures of her, Tim, and her parents in a range of poses were scattered across every flat surface and I remembered being present at the taking of more than one of them. Each one contained a coterie of smiling faces that chronicled the birthdays, holidays, vacations, and spontaneous moments of the Price family over the years. Buried among them on a shelf lined with books and interspersed with the souvenirs and curiosities that you accumulate over time, was a picture of us that had been taken a lifetime ago. I smiled to myself at the memory.

Olivia ruptured the silence by volunteering to make us something to eat. My Rodeo Burger had worn off quite a while ago, so faced with immediately beginning to read through a stack of scientific journals or quelling my growing hunger pangs, I felt that dinner was the more prudent choice.

"I can make spaghetti if that sounds good to you," she said as she walked toward the kitchen, "and you can help. You can start by opening a bottle of wine. I have a couple of bottles of Pinot Noir in the rack on the counter."

I found some red wine glasses in the cabinet over the rack,

grabbed two of them, opened the bottle, and poured some for each of us. I'm not much of a wine guy—anything that doesn't come with a twist-off top, a free ballpoint pen, or in a box is suitable to my palate—but this had a rich earthiness that told me she hadn't gotten it as part of any "two-for-one" special.

Olivia stood at the stove mixing a conglomeration of tomato sauce, ground beef, and Italian sausage, along with a variety of spices in a pan, resulting in an aroma you just don't get from a microwaved meal. Along with keeping our glasses filled, I was working diligently performing my assigned task—chopping the onion, celery, and green pepper that was going to be added to the now-simmering sauce. I finished up and carried the bowl containing my vegetable medley over to Olivia and the waiting saucepan. I watched her absent-mindedly push an errant strand of hair behind her ear.

She was beautiful. I caught the scent of her hair as I emptied the bowl into the sauce. I held back the urge to put my arms around her. Maybe it was the wine that helped her step over the threshold of what had lingered between us all day.

"Why did you shut me out? You just left school and I never heard from you again. I called and left messages with your parents. I even came to your house, but your mom said you weren't home. We both knew she was lying. I don't understand why you felt you needed to go through it all alone. I loved you. I know you were hurt, Mitch. I can't even imagine what it must have been like for you, but you didn't need to hurt me, too."

Sometimes you imagine a situation and what you'd say. This was one of those times. In my version, I was repentant—that much was the same—and I say something so profound that ten years instantaneously melts away and we embrace and share a long, lingering kiss. So, with that in mind, I drained my glass and began.

"It was the worst time of my life. I just shut down. It seemed like our front lawn was filled with reporters for days. My mom and dad had to push through them just to go to work."

I paused for a moment remembering the disappointment I saw in their faces, and I can only imagine how many times they had to stop themselves when some idiot called their son a bum, a cheater, or worse.

"I couldn't go out. If someone said something or asked me about what happened, what could I say? I couldn't deny it, or blame someone. I cheated. I blew everything that I'd worked for. I still don't think anyone could have said anything worse than what I told myself every day. I didn't want to talk to anybody, especially you. I deserved what happened to me and that meant I didn't deserve you."

There it was. I had fucked up and then had been too afraid to face the person that I loved more than anything in the world. Not exactly a profile in courage.

She turned quickly to the stove and turned the heat down under the saucepan and then turned back and stepped toward me and said, "You never even tried. What happened to you was horrible, but you've obviously moved on. But in all that time, you never even picked up the phone."

She briefly paused to catch her breath before revealing, "I was in love with you, and I thought you loved me, but you weren't man enough to let us face it together. That's what people do. I waited, waited until it was obvious that there was no point in waiting anymore."

I mumbled through a reply that even I thought was lame.

"I'm sorry. As time went by, I figured that you'd moved on, and I deserved that. It wasn't right. For what it's worth, I think I'll always be in love with you."

For a moment, everything was still. I heard the neighbor's dog bark and a lawn chair screeched slowly as the wind blew it along a concrete patio, and then what seemed like ten years' worth of tears began to flow down her face. I put my arms around her and held her there in the middle of the floor. I don't know how long we stood there, but as sobs gave way to silence, she raised her face toward mine. We shared the kiss that I'd imagined. Then she took my hand and led me to the bedroom.

Chapter 12

Around midnight we emptied the saucepan and put it in the sink to soak, ordered a pizza, and began working through the stack of paper we'd left in the living room. Olivia was curled up on the couch wearing a well-worn number 2 Michigan State jersey with "McKay" on the back.

"I couldn't get rid of it. It's so comfortable to sleep in," she confessed as she intently scoured Tim's dissertation. Out of 25 possible titles, I had chosen to begin the evening's reading with a pithy article entitled, "A Review of Climate Vectors and Seasonal Anomalies in Sub-Saharan Africa" in the *International Journal of Climatology*, a choice that necessitated my getting up every five minutes to walk around to stave off the possibility of waking up with a drool-infused page attached to my face.

After an hour or so, I had progressed to page five and determined that the gist of the article was that it's very hot in Africa—a scientific fact I think everyone can agree with. I glanced over at Olivia and it looked like that, as much as she loved her brother, his dissertation was about as enthralling as climate vectors in Africa. I walked over and began to rub her shoulders.

"Mmmm, that feels good," she said. "How are you coming with the journals?"

"Not too good," I confessed. "In fact, I was about to ask you the same thing about Tim's dissertation."

"I've read through it twice. His general thesis is, was, that cloud formation is an independent process from both the

Earth's geological activity and atmospheric composition. It also looks like he thought that from a longitudinal perspective the density and type of cloud formations is a cyclical function with the fluctuation of the water vapor they contain at the time acting as either an insulator or a shield if you will, based on periods of high or low solar activity."

"And that means what exactly?"

"Essentially, it would mean that the concept of anthropomorphic activity on the climate is negligible to nonexistent."

I sat down next to her on the couch. "What about 97 percent of scientists agree, and it's settled science? If he was right, that would have made a lot of people *very* unhappy. The green industry would essentially collapse, and scientists like Knowles would be publically discredited and humiliated. Their careers would effectively be over. But Knowles said he'd hit a wall. I guess he couldn't prove it."

"I can't tell by what he's written so far. There are a bunch of data charts and calculation explanations, but I'm not sure what they mean or prove. I was just about to start looking at his bibliography to see if the works he cited provided some direction as to the methodology that he was trying to use to construct a testable model. Why don't you look at it? I need something to drink."

She handed me about ten single-spaced typed pages that made up Tim's list of sources up to that point, and walked into the kitchen.

The sources were in alphabetical order based on the last name of the author, although many had more than one. The listings were both books and periodicals, none of which you'd find in a doctor's waiting room. I was almost to the bottom of the first page when I saw it. I called out to Olivia, "Hey, what was the name of that roommate of Knowles. The guy who died?"

"Adams. Kevin Adams. Why?", she replied as she walked back into the room carrying a bottle of water.

"Well, he's right here," I said pointing to the second listing from the bottom of the page, "Cycles of Cloud Formation and Historical Variations in Global Climate Patterns" in the *Journal of Earth and Planet Science*. We must have been too busy to make the connection when we were at Tim's. I crossed the room and rifled through the stack of articles that I'd left by my chair and found Adams' article halfway through the pile. The text was skewed on the pages, so Tim must have copied it directly from the publication itself. What might have been Adams' first—and possibly only—published paper consisted of 20 pages held together by a staple in the upper left-hand corner.

I handed it to Olivia and she began flipping through its pages and then sat down to begin reading.

"I wonder if Knowles knew about this, and, if he did, why he didn't bother to mention it? You'd think that he'd have thought it was an interesting coincidence or been pleased that Tim was somehow incorporating his friend's work into his own research."

"Could he have missed it?" I asked. "Maybe he was just focusing on what Tim had written to this point."

"It's possible," Olivia answered, "but I doubt it. Part of what Knowles would have been doing in his review is checking the accuracy of Tim's citations and he would have had to use the bib to do that. I suppose it might not have occurred to him to mention it."

"I think it's at least worth asking him about. While you read that, I'm going to write down a list of who else we should talk to. Maybe I'm just being cynical, it comes with the territory, but most of the time people do or don't do things for a reason."

It took Olivia about forty-five minutes to read Adams' paper. During that time, I came up with a list of people who I'd begin talking to in the morning: the two Planet Action leaders, Tyler and Stewart, and the Dean of the Geosciences Department, Devin Mallory. I'd also try and talk with Ward. Harley had made it clear he wasn't a sharing kind of guy.

I asked Olivia again if Tim had ever talked about any other Ph.D. students in his department, someone who might have more of an insight regarding what he was working on. After a few minutes, she remembered one name—Steve Atkinson.

"He's the only doctoral student I can remember him mentioning by name. They shared an office." It was a start.

I was finishing my list when Olivia put down Adam's article. She stood up and stretched, a sight that enhanced the room décor dramatically.

"A lot of this is pretty technical, but this must be where Tim got his idea for his dissertation. Adams hypothesized that cloud patterns and density followed long-term cycles, 100 years or more. He didn't go as far as Tim did in attributing these cycles to related patterns of solar activity, but he did speculate that they had the greatest impact on climate as opposed to any other potential variables like atmospheric composition, the amount of CO_2 for example, ocean temperatures, and other factors that are found in climate models. Tim must have believed that he was on the right track. His research builds on what Adams proposed 25 years ago."

"I suppose it's possible that Knowles didn't know what his roommate published back then, but it's hard to believe that he didn't have any idea of what he was working on. And if he did, he would have had to put things together to see why Tim chose to make this as his research topic, especially when he saw his article in the bibliography." I said. "We need to talk to him again."

By the time we'd finished going over my list and determining what we wanted to find out from each one, it was after 3:00 a.m. Olivia had to teach an eight o'clock class in the morning, so we went back to the bedroom—to sleep this time.

Chapter 13

It was still dark when my internal clock woke me up at 5:00 a.m. Carefully, I slid out of bed, put on my jeans, grabbed a sweatshirt from my suitcase, and took my laptop to set up shop at the kitchen table. I'm not a coffee drinker, but the Keurig on the counter was a pretty good indication that Olivia was—deductive reasoning is an important skill for a private investigator—so I rummaged through the cabinets until I found a box of those little plastic containers and got it started.

I'd been working for over an hour when Olivia came in. Even wrapped in an old pink robe and wearing a pair of gray thermal socks, she was still beautiful. She grabbed a mug, poured the product of the Keurig into it, and then sat down at the table with me.

"Thanks for making coffee. You still don't drink it?"

"No, I'm still more of a Diet Vernors in the morning kind of guy."

"I can't help you there, but I did buy some cereal the other day. It's in the cabinet next to the refrigerator. I'm running late, so you'll have to fend for yourself. What have you been working on?"

"Reading the background stuff Nikki sent you and checking up on the folks that I'm going to talk with this morning. She even found the arrest reports, including their mug shots, of the Planet Action members arrested that night. You couldn't find a nicer-looking cross-section of American youth. Here, look. They all even wore the same hoodies, well except for one of their leaders, this kid Tyler. He's one of the kids I'm going to try and talk to today. I checked Knowles' schedule and he's got classes until mid-afternoon, so I'll start with the two Planet Action people. You've got classes until noon, so why don't we meet at the Student Union around 12:30, grab something to eat, and then we can both go to meet with Mallory."

"Okay. I've got to get moving. You going to be okay here by yourself?"

"I missed my morning workout, so it would be nice if you stayed but if you've got to go, you've got to go."

She leaned over and kissed me, then walked out of the kitchen and a minute later, I could hear the shower. Feeling hungry, I scrounged up a bowl and opened the cabinet where she had put the cereal expecting to find Kashi or one of those other healthy breakfast offerings that give new definition to the word bland. A quick flash of red caught my eye as the opened cabinet door revealed a new box of Cap'n Crunch.

Since I hadn't been able to indulge in the Cap'n for a while, I splurged and treated myself to two bowls while I checked the online version of the *Lansing State Journal* to see what they said about the arrest of the three Planet Action members. What looked like the high school photos of three earnest-looking young adults stared back at me underneath the headline "MSU Students Arrested in Library Murder."

At twenty, James Koslowski was the oldest of the three. He had a pleasantly plain face with short, dark hair and appeared to have only reluctantly acquiesced to the photographer's request to "smile." He'd been a member of the band at Rochester Adams High School and was currently a junior biology major. His parents and the friends whom the paper had contacted described him as a "quiet guy who was passionate about the environment and never could have done something like this." Richard Black and Jaclyn Davis were both nineteen. He was a good-looking kid with a square jaw and a set of teeth that would have made any orthodontist proud. As class president and captain of the football team, he must have ranked high in his high school's hierarchy and was currently listed as majoring in pre-law. Jaclyn Davis looked like the kind of girl who would be forever referred to as "cute." She was blond with elfin features and a big smile who'd been both a cheerleader and homecoming queen and was now a sophomore psychology major.

Football had consumed virtually all my time outside of the classroom and insulated me and my teammates from the day-to-day activities of regular students. We ate all our meals and attended meetings, practice and mandatory study sessions together. There was no time to do things like participating in protests like these kids had, and although most of my teammates have gone on to successful careers, the average locker room isn't exactly a hotbed of political discussion. Based on my experience, I couldn't imagine how any pampered progeny of suburban Detroit could arrive on campus and in a few short years become part of an unruly mob bent on committing vandalism in a school library. Misguided maybe, violent radicals, no. They hardly appeared to fit anyone's idea of a rogue's gallery, and, as Ward had observed, weren't exactly cut out for prison life.

After I'd showered and dressed, I decided to make my rounds on foot. My only experiences with college campuses were those of the schools in the Big 10 and the others I'd visited when I was being recruited. Each of them deserved to be considered the pride of their state's educational system. I'm sure that most every university in the nation feels they could lay claim to being one of the most beautiful campuses in the country. All I know is that from the first time I set foot on the Michigan State campus, I felt that was where I belonged. When you're a kid, you imagine what college would look like or at least I did, and the home of the Spartans was the real-life version of my college vision, and even though I hadn't been there in ten years, I hadn't seen anything to make me change my mind.

Greyson Tyler lived on Grove Street, which was only a couple of blocks from Olivia's place. I realized that calling on him at 8:00 a.m. was a dicey proposition, as it would be for just about any college student I've ever known, but it gave me more than a decent chance of catching him before he headed off to class. It was somewhere in the 60s when I left the house, and the sun had the sky all to itself. As I walked over to Tyler's house, the student pilgrimage towards campus was well underway. Not much had changed since I'd left. Baseball caps were still the headware of choice, although the unwritten rules of collegiate style now dictated that the bills be worn in the front, rather than backwards like when I was trudging my way to class. Beats earphones outnumbered the earbuds I'd worn, and North Face seemed to have cornered the backpack market, albeit with versions that seemed better suited for summiting Everest than attending Humanities 201.

The house Tyler and his roommates lived in was a classic student rental, a few years overdue for painting, steps that showed the wear of hundreds of visitors over the years leading up to a porch adorned with two overstuffed chairs that no one who hadn't downed at least a six-pack would dare sit in. I noticed that the shrubs featured a plethora of discarded Solo cups, red of course, possibly the remnants of one of the block parties that the street had been known for back in the day.

I added my legacy to the steps and knocked on an unusually filthy front door. After trying the broken bell and repeating the knocking process for another five minutes, I was about to chalk it up to an exercise in futility when a well-dressed young man answered the door.

Based on the similarity in his appearance to his mug shot, I was looking at Greyson Tyler. He was a little shorter than me and about twenty-five or thirty pounds lighter. A permanent look of contempt was etched into his face. As my mother used to say, it was a face that "you just wanted to punch," with the brown eyes, thin nose, strong chin, and emaciated cheekbones usually found on an Abercrombie and Fitch catalogue model. He was dressed in what you might describe as radical chic, a red-and-black checked L.L. Bean flannel shirt, $200 jeans, and an unscuffed pair of $300 hiking boots. Combined with the callus-free hand he extended after I introduced myself, it was obvious the most strenuous outdoor activity this kid did was waving to the gardener.

I explained that I was working for the Price family to help piece together the events on the night Tim died. He hesitated for a second. The gun tends to put people off.

His initial "I really don't think I'd be of much help," was meant to push me off, but when I explained I was only looking for some background information to help provide a narrative for the family, he relaxed and invited me in. A quick look around the living room demonstrated that the principles of college decorating are timeless. The room was dominated by two couches that had been preserved in someone's basement, accompanied by a mix-matched set of arm chairs, two used end tables, and a coffee table from Ikea, with the focus of the decor being a flat screen as big as a boardroom conference table hanging on the wall. The place itself reeked of weed, beer, last night's pizza, and inconsistent personal hygiene.

"Maybe it would be better if we talked in my room," he suggested. I agreed.

His room appeared to be the largest of the four upstairs bedrooms. It was a mixture of the expected and expensive. The walls were decorated in what you might describe as the "righteous radical school," and would fit in with the most progressive young collegian, be they in East Lansing, Cambridge, Austin, or Berkeley. The obligatory Che Guevara poster ("chicks dig it") hung over his Ralph Lauren duvet-covered bed, accompanied by a couple of placards in support of the "Occupy Movement," a sign declaring the premises a "Gun-Free Zone"—for obvious reasons there appeared to be some flexibility on that—and a framed campaign poster for Congressman Brian Perkins was mounted above his desk.

A silver Rolex President rested on the nightstand—probably for those black-tie protests—and a Persian rug dominated the floor. Judging by the intricacy of its design and colors, it hadn't come from the College Dorm Design section at Target. Tyler invited me to sit down in one of the room's upholstered armchairs as he sprawled in the other, while casually picking at a flesh-colored Band-Aid in the middle of his hand.

"Man, Mitch McKay," he said with actual enthusiasm, "I remember you. My dad has season tickets and he took me to all your games. You were a big deal. It sucked when you got kicked out. I thought my dad was going to have a stroke when he heard the news. For about a week every time he saw something about it on "Sports Center," he'd get this pissed look on his face and say, 'There went our chance at a national championship.'"

"Yeah, it sucked", I answered, "Having the fact that you were a fuck-up broadcast every couple of hours isn't a real ego booster. Something wrong with your hand?"

"It's nothing. A friend of mine just broke up with a guy she was living with and I helped her move her stuff. She'd packed it all in some old milk crates. While I was moving one from the kitchen, I got stabbed by one of those meat thermometer things. Kind of ironic. I haven't eaten meat since I was fifteen. I'm a full-on vegan."

A crumbled McDonald's hamburger wrapper perched atop a desk-side wastebasket begged to differ with that statement, but if I had to eat nothing but microwaved Green Giant vegetables for every meal, I'd probably fall off the wagon every now and then, too.

"It was one of those days", he continued. "Later, she locked the keys to the place in the apartment, and I had to pick the lock to get us back in. I guess those summers working for Lock Tite Locksmiths paid off."

Since Tyler appeared to be a chatty young man, the best way to proceed was to appeal to his obvious commitment to the cause or in his case, causes, and let the conversation flow so that he'd feel comfortable answering as my questions about what happened in the library became more specific. "Looks like it's not just about climate change with you."

"You've got to be involved, man. A lot of people like to talk big about where they stand on this issue or that, but when it comes to doing something about it, they've got something better to do. Don't get me wrong—everyone does their part."

Tyler was really getting into it now, his voice taking on the timbre of a revivalist preacher in the pulpit of tent crusade. "But just like with this fossil fuels-divestment vote coming up, action is what helps people understand how important the issue is. That's the reason why we're having a massive rally the day before this week's vote. It's going to be huge. All different groups coming together for a common cause—LBGT, Pro-choice, the Black Student League, you name it, making the board of regents know that it's time for this school to start walking the walk. People like Professor Knowles, Dean Mallory—he's going to be the secretary of the EPA—will be speaking. I'm even driving Professor Knowles' father and his wife there. They're both going to be on stage with the professor. He's got to get there early, so I volunteered to drive them. His wife doesn't drive, can you believe that, and his dad has Alzheimer's."

"What about the protest in the library? Why do that if you've got something bigger planned a few days later?"

"It was part of an overall strategy where we'd hold smaller protests around campus to help build up excitement for Friday's demonstration. Things were going fine until some of the people in the library started getting in people's faces; everything just got out of control. Then somebody called the cops."

"I don't know, Tyler. Seems like crashing the library the weekend before mid-terms when people are there to study, was asking for trouble. If you were going to do it, why not just protest outside the building?"

"We needed something bigger. The library was perfect—"

I interrupted. "So, what you're really saying is that protesting in the library would ensure some type of altercation." It was obvious that the purpose of the protest was provocation. Although no one could have predicted what happened, he knew that they were setting the stage for a violent encounter. "Someone died, because you wanted something bigger. Don't you feel you have some responsibility for that?"

My question hit him like a slap in the face. The smug righteousness retreated, and a defensive petulance took its place. I guess in the circle that Greyson Tyler runs in, good intentions are all the justification needed.

"We don't condone violence and vandalism. I'm sorry about what happened but that's not something that I'm— we're—responsible for. I don't know why James, Rick, and

Jackie did what they did, but it had nothing to do with why we were there."

My urge to toss this kid through the window was growing exponentially, but I maintained my composure and preceded to ask him about how the remainder of the evening played out.

"How did everything end up? You were arrested, right?"

"Yeah, they tried to charge me with inciting a riot, but my old man got that thrown out immediately. I'm still up for criminal trespassing, but that's no big deal. Probably a fine."

"I guess that won't look bad on your resume. Probably a plus."

"I've already got a job with Congressman Perkins when I get out of here. I've worked on his last two campaigns and my parents have been big contributors. He's not like those obstructionist flat-earth Republicans. He understands that climate change is not just the biggest issue facing this country but the world. His proposed legislation on corporate and personal carbon taxes is revolutionary. The personal element is a step that not even the Europeans have taken. The pay sucks, but he's a rock star. A lot of people think he's going to be our next senator."

I couldn't help but think that Greyson Tyler was a living cliché. He was just another indulged, clueless kid who felt the strength of his convictions and the soundness of his arguments would prevail through theatrics and shouting the loudest. Tim's death wasn't so much a tragedy as a career booster. He'd probably do well in a career built on exploiting perpetual grievances.

"Sounds like you've got it all worked out," I responded. "I'm sure your parents must be proud."

"They've raised me to stand up for what I believe in, no matter what the cost. I'm committed to that."

Sarcasm was lost on this kid.

Tyler said he had a paper to finish, and I'd had all I could stand, so I told him I might have a few more questions later and left before the bad taste in my mouth could get any worse.

Tyler's Planet Action co-founder, Randy Stewart, lived in an apartment complex about twenty minutes away on the edge of campus. As I began my walk over, I called Ward to see if they'd learned any more since the arrests yesterday afternoon. He answered on the second ring.

"Hey, it's Mitch. I just got done talking to Tyler and I'm on the way to his buddy Stewart's apartment. Thought I'd check and see if any of those three you arrested offered any more insight into what actually happened."

"Nothing more than what I told you yesterday. Before their lawyers got there, Harley threatened them with everything but the proverbial rubber hose. Within five minutes, each of them was crying so hard they could barely talk. I guess he thought he could get them to roll on each other. The Kozlowski kid wet his pants, for God's sake. The DA's going to hold a press conference at 11:00 this morning, but it's only going to be a reiteration of what we already know. Each of them denies being on the fourth floor and say they didn't see anyone else in the stairwell. They're sure to ask her if there's any link between this and the Walker murder, but each of them said they didn't know anything about it. You've seen the pictures. Do any of them look like they could bash someone's head in? I don't know how she's going to finesse it since we've still got zip. The chief will love that. What did you think of that Tyler kid?"

"He's an asshole", I said as I made room on the sidewalk for a girl on a skateboard, "and he definitely knew that there was no way that staging a protest in the school library the weekend before mid-terms wasn't going to cause, shall we say some hurt feelings. That makes him a prick, but not a guy who told those three to start trashing the place. They went off the reservation on their own on that one. No one saw anyone else head toward the stairs?"

I could hear Ward shut a door. "Just saw Harley. His head would explode if he knew I was talking to you. To answer your question, we've talked to everyone who was there that night. As you'd expect, we've got all kinds of conflicting statements because of the chaos. Most say they didn't see anything, and some say they did. Naturally, those who say they did see one or more people near the stairwell describe who or what they saw differently, and, since the stairwell is located behind a bunch of shelves, it isn't visible from most of the places in the room, which, of course, means they're probably full of crap. Let me know if Stewart has anything interesting to say. We talked to him, but it seemed like he's just Tyler's yes man. In the meantime, I need to go and prepare to stand behind the DA at the press conference with my 'justice will be served' face."

The Cedar Village apartment complex is well known to both the university and the local law enforcement community, and for the same reasons. Located along the Red Cedar River and directly across from the campus, the collection of sandy-colored brick buildings has achieved a reputation for "rambunctious" student behavior that has often received national attention. Beginning in the '70s, the complex became known as the home of two—one in May, the other in October—social events of 4,000 or more students gathering for an evening of public intoxication, drug consumption, and general misbehavior that have historically defined the student experience on campuses throughout the country.

Unfortunately, an increasing schism regarding the

parameters of acceptable social gatherings led to Cedar Fest being banned by a judicial injunction in 1987. The intervening period of stasis abruptly ended when the men's basketball team made the NCAA Final Four in 1999, resulting in a spontaneous demonstration of school spirit that culminated in tear gas, eight incinerated automobiles, twenty-four broken windows, and an equal number of arrests. The continued rising fortunes of the Spartans on the hardwood has subsequently led to an increasing level of antisocial behavior that has come to include large conflagrations featuring couches and other assorted furniture.

Fortunately, basketball season was long over, and there were no flaming divans to greet me as I walked toward Stewart's apartment. He opened the door on the third knock. At 5'10 and about 130 pounds, he looked like the "before" picture in an old Charles Atlas ad. Unlike Tyler, he was dressed in the standard collegian uniform of torn Levi's, a well-worn T-shirt featuring the Obama "Hope" graphic, and an old pair of Nikes.

I explained why I was there which prompted him to immediately declare his innocence, "I had nothing to do with that. I never left the ground floor. I even tried to get away, but the cops got me as I was running out the front door."

I told him to calm down and explained that I just wanted to talk to him about what he'd seen that night. He didn't see any harm in that and invited me in.

The apartment was pristine. No blemishes on its white walls, no food-encrusted dishes had found refuge in the sink, and the furniture didn't appear to present a risk of catching a social disease, if you sat on it. In contrast to Tyler's place, no odor of illicit activity hung in the air; perhaps it was masked by the lemon-scented plug-ins I noticed in some of the wall sockets, and there wasn't a bong serving as a conversation piece on the polished wood top of the coffee table.

"Wow. This place doesn't look like any college apartment I've ever been in. Do you have a maid come in a few times a week?"

"Nah, I guess I'm kind of a neat freak," he said as he ushered me toward the couch. I sat down and he took possession of a chair that at one time would have been described as plush. "Just because you're in school doesn't mean you have to be a slob."

"I'm going to guess and say that I don't think you'll have a problem getting your security deposit back."

He laughed at that and swept a shock of brown hair off his forehead. "I'm not sure how much I can help you," he said. "I mean, I was there and all, but once things started to get out of hand, it was pretty much every man for himself."

The sound of steps in the carpeted hallway followed by an inquiring "Randy, who's here?" preceded a young girl's entrance into the apartment living room.

I stood up and Stewart did the introductions. Her name was Emma Williams. She was petite, had a face with so many piercings that it looked like she'd fallen into a tackle box—TSA employees probably run away when they see her in the security line—and she and Nikki shared the same thoughts on colored coiffures, with hers a shade of green that reminded me of the Hulk. Like Stewart, she was wearing ripped jeans which she accessorized with scuffed black combat boots and a top that offered up the question "With a shirt this cool, who needs pants?" She had an old army backpack slung over her shoulder that she tossed onto the couch next to me.

"Emma's a women's studies major" said Stewart. I guess to prove her radical bona fides. I'm not sure what a degree in women's studies qualifies you to do. Seems like you probably either end up driving the kids to soccer games in a mini-van, with your major act of rebellion being eating gluten-free bread, or teaching feminist literature to clueless suburban kids while publishing diatribes against the patriarchy and Camille Paglia on your blog. But what do I know?

I stood up and introduced myself to Emma and shook her hand as Stewart explained that I was trying to gather some information about what had happened on the night of Tim's death. She responded with a somewhat apathetic "Uh, huh" and complaining that "It's cold in here," reached into the backpack and pulled out a black Planet Action hooded sweatshirt.

As she put it on, I asked, "Does everyone in your, er, organization, have one of those?"

"Yeah", she answered. "We wear them to all our protests so people know who we are."

"What do you wear when it's hot?" Her blank stare indicated that they hadn't thought about that.

"So you all were wearing them last Saturday night?"

It was Stewart who answered, "Definitely. The protest at the library was the last in a series of demonstrations that we were holding leading up to the rally on Friday before the divestiture vote. It's time for the university take the lead in demonstrating that fossil fuels are going to kill our planet. Do you realize that over 1.5 million metric tons of CO_2 were generated last year in this country by cars alone?"

Can't say that I did. "Sounds like a lot. Look, I appreciate your passion, but didn't you ever think that staging a protest in the middle of the library the weekend before mid-terms maybe wasn't such a great idea?"

Emma's face looked like she'd just bitten into a bad burrito as she acidly replied, "That was all Tyler's idea. He and Randy had agreed to have it on the front steps, but at the last-minute,

Tyler decided it would have more impact if we were in the library. What an asshole. Told us he'd had someone already call the local TV stations and the newspaper. It never should have happened—" her voice trailed off as she pulled her knees up to her chest and held them there.

"I told him that he was just asking for trouble," Randy began. "If I'd have been there to study, I would've been pissed. Me and Emma almost said 'Fuck it' and bailed. We should have, but I'm a co-founder and I knew it wouldn't look good if I left. Tyler just never knows when to stop. Everything's always got to be bigger. 'It's the only way people will know' he says. Yeah, they all know now. Not that it will do any good, but please tell Ms. Price how sorry we are."

Unlike Tyler, whose sincerity was about as real as a Hollywood agent's, I believed they were both genuinely remorseful about what had happened. But they'd been right in the middle of it, and it wasn't me who would or could absolve them of their guilt.

"I think you need to do that yourselves," I said. They both nodded silently. Emma used her sleeve to dry her eyes.

"How long have you known Tyler?" I asked.

"We both sublet rooms in the same house two summers ago," Stewart answered. "He saw me reading *Silent Spring*, you know, the book by Rachel Carson, on the front porch one night. We started talking and by the end of the summer, we'd fleshed out a basic idea of what we wanted Planet Action, I came up with the name, to be. We'd even written a mission statement and decided what each of us would focus on. Obviously, I'm not the dynamic follow-me type of guy, and you've met Tyler, so he focused on recruitment, Emma was one of our first members and pretty much became the face of the group. We're a 527 organization, so I handle all the organizational and administrative activities—getting permits, arranging transportation, keeping track of our accounts, and filing IRS documentation. The behind-the-scenes stuff."

Stewart paused for a moment, and Emma got up and asked us if we wanted something to drink. I declined. Stewart said, "A Coke please, babe." They were a couple. I wondered if she'd met his parents, maybe for the holidays. "Mom, dad, I'm bringing a friend home for Thanksgiving. Could you please take those magnets off the refrigerator?"

Emma returned and handed Stewart an open can of Coke. He took a long sip.

"Maybe you could tell me about what happened on Saturday night", I said.

Stewart answered first. "It's like we told the police when they busted us."

"You were both arrested?"

"Yeah". It was Emma this time, with just a hint of enthusiasm in her voice. "They fingerprinted us and took our mug shots and everything. Man, was my dad pissed."

"I can imagine. Parents are funny about things like that."

"No shit. It was worse than when I got my nose ring." Based on the amount of metal melded to her face, I imagine that Mr. Williams probably didn't think the outrageous behavior bar could go any higher and then it did.

I turned my attention back to Stewart, "So you were saying?"

He continued, "It started out like most of our demonstrations. We all met at the gardens. I guess there were about fifty of us. Tyler had us break into two columns and said that when we got into the library, the guys on the right would circle to the right and the left column would do the same thing on the opposite side so that we'd encircle the entire study area. From there, it was going to be the usual thing. You know, chants and sign waving until the campus cops came to break things up. As we were walking in, I saw two news vans pulling up. Anyway, things started just like they were supposed to, until I'm not sure what happened, but suddenly fights were breaking out all over the place."

"What happened then? Did you get mixed up in any of it?"

"Man, I weigh one hundred thirty pounds. Getting the crap kicked out of me wasn't on my agenda. I grabbed Emma and tried to get out the door. At first, there was nowhere to go, but then I saw a couple guys crawling under the tables to avoid the mob. Seemed like a good idea, so we jumped under a table and followed them. We got to the front door and tried to run, but the cops had the place surrounded."

"So did you see Black, Koslowski, or Davis at all?"

"I saw them when we were at the gardens, but after we got inside, things went bad pretty quickly and I wasn't looking for anyone. But what they did was never part of our plan. I still don't know why they did it."

"That's not what we do," Emma interjected as she left her seat on the couch and walked toward the door wall on the far side of the room. She cracked it open, lit a cigarette, and blew the smoke out the opening before continuing. "If you go around trashing things, no one takes you seriously. Everybody just thinks you're no better than a bunch of drunk college kids burning a couch."

Considering where she lived, I wonder if she realized the irony of what she'd just said.

"Where was Tyler during all of this?"

Stewart took another drink from his Coke, paused a moment, and closed his eyes like he was trying to visualize the events of the night, "As soon we got in, he jumped on top of the counter at the head of the room. It's funny, I've seen him at a bunch of these things over the last year or so, but he was more jazzed about this one than I've ever seen before. The last I saw of him was when he leapt into the crowd."

Emma took a last hit on her cigarette and tossed it out the open doorwall, closed it and walked back to the couch and said, "I don't know about Saturday, but he must be really pumped today. He got a 96 on the mid-term. How'd you do by the way?"

"Eighty-one. He got a 96?" Stewart seemed incredulous. "Talk about saving your ass."

"Tyler wasn't doing well in a class?" I asked.

"I'll say", replied Emma. "He was failing. We're all in or were in Dr. Walker's class—the guy who was killed."

"You were all in the same class as the professor who was killed? That's a pretty big coincidence."

"Not really", said Stewart. "All of us, I mean everyone in Planet Action, try to coordinate our schedules when we can. We look for professors who are deniers, and try to make sure that students hear the other side of the story, and Walker was one of the biggest. He's written editorials in the *State News* talking about how science has been hijacked and the whole climate-change movement is a form of neo-fascism. We try to push back as hard as we can, but you need be careful since they are the guys who give you your grade. This class looked like a blow-off, so we figured, two birds with one stone, you know. Turns out it's fucking hard. Emma and I were doing okay, but Tyler was getting hammered."

"Sounds like he really pulled one out of the hat."

"I'll say. He's a really smart guy, but I don't think he usually tries very hard. He must've busted his ass on this one."

We talked for a few more minutes, but neither of them had much to add to what they'd already told me. Before the silence could reach the level of uncomfortable, I said that I had another appointment and prepared to leave.

"I think I've taken up enough of your time," I said as I got off the couch and began heading to the door. "It was nice to meet both of you" and, just to make sure they'd didn't think they'd shed all responsibility for Tim's death, I continued, "Think about what I said about Ms. Price."

They mumbled a duet of "we wills." I hoped they would.

Stewart walked me to the door and I gave him my card and told him to call me if he thought of anything else.

Chapter 15

I didn't have to meet Olivia for another couple of hours, so I decided to take a walk across campus. Truth be told, I was going to the Duffy Daugherty Building/Skandalis Football Center, but I did have to walk through campus to get there. The sun was warm against my face as I walked along the path that bordered the Red Cedar. I could hear some laughing and splashing, and when I looked, I saw two canoes, each with a guy and a girl attempting to navigate the gentle current of the river's muddy, brown water. The river's not deep and its most threatening obstacles are student contributed, and since a stray shopping cart is a lot less precarious then a Class Five rapid, the university has decided that it's safe enough to rent steel constructed canoes to students who don't show any outward signs of impairment. Although it was probably still too early in the day to attribute the futility of their efforts to the ingestion of one or more intoxicants, the occupants of both crafts seemed to be having trouble synchronizing their paddling efforts, causing each to traverse the water by weaving from one bank to the other.

It was getting warmer as I walked. I contemplated taking off my jacket, but today's college students tend to have adverse reactions to guns. Kids. I went over what I'd learned from my discussions with Tyler and Randy Stewart and Emma Williams. Tyler was obviously the driver behind the group's activities, but based on Randy's and Emma's commentaries, he wasn't necessarily popular with the troops. I wondered how many other members of Planet Action felt that their leader's strategies and tactics were a little less genuine than their own. In his desire to go big, he clearly knew that moving the protest inside the library would have violent repercussions, and if the other participants were anything like Randy and Emma—well, maybe just Randy; Emma looked like she could handle herself, then slugging it out with other members of the student body isn't part of their preferred modus operandi. Despite all that, I didn't think Tyler had planned for what happened on the third and fourth floors. He was certainly Machiavellian, but even though I'd taken an instant dislike to him, he didn't seem malevolent. It was becoming more and more apparent that Tim's death wasn't due to the Planet Action demonstration. The fact that all three of them had been in Walker's class bothered me, but the timing of his death didn't offer an obvious link between the two events. Unfortunately, based on recent events around the country, bad grades sometimes elicited more than a shouting match or a nasty email on the part of a disgruntled student.

The Duffy Daugherty Building/Skandalis Football Center is named after the coach of the powerhouse Michigan State teams of the '60s and a family who made a substantial donation to the athletic department. The building sits across the street from Spartan Stadium and houses the football team's training facilities, coaches' offices, meeting rooms, and pretty much everything else connected to the program. I'd probably spent more time here than in my various campus' residences.

To play for a major college football team is a full-time job. Although the rules say that no more than twenty hours per week can be devoted to your sport, there's no time clock for you to punch in and out. At any time of the day or night, you'll find players and coaches attempting to gain that last tiny bit of a competitive edge, whether it's noticing the strong safety over-commits on short yardage play action or maybe it's possible to hit on the 9 route when going four wide forces them into man coverage. More wins result in going to a bigger bowl, becoming more attractive to that five-star recruit, making more money for the athletic department, and increases the profile of the university.

Except for the preponderance of very-large young men clad in all manner of workout attire and the periodic concussion of weights being slammed into place, the building's lobby could be found at the headquarters of any Fortune 500 firm. Metal and glass dominated the décor and a nice-looking young woman sat behind a large desk with a large burnished-metal Spartan emblem on the wall behind her. I gave her my name and was greeted with smiling indifference—probably too young to remember my glory years—and asked to see Coach Tolliver.

After informing me that "Coach Tolliver does not see anyone without an appointment," she prepared to go about doing whatever business it is that receptionists do, thereby forcing me to play my hole card.

"Is Mrs. Poole still Coach Tolliver's admin?" I asked. Jean Poole had been the coach's administrative assistant since the year I'd arrived. She maintained his schedule, coordinated his meetings with everyone from his players and assistant coaches to the press and even the growing number of companies that thought people would buy more of what they had to offer if Jim Tolliver attested to the fact that he did. So effectively did she serve as his one-woman praetorian guard that it was the common belief that "For the Xs and Os you talked to the coach. For everything else, you talked to Mrs. Poole." Maybe because as the quarterback you tend to spend more time with the head coach than other players, or because she liked the fact that a Heisman Trophy candidate was still polite enough to say "Yes, ma'am" and "No, ma'am", I'd always gotten along well with Mrs. Poole and I was hoping she still felt the same way. I asked the receptionist to call her and tell her the "Mitch McKay was here to see the coach."

She did, and a minute later Jean Poole walked into the lobby.

She was wearing a lavender blouse with a black pant suit that featured a Michigan State block "S" pin on her lapel, and she engulfed me in the best iteration of a bear hug that a person can give to someone who's a foot taller than them.

"Mitchell, it's so good to see you. It's been so long," she said as she directed me toward a long hallway to the right of the receptionist's desk. The girl at the desk looked perplexed until Mrs. Poole informed her that I was "Mitch McKay, the greatest quarterback in Spartan history." She looked back at us and gave a cautious smile. I guess being an actual football fan wasn't a requirement for the job.

We walked down a long hall featuring the photographs of all the schools' All-Americans arranged by decade. I checked and the 2000s were one shy. Mrs. Poole must have noticed as she said, "The president insisted. He was so mad. He told her, 'You can't just make over 9,000 yards passing and eighty-five touchdown passes disappear from everyone's memory.' She wouldn't listen." She lowered her voice, and in a conspiratorial whisper, added, "I always thought she was a bitch. This new one seems better."

The double doors to Tolliver's office were closed when we arrived. She said, "Don't worry, he's on the phone with some reporter. You're the perfect excuse for him to get off and with that, she knocked twice on the door before opening it and escorting me in.

Tolliver looked up and saw me. He held up a finger and turned back to the phone, "Hey, I've got someone in my office. Let me transfer you to Mrs. Poole to reschedule."

Demonstrating the agility that had made him an All-American running back at Tennessee thirty years ago, he made it from his chair to where I was standing in under a second to shake my hand and give me a pat on the back that involuntarily expelled all the air from my lungs.

"Mitch. I can't believe it. C'mon and sit down."

His office was the size of a basketball court, so I sat down in a chair that would have been somewhere around the foul line. A quick glance around the room found it filled with the game balls, awards, and team photos he'd accumulated during his 30 years of coaching. I couldn't help but notice a picture of he and I surrounded by my teammates and holding our first Big 10 championship trophy prominently featured on one of the shelves behind his desk.

He was a little grayer than the last time I'd seen him that day in the president's office, and had gained a few pounds around the middle, but for the most part, still looked like the same guy who'd sat in my living room a decade ago.

"So how are you, young man?" he asked as he sat down in the chair opposite me. "I heard you're a PI. I've gotta' say you're the first one I've ever met."

"It's not as glamorous as it looks on TV," I said, "but I like it. It suits me. Turns out, I'm not a big fan of structure."

That prompted a deep, throaty laugh. "Now there's a shocker. What brings you back here? What's it been? Nine, ten years?"

"A case actually. I don't know if you remember Olivia Price, but I'm looking into her brother's death. He was the one killed last Saturday in the library."

"I remember her. Beautiful girl, you were punching way

above your weight class with her. That was *her* brother?" he asked incredulously. "I thought the police arrested the kids who did it."

I didn't want to get too deep into things, so I explained that the family had just wanted a second set of eyes to look at things. "You're right about the out-of-my league thing."

I guess I'd planned on saying it, but then I blurted out, "Coach, I just want to say I'm sorry again, and thank you for all you did for me. I know it made things hard for you –"

He cut me off mid-apology with a wave of his hand. "No need to apologize. You were a good kid who made a mistake, but you've overcome it," he said. Gesturing around the room, he continued, "None of this happens without you. You could've gone anywhere, but you came here and worked your ass off. Every kid whose played quarterback for us since you left knows you're the measuring stick. We've had some good ones since, but no Mitch McKay's."

I said, "Thank you," and we talked for the next half hour about the potential for this year's team and about Michigan's new head coach before Mrs. Poole popped her head back in to remind him that his meeting with the defensive coaches was about to start.

Chapter 16

"It's 10 a.m. and he's drunk," thought Devin Mallory as he listened to Arthur Knowles slur his way through some sort of rambling apology, or at least that's what it sounded like since "I'm sorry" was about all he could make out. After Knowles ceased talking— "maybe he passed out" he thought, he hung up his office phone and told his admin that he had some business to attend to and that he'd be back in a few hours.

Twenty minutes later, a clearly distraught Sara Knowles was leading him back to her husband's study. "I don't know what's wrong with him, Devin," she said while dabbing at her red-rimmed eyes with a Kleenex. "He hasn't come out of there since yesterday afternoon, and he's been drinking the whole time. He wouldn't come to bed; I don't think he's slept at all. I've tried to ask him what's wrong, but he won't talk to me. I've even heard him crying. Please talk to him."

The overwhelming combination of sweat and alcohol assaulted Mallory as he entered the study. An empty vodka bottle sat on the glass coffee table, with a second that appeared to be no more than a drink away from joining its comrade situated atop a pile of papers on the desk. Arthur Knowles was standing in the corner looking out one of the room's floor-to-ceiling windows.

"Arthur?" queried Mallory.

He had to repeat himself twice before his statement registered with his friend. As he turned to face him, Mallory was struck by his transformation. If asked, he would have normally described his friend as having the look of a

"Homeric hero." This wasn't the man he knew standing before him. His unwashed hair hung lankly over a face that was drawn and pinched, and his olive skin tone had been replaced by a gray pallor. His cashmere sweater was stained and clung to him with desperation, while the normally sharp creases in his pants had lost the battle with the wrinkles and featured broken lines typically found on garments exiled to the nether regions of a laundry hamper.

In his right hand, he held a glass so tightly that it appeared the blood had ceased flowing to his fingers, while his left hand gripped his wrist in a vain attempt to stop the tremors that caused the liquid in his drink to quiver violently inside the walls of the tumbler.

Knowles moved unsteadily away from the window, prompting Mallory to help guide him to the nearest chair, taking the drink away from him in the process. Taking a seat near him on the couch, the only question he could think to ask was, "My God, Arthur. What's happened?"

At first, no answer emanated from the figure slumped in the chair, but the silence was soon interrupted by the barely audible repetition of "Kevin, Kevin—"

"Arthur, who is Kevin?" Upon hearing the name repeated back to him, Knowles sat up a little in the chair, and seemed to emerge from his alcoholic fog.

Although his speech still bordered on the indecipherable, Mallory was able to piece together a narrative that began with an article by Knowles' late roommate that had been published in an obscure journal that had ceased publication years ago.

"I don't understand. The guy you lived with over 25 years ago published a paper that said climate variation was the product of some cloud formation cycle. Maybe three people ever read the thing, and we know it's not true."

Upon hearing this, Knowles suddenly became agitated and

stood up and began to move clumsily around the room.

"It is true, Price's dissertation work proves it."

"Arthur, you're drunk, and I'm sure you're upset about Price's death. He was your student, and we all felt that he'd do great things."

"No, no. You don't understand, Devin," he said, as he leaned against the arm of the couch for support. Regaining a sense of clarity, he continued, "He proved Kevin's theory and expanded on it. Tim Price developed an algorithm that proves that there is a longitudinal pattern of cloud formation that is related to a similar pattern of solar activity."

"Arthur, please. You're talking gibberish. That would be contrary to all we know, every study that's been published. Tim Price was brilliant, but he can't change years of incontrovertible evidence."

Staggering over to his desk, Knowles vomited violently in the general direction of a trash can, hitting himself, the rug, and part one of the windows in the process. "See for yourself," he said as he pointed to a copy of the dissertation and the dog-eared journal on the desktop.

Mallory stepped out of the room and asked Sara Knowles to please make some coffee and to bring some towels and a bucket of water, and returned to the study and began to read.

It took him a little over an hour to realize that he was holding direct evidence that could invalidate the "accepted wisdom" of anthropomorphic climate change in his hands. From a forgotten article written in a little-known, extinct publication, Tim Price had built upon a postulation to make one of the biggest scientific discoveries of the last 100 years. His findings would have ramifications that crossed all scientific, economic, and political boundaries. Careers would be devastated, with men like himself, Knowles, and countless others relegated to the position of those whose disproven theories and beliefs continue to exist only in the realm of the unbelievable and are forever prefaced with the phrase, "It was once thought …"

He felt a cold finger of panic along his spine as he rose to rouse Knowles from his alcohol-induced state of semi-consciousness. Three cups of coffee and an impromptu nap had helped Knowles reach a mental state a couple of steps above a coma, and through focused effort, he sat up in his chair.

"Arthur, listen to me. Has anyone else seen this article and Price's dissertation?"

Knowles belched out a foul-smelling cloud of bile, coffee, and vodka. Collecting himself somewhat, he mumbled, "It's not finished. That's all he gave me."

"I realize that, Arthur, but does anyone else have copies of these? Do you know what would happen if even this portion of his dissertation was made public? So again, has anyone else seen these?"

"No, no. I'm the only one, but he probably had it on his laptop. I stole the only copy of the journal from the library."

"Good, good—that can be taken care of—" but Mallory's momentary sense of relief was dashed when Knowles said, "but I think his sister and that football player suspect something."

"What, why, Arthur? What would they suspect?"

For just an instant, he looked straight ahead, and in a clear voice said, "They know what happened." Then he buried his face in his hands, and between fits of convulsive sobbing, he narrated the events that took place in the library to his confessor.

As he drove away from Knowles' house, Mallory punched a number into his phone and dialed. "I need your help" was all he said to the voice on the other end.

Chapter 17

I met up with Olivia on the steps to the Student Union. It was noon, so the place resembled a mini-Grand Central Station with students coming and going. We made our way to one of the multiple food shops, making our selection based on which one had the lowest volume of erstwhile consumers waiting to pay for their selections rather than cuisine, and picked up a ham and Swiss for me and a chef's salad for her. After surveying the area for available seating, we identified a couple who were nearing the end of their meal and through precise timing, took possession of their vacated table.

Quickly, I updated her on what I'd learned from Tyler, Stewart, and Emma. "The Tyler kid is a real piece of work. He calls the shots. Originally, they were going to hold the demonstration outside, but he changed things at the last moment because he knew that an altercation of some type was bound to happen. Stewart is his number two, but I don't think he's a big fan—Tyler runs right over him. His girlfriend pretty much confirmed that. They all agreed that there was no plan to do anything outside of the main floor, and the three members in custody acted on their own. I think between them and the statements of the other three, they had nothing to do with what happened to Tim," which came to me even as the words were leaving my mouth.

Olivia looked quizzically at me, but I think she needed to hear me say it to let her mind go there.

Tears began to form in her eyes. Her worst fears were being confirmed. Someone *had* killed her brother. I've seen the same look on the faces of a victim's loved ones too many times. Fear, grief, and the final loss of hope all collide with devastating effect and irreparably alter the course of a life She struggled to maintain her composure as I quickly cleared away the remnants of our lunch and guided her out of the building.

I found a quiet spot on the lawn outside of the Student Union, and we sat until Olivia's tears subsided. After a few minutes, she looked up at me and whispered, "Why?"

"I'm not sure yet, but what if your brother didn't hit a dead end? That would explain why he was the target. I think whoever pushed over those shelves on the fourth floor wanted your brother out of the way. I doubt that was their original plan, but they must have heard the shelves crash on the third floor and figured that the police would blame the Planet Action people, because their actions were the same. I think we need to get a second opinion on his dissertation. If Tim was right, there are quite a few people here whose worlds would be rocked."

She leaned back and raised her hand to shield her eyes from the sun and said, "That makes sense, but how do we find someone who we could trust to tell us if he was right? Anyone we talk to would be a potential suspect, and we've got a meeting with one of them in ten minutes."

"That's true, but we still have Tim's laptop and the copy of the Adams article. Would everyone in his department know what he was working on? When you were working on your dissertation, how many people knew what your topic was?"

She smiled to herself. "You won't believe this but the competition in the academic world can be ruthless. Everyone wants to get a job at a Tier 1 school. The prestige alone adds to the credibility of your future research. There's a number of things that can influence one of those schools' decision to hire you, but as a new Ph.D., the originality and quality of your dissertation carries a huge amount of weight. People's ideas are stolen all the time, so you don't do a lot of sharing. The only people who knew about what I was working on were my faculty advisor and the other three professors on my committee."

I'd never imagined that the professors I'd had in school were the product of some type of academic survival-of-the-fittest Darwinism. "Really? I never gave it much thought, but I guess I always figured things were congenial — community of scholars and all that."

She laughed and said, "You'd think so, but it can be really hardcore. I guess it seems silly. I can't remember who said it, but someone was asked about it once and said, 'Academic politics are so vicious precisely because the stakes are so small. So, there you are.'"

We had ten minutes before our meeting with Dean Mallory. I waited while Olivia checked her makeup and then we walked over to the Natural Science Building. Dean Devin Mallory's office was on the third floor and we were ushered in as soon as we arrived. Although he wore a brown tweed jacket over his button-down shirt, tie, and sweater vest, no one would describe him as looking professorial. His 6'2" solidly built frame, closed-cropped style haircut, and overall demeanor indicated he'd spent time in the military before devoting himself to the life of an academician. His skin had the weathered look of a man who spent a great deal of time outdoors, and the pictures throughout the office of him proudly displaying a cross-section of dead animals confirmed my suspicions.

After he had shaken my hand hard enough to fuse bone, he gestured toward two unpadded, wooden straight-back chairs, and we sat down while he returned to the large well-padded chair behind his desk. Before either of us could speak, he said, "Spartan football hasn't been the same since you left, son. I have season tickets. Don't miss a game. I remember that Michigan game. You must have completed forty passes that day. Every time they'd score, you'd march us right back down the field. I just knew we were going to the Rose Bowl, before, you know, the incident."

He said "the incident" in the same way someone might describe a dog peeing on a rug.

"No one was sorrier about that than me, sir. We don't want to take up a lot of your time. We're trying to learn more about Tim's dissertation research."

He paused a moment, adjusted his tie, and, somewhat incredulously asked Olivia, "You think your brother's death had something to do with his dissertation? Ms. Price, I'm very sorry about your loss, but I don't see how his research was responsible for his dying in a terrible accident. In fact, I understand that the police have arrested three people."

Satisfied with his pronouncement, he leaned back in his chair. I've read about people who consciously manipulate the environment, like raising their chairs so they are looking down on whoever they're speaking with to put themselves in a dominant position in a discussion or meeting. I'd always thought that was more myth than fact, but as I found myself half blinded by sunlight radiating through the window on the wall behind his desk while sitting in a chair that could have served as a medieval torture device, I was starting to reconsider my position.

"They do. But no one can explain why. They admit they were the ones who vandalized the third floor, but they say they weren't the ones who killed Tim. Ms. Price and I can't see how anyone else could have done it," I retorted, ,"but it doesn't seem like it could have been an accident. Why knock over only the three shelves closest to him if he wasn't a target? Doesn't that strike you as odd?"

Out of the corner of my eye, I saw Olivia looking at me with a puzzled expression.

He got up from his chair and closed the blinds behind him. If nothing else came out of this meeting, at least my retinal function wouldn't be permanently damaged.

"Excuse me, but it can get very hot in this office, particularly in the afternoon." He took off his jacket and hung it over the back of his chair before continuing, "Unfortunately, in my experience, student enthusiasm, as it were, can be very unpredictable. I'm sure you've seen reports asserting that the human brain isn't fully developed until age twenty-five, specifically, the area responsible for impulse control. Now there is a great deal of debate about this, but my point is that it's not improbable that the students in question became caught up in their enthusiasm and felt that their actions would contribute to the overall purpose of their cause. In a sense, their actions are not unlike the behavior we've seen in response to our recent sports successes."

"Unfortunately, professor, this time there's a body count. And wouldn't the fact that only the three shelves nearest Tim were knocked over demonstrate rational behavior?"

"Sorry, but I'm not a psychologist, Mr. McKay, but I find it difficult to imagine how Mr. Price's efforts to identify a linkage between cloud-formation cycles and long-term climate fluctuations and trends would make him a target for retribution at the hands of a bunch of overzealous undergraduates."

"Dr. Mallory," Olivia interjected, "what was your

impression of what my brother was working on. I mean, would it have been considered controversial in any way, for example?"

He swiveled in his chair so he was facing her and moved himself closer to his desk. "Dr. Knowles was the head of committee, and I don't think it would be unfair to say his mentor as well. Have you spoken with him?" he replied.

"We have," she answered, "He told us a little, but he said that my brother had determined it to be a dead end. I guess I'm a little confused, since the last time I saw Tim, he was very excited and said it would help make climate-prediction models much more accurate."

Mallory answered: "I'm not sure that I can tell you any more than what Dr. Knowles told you. Although I spoke to your brother on more than a few occasions, I only had a cursory familiarity of the progress of his dissertation. I can say that Dr. Knowles, who has been a friend and a colleague of mine here for over a decade, considered him to have a uniquely insightful mind with a very promising future. I agreed. I heard about the problems he had encountered, but as you know, scientists run into roadblocks all the time, so your brother's experience was unfortunate but not uncommon."

I couldn't disagree with what he was saying—maybe it was the perfunctory manner of his delivery, but I couldn't help thinking that, to him, Tim's death was more an inconvenience than a tragedy. The frown on Olivia's face indicated that she agreed.

"Could anyone outside of the department have known what he was working on?" I asked.

"I wouldn't say that it's impossible. Perhaps Mr. Price talked to someone else about it, but from a department standpoint, only his committee would have any real knowledge of what he was pursuing, and dissertation topics aren't usually stimulating topics for dinner-table discussions. So, I would say no. I'm sorry that I couldn't be of more help to you."

Olivia nodded and then we both stood up and thanked him for his time.

Chapter 18

"He knows more than he's telling us," I said to Olivia as we walked out of the building. "He was pretty specific when he described what Tim was working on, and he didn't seem surprised when you told him that Knowles had said he'd hit a dead end. But there was also nothing that he said that disputed the fact that the three kids did do it."

The late afternoon sun danced through her hair as she turned toward me and asked, "I agree, but where does that leave us? We still aren't any closer to knowing why someone would want to kill Tim."

"We need to understand more about his dissertation and what he found. Mallory didn't want to talk about it, but he seemed to have a better grasp of what your brother was attempting to prove than he was willing to admit. And no offense to your brother's intellect, but if he and Knowles were so close wouldn't you have expected him, especially as a scientist, to have wanted to understand why his research had hit a wall? Of course, strange behavior doesn't provide an alternative theory regarding who killed your brother, but it does make learning about Tim's dissertation more important. What was the name of that grad student he shared an office with?"

The disgorgement of students from the surrounding buildings indicated that some afternoon classes had concluded. As we stood on the sidewalk, Olivia concentrated on recalling the student's name. "It was Steve something, I can almost see it. Atkinson, that's it. Steve Atkinson. Let me see if he's listed in the student directory or the Geoscience Department website."

"Would they even have a number for him since everyone uses their smartphone for everything?"

"He'd have an office number and email address. Here it is—let's try that first." She dialed the number. After a few rings, she shook her head and then recorded a voicemail leaving her number and asking him to call her as soon as possible. She'd just finished typing out an email to him when her phone rang and Steve Atkinson was on the other end.

He explained that he'd just stepped out of his office and saw the message light when he returned, and he could meet us right now, if that would work. Olivia thanked him and told him we were right in front of the building and would be there in five minutes.

The office that Tim and Atkinson had shared was on the fourth floor of the building and Atkinson was waiting for us when we arrived. Clad in a flannel shirt, an old pair of Levi's, and well-worn hiking boots with long hair and a beard, Steve Atkinson looked more like a lumberjack than a doctoral candidate. He ushered us into the tiny two-person office and took a seat at a small desk that featured an open laptop and enough stacks of journals and papers to constitute a fire hazard. Olivia pulled up the room's one visitor chair and sat down, while I borrowed the chair from Tim's old desk and did the same.

"Like I said on the phone, I don't know how much I can help you," explained Atkinson. "I didn't know your brother all that well. He wasn't exactly the easiest guy to talk to, so mainly any discussions we had were on the technical aspects of what we were working on."

Olivia nodded her head, and a small smile crossed her lips as she admitted, "Socially awkward is probably the nicest way to describe him. I know he loved his work. The last time I spoke with him, he was very excited."

"Yeah, awkward would be one way to describe it. Your brother was a good guy, and in our world, he was already a 'rock star.'"

Since I wasn't exactly sure about the criteria that defined an academic rock star, I asked Atkinson to elaborate—"Just because I'm curious, how does one become a geoscience rock star?"

He laughed. "Yeah, you wouldn't think a geek, no offense, Ms. Price, would have much in common with Mick Jagger, but in the geoscience and climate-research community, he couldn't go to a conference without being surrounded by people hanging on his every word. Let me explain it to you this way. What you hear about the academic world, the whole publish-or-perish thing is true. I'm sure Ms. Price would agree with me."

Olivia offered her agreement, "More than you'd ever want to believe."

Atkinson continued. "I'm working on my dissertation which, if I'm lucky, I might be able to get one good paper out of. He's already published three papers in major journals and presented to the IPCC. I heard he was already getting offers to publish his dissertation and no one's even seen a chapter. I'd be lying to you if I said I wasn't jealous. Think about how you would compare yourself to him if you were another doctoral student. As far back as you can remember, you've always been the smartest one in the class and all your teachers and professors have told you how brilliant you are, and then you meet someone like Tim and you realize you're not even in the same league. It's pretty sobering."

"Thank you for that", said Olivia. "The focus of my brother's dissertation seems to be that there is some type of extended period of cloud formation. He finished about 100 pages, and I read those. As best as I can tell, it seems that if he was right, then it would impact the accuracy of existing climate models, but that's about all I can tell you. I've got a copy right here."

She reached into her purse, and pulled out the pages that we had looked at last night, and handed them to Atkinson.

The room was silent for about fifteen minutes as he quickly rifled through the pages, with the odd "Interesting" and "Uh-huhs" providing some commentary as he completed his perusal. "There's actually a lot of analysis in here. I need to take more time to read through it, but if I'm going to be able to tell you what he found, I'll need access to the calculations and models that he made to develop what he's written here and maybe see how much more work he's done on this. And that means I need to access his mainframe files."

"We've got his laptop", I said. "Couldn't we just copy them and give them to you on a thumb drive?"

He and Olivia gave each other knowing glances, before he responded, "No. The complexity of the calculations, and the sheer size of the models themselves would crash a laptop. To do the analysis that Tim was doing here, he would have had to use Laconia, the school's supercomputer. It's in the Computer Science Building. In fact, in the days before personal computers, something like it supported the entire university. You'd go to a dumb terminal somewhere on campus, input your program instructions, and then come back to the CSB to get your printouts. I can't even imagine what that must have been like."

I felt like I'd asked him to program a VCR.

Olivia rescued me. "Laconia can be accessed from a laptop. Since we don't know what Tim's password was, we'll have to hack into it to access his files."

"I'm sure I can do it, but it might take me awhile," volunteered Atkinson.

Instead, Olivia told him to "move over" and sat down in front of his laptop and said, "That's okay. It will be faster if I do it. I mean, after all, I do teach computer science."

It took her about twenty minutes. I think that was longer than she expected, but after Atkinson admitted he couldn't have done it anywhere near as fast, her reputation remained intact.

"This is going to take awhile. If I could hold onto this," he said, pointing at the copy of the abbreviated dissertation on the desktop, "it would help me use his files to interpret what he's done. I'll call you when I've got something for you."

I was reluctant to give him our only copy of Tim's work, but Olivia said we could print out another copy when we got back to her place and slid the paper over to him.

"Great", he said. "I'll try to give you at least some preliminaries later tonight. I don't have any more classes today, so I can start on this right away."

Before we could even say good-bye, his fingers began to traverse his keyboard.

Olivia had grading to do, and I was hoping Atkinson would find something to fill in the missing portion of my emerging theory of the cause of Tim's death and, more importantly, the person or people behind it, so we went to back to her office to grade and wait. Her office was in the Computer Science and Engineering Building. Compared to the structures north of the Red Cedar, it was a newer building, and subsequently, the offices resembled those of your average government employees rather than the wood-shelved, book-lined scholarly sanctuaries found in the classical structures north of the river. Despite having a poor foundation to start with, Olivia had done a good job of softening its hard edges and making it more welcoming to the intellectually curious student seeking professorial guidance.

Since her office was devoid of a window, she'd chosen to use a variety of lamps strategically placed around the office to spare her and her visitors the retinal assault delivered by the overhead fluorescent lighting. The starkness of its light-green walls was muted by a large multihued fabric wall hanging and a few well-placed framed prints of the insides of computers photographed to appear as articles of abstract art. A trio of well-stocked floating wood bookshelves clung to the wall behind her gray metal desk. As she began grading a stack of student-generated Python programs, I took a seat in one of those wood and vinyl—pea-soup green in this case—chairs that only institutions that buy furniture in bulk would procure, and wrote down what we knew so far.

It was apparent that Tim's death and likely Dr. Walker's were related to Planet Action's protest in the school's library. The chaos that took place that night would have provided sufficient "cover" for the killers. Most importantly, the timing of both killings couldn't have been coincidental. Maybe it was opportunistic, but whoever killed Tim must have either seen or heard what happened on the third floor and decided that pushing over those shelves would lead the police to think it was the unfortunate result of the actions of the three Planet Action members who decided to do the same thing on the fourth. The motive appeared to be linked in some way to his dissertation research. Had he proven Adams' theory? Hopefully, Atkinson would be able to tell us, but if he did, that would expand the suspect pool instead of narrowing it.

Obviously, people like Knowles and Mallory would be obvious candidates since that would be devastating to their careers, but they weren't the only ones who would be negatively impacted. Even if the three suspects that the East Lansing police arrested didn't do it, that left the remaining members of Planet Action, any number of like-minded students, and even the regents planning to vote "yes" in Saturday's divesture vote. Of course, if he hadn't proved his theory or if Atkinson couldn't find anything conclusive, we were back to square one and the odds of the three kids in custody doing serious jail time would increase dramatically. All we could do was wait for Atkinson's call.

Olivia said she needed another half hour, and I hadn't checked in all day so I decided to use that time productively and called Nikki. She answered on the third ring. I explained where we were in our investigation of Tim's death and then asked her what was going on in the office and with Fang.

"You had three calls from prospective clients. I put them on your calendar for next week. I'm assuming you'll be back by then, because if you're not, I'm going to have to hit the grocery store. You're out of Milk Bones, dog food, popsicles, and beer."

"I knew we were low on dog food", I began but before I could go on, she interrupted me.

"Yeah, I had to get Fang a Whopper Jr. for dinner last night. You should have seen her tear into that thing. I gave her some of my fries, too."

"You gave her a Whopper?"

"No. Even I know that would be too much for her. I stopped at Burger King to pick up some dinner, so I decided to get her something," she replied with a slight laugh.

"I'm not even going to ask about the popsicles and beer, but there had to be fifteen or twenty Milk Bones in the box when I left. Fang ate all of them and a Whopper in a day and half?"

"I told you, it was only a Whopper Jr., and as for the treats, I don't think you reward her enough. She's a good dog."

Visions of finding Fang in a food coma when I got home flashed in front of me, so I decided to turn the conversation back to business. "So we've got three appointments for next week. Anything else I should know about?"

"I've been working on clearing up our receivables. Remember that Kalinowski guy that wanted us to do a background check on his fiancé?"

"Yeah, everything about her checked out. No hidden marriages or divorces; financial history was clean. Last thing I heard was that she'd signed the pre-nup. Looks like she loved him for him. What about him?"

"He was stiffing us. Not returning my calls or emails. I finally got ahold of him today. I called from that lawyer's office down on the first floor so he wouldn't see it was me on the caller ID. Figured he probably deals with lawyers quite a bit. He picked up. Anyway, he answers the phone and I nicely explain that his invoice is way overdue. Well, he starts giving me attitude, says we didn't find anything he didn't already know. Pissed me off. Guy makes a half a million a year and he's trying to weasel out of paying us? Really? So, I tell him that while we were doing the background on the fiancé, we got a picture of him that he probably doesn't want *her* to see."

"Wait, what?" I said. "Are you telling me that you blackmailed a client?"

"It's only blackmail if you're trying to get money for nothing. This was just a particularly effective collections technique. Plus, the guy was being a dick."

"Nikki, you threatened to show his fiancé a picture that we didn't even have. Collections or not, that's still blackmail."

"I think it could go either way. But I wouldn't worry about it—as soon as I said that, he got real quiet. I told him he had until 5:00 to pay up. I already deposited his check. What a prize that gal is getting. He demanded the pictures. I told him there was only one and I gave it to him."

"What picture did you give him? We didn't have any."

"Sure we did. I never said what the picture was. You know how we always get one of the client to keep with their background information? I gave him that. He looked like shit. If it were me, I wouldn't want anyone to see that."

I thought I'd taken this as far as I could over the phone, and that maybe this was more of a face-to-face type thing. "Okay, Nick. We'll talk more about collection techniques when I get back to the office, but good job on cleaning up the receivables, I guess".

"Hey, that's what you pay me for."

Sometimes she frightens me.

Chapter 19

Greg Pardington hit the *submit* button on his laptop and his story on the Spartan baseball teams' 5–4 loss to Illinois instantaneously flashed through a fiber-optic cable to the offices of Michigan State's student newspaper, the *State News*, to appear in tomorrow's issue. He took another swig of Red Bull, the stuff tasted like panther piss but you couldn't beat it for keeping your eyes open when you pulled an all-nighter or were writing about something as mind-numbing as baseball. He loved, no, he was passionate about sports.

Ironically, as much as he'd tried throughout his life, he was never very good at them. Despite his enthusiastic efforts, his 5' 7" 140-pound frame, which seemed to be immune to adding muscle, and his general lack of athleticism had resulted in his being cut from the JV football, basketball, and hockey teams during high school, and he still wasn't anyone's first choice when choosing sides for touch football or pickup basketball, but writing about them put him as close to the action as possible without being on the field or court. Baseball, however, with its lack of a time limit and often-somnolent rate of play, had never appealed to him. In fact, he had once written a column proposing the only reason soccer had been invented was to make baseball look exciting. Fortunately, the team wasn't very good this year, and was in no danger of advancing to the play-offs for the College World Series, so only a few more weeks remained to endure.

Maybe it was a baseball hangover, or he'd had one Red Bull

too many—his body felt like it was vibrating, but Pardington was stuck trying to come up with an idea for his next blog post. Writing for *State News* was good experience, and was helping him build up a portfolio; he'd even written some small stuff as a stringer for the *Free Press* and the *Chicago Tribune*, but everyone knew that print media was on life support and the future of sports reporting, or any reporting for that matter, was online. He religiously published new posts to his blog, *Always in Season*, Monday, Wednesday, and Friday. Since a key requirement for building a network of followers—and he was up to 25,000—was to provide them with a regular schedule of content so that reading him became part of their routine, now was not the time to do anything that would negatively impact the steady growth of his follower base. He'd had two calls in the last three weeks from ESPN asking him about his post-college plans, so he needed to keep up the momentum.

Staring at his blank computer screen, Pardington ran through recent events in the sporting world seeking the spark of an idea. Rarely was this a linear process. Most of the time, a tiny scrap of one thing led to a 500-word essay on something else. For instance, when the NCAA mandated that schools had to provide athletes not only three meals a day but also to make snacks available for them 24/7 as well that led to a screed contrasting that with the Ramen noodle-laden diet of the average student. Unfortunately, the NCAA hadn't issued any mandates lately. He was just about to head downstairs to grab a bottle of water—sometimes getting away from sitting in front of a blank screen re-started the thought process, when his roommate Keith Starnes walked into the room and slumped into the chair nearest his desk.

"Any dope left?" he asked as his heavy-lidded eyes

canvassed Pardington's room for evidence of any remnants of the contents of the bag they'd purchased the other day.

"Nope," answered Pardington. "You smoked the last of it last night. You might want to think about pacing yourself a little more the next time."

"That sucks. We just bought that. I think that guy shorted us. Next time, we should weigh it before we leave."

Pardington turned toward his roommate, who was now attempting to recline across the chair by throwing one leg over its right arm, while simultaneously lighting a cigarette and pulling an empty Molson's bottle toward him to use as an ashtray. "Are you serious? It was the same as we always get, but lately you've been getting high like you're a Rastafarian in training. I think I maybe smoked one joint out of that bag, and you still owe my $50 bucks. Did you ever hear the phrase 'everything in moderation'?"

Starnes blew a couple smoke rings, and missed the top of the bottle while ashing his cigarette before replying, "I'm more of a go big-or-go home kind of guy. You know—too much is never enough."

"I don't know, dude. Based on your grades, you're a lot closer to the going-home part. The last time your dad was here, he wasn't too happy. I think his exact words were, 'If shit were brains, you'd be Einstein.'"

"Said with love my friend, said with love. Anyway, I forgot to tell you who I saw in the Peanut Barrel yesterday. I walked in and sitting at a table with this professor I had for Computer Science last year—man, she was hot—was Mitch McKay."

Pardington rolled his chair a little closer. "Mitch McKay. Are you sure? I heard that he's never been back here since they kicked him out."

Starnes swung his leg around to sit up, brushed some stray ashes off the front of his old, black Metallica T-shirt and shoved the remainder of his smoldering Newport down into the Molson bottle, where it was extinguished with a brief sizzle, and reaffirmed his siting. "Dude, I saw him a million times while my brothers went here. It was him. He looked exactly the same. Guy's a stud."

"What was he doing?"

"Well, since it was the Peanut Barrel, I'm pretty sure he was eating but he was sitting with this really big guy, I think he's the owner, when I saw him."

"I wonder what he's doing here?" said Pardington, as he moved his chair back behind his desk and googled McKay's name. After skipping the first few entries that all were related to his football career, he clicked on the link for "McKay Investigations" and pulled up his website.

"Check this out. He's a PI. Says here he graduated from Wayne State with a degree in criminal justice and was a Detroit cop after that. What the heck is he doing here?"Pardington thought for a few seconds and then asked, "What was the name of that professor he was with?"

Starnes searched his man-handled Newport pack for another cigarette and finding it empty, balled it up and tossed it in the general direction of Pardington's desk-side trash can, missing it by a couple feet. "Oops. Sorry, I'll get that. Price. Dr. Olivia Price. I won't forget her. I never missed a class. Got a 3.5. If every professor looked like her, I'd be a Phi Beta Kappa."

"Price. You mean the one whose brother was killed last week?"

"I didn't know she had a brother—"

Another quick search on Google answered Pardington's question. "It must have something to do with her brother's death. I wonder if he's still here?" he asked himself as he searched White Pages.com. Finding what he was looking for, he grabbed his backpack and moved to the door, leaving Starnes' "Where are you going?" hanging in the air.

Chapter 20

After Olivia's half hour had turned into three, I was able to use my powers of deduction to conclude that grading computer programs is extremely detail oriented. It's important to stay sharp. I guess maybe I sighed too deeply or made too much noise squirming in my chair, but something alerted Olivia to the fact that one of us felt we'd been there longer than expected.

"Getting restless over there?"

"Me? No. Whenever you're ready. We still haven't heard from Atkinson, but *you* look like kind of hungry."

"Oh, really," she said looking up from her laptop screen. "How exactly does hungry look?"

"Well, maybe it's the glow from your screen, but you're looking a little emaciated. Not like starving children in Africa, but you're definitely throwing off that 'I-need-nourishment' vibe."

She leaned back in her chair and pulled her hair back from her face. God, she was gorgeous. "Lucky for both of us I just finished up. I wouldn't want you to have to see me gnaw off a limb or anything."

"Well, since you put it that way. Where do you—"

My dining inquiry was interrupted by the ringing of Olivia's phone. She answered it, and after a second, mouthed to me that it was Atkinson and then put him on speakerphone.

"Steve, I've got you on speakerphone. I'm here with Mitch. Did you find anything?"

On speaker, Atkinson's voice sounded like he was sitting in a diving bell. "I'm sorry I didn't call you sooner, but I wanted to make sure I was interpreting your brother's results correctly. I still want to keep working through his calculations and the model he developed, but it looks like he was right."

Olivia was still for a moment, and then she covered her mouth and turned away from the phone.

Her phone was laying on the middle of her desk, so I moved closer in order for him to hear me better. "What exactly does 'right' mean? *Is* there some relation between solar activity and cloud formation?"

"Yes," he responded, "but it's more complicated than that. We've always known a relationship existed between the sun and how clouds are formed. Basically, it's pretty much what you probably learned in school—sun makes water evaporate, water molecules in the atmosphere combine to form a cloud, and after reaching a saturation point, it rains and the cycle repeats itself. Obviously, there's more to it than that, but that sums it up in a nutshell. What we didn't understand, or at least hadn't been able to account for was if there was a longer-term relationship, and if there was, what if any impact did it have on long-term temperature patterns."

I grabbed a pen and began to take notes as he continued. "What Tim, Ms. Price's brother, appears to have determined is that a direct relationship has existed between cycles of cloud formation and solar activity and that it's much longer than anyone would have ever thought."

"You mean like a decade?" I asked as I continued to scribble furiously on the page.

"Way longer than that. Based on his calculations and the scenarios he ran, it appears that the cycles last for approximately 150–200 years, give or take a decade."

"What does that mean in terms of the weather, I'm sorry,

changes in climate?"

"Quite a lot actually," he began, "but again, to put it in simple terms, it means that fluctuations in climate are dictated by the amount of cloud cover produced during the period. Naturally, there are variations over that length of time that can lead to decades of warming or cooling. The key driver is the intensity of solar activity during the period. This is where it starts to get complicated. Think of the sun as a giant nuclear reactor than turns hydrogen into helium. That transference is what generates heat. What Tim's research indicates is that there are historically predictable patterns of the 'amount' or intensity of this process based on changes in the volume of hydrogen available over a defined period of time. The rate of cloud formation and the corresponding density, which is important due to their reflective and insulating capacity, follows this pattern of helium production."

Olivia had been following the conversation and now turned her chair back toward the desk and asked him a question I wouldn't have thought to ask, "What about the validity? How could my brother have been sure that he was correct?"

"That was the first thing I checked once I understood what he had done. Effectively, your brother had developed an algorithm that accounts for these cloud cycles that could be incorporated into existing climate models like those that the IPCC uses. If you know anything about astronomy, it's like the concept of the Hubble Constant. Astronomers use it in their models to determine the rate of expansion in the universe. The most common way to verify climate models is to use them to see if they can replicate past climate trends, particularly things like the Little Ice Age and the Roman Warming Period, and of course, the last 150 years of global climate variation—the only period that we have detailed records for. Most of the models used today were tested that way, but they needed certain variables, like CO_2 production, to be manipulated to duplicate the trends. With your brother's cloud constant, my term not his, added, the models he tested didn't need any variables to be manipulated. They were more accurate, with variations measured in years not a decade or generation than anything currently being used."

"Well, wouldn't that be a good thing?" I interjected. "From everything I've seen, isn't that the major complaint—that their accuracy is so off that its uncertain how reliable their predictive value is?"

"That's right", he said, "and that's why his 'cloud constant' is so major. Once he had validated the historical accuracy, he ran predictive simulations where he added his cloud formula to multiple existing models."

"So, what happened," asked Olivia.

"Well, you've probably seen things in the news and on TV talking about temperatures rising as much as 2–3°C by the end of the century. Your brother compared their predictions to those generated using the constant. They were amazingly consistent, less than .25° variance between all of them. They all showed that by 2100, the average global temperature will 1–2°C *cooler* than it is now. And most, importantly, he varied the CO_2 volume in each scenario, making its production higher than predicted. The results didn't change. If your brother is correct, anthropomorphic activity has little to no effect on climate. All fluctuations are the result of natural occurrences."

"In other words, all this climate change stuff is crap?" I wondered aloud.

"Well, I wouldn't say that," Atkinson responded, "Tim's work does seem to offer a powerful counterpoint to current theory, but he definitely had more work to do. There are a multitude of scenarios he would have needed to address, and it looks like that was what he was working on to complete his dissertation. And like any scientific theory, its validity would have to be demonstrated through testing by other scientists. I'll be honest,—if your brother had published this, Ms. Price, the rush to discredit his findings, and him quite frankly, would have been enormous. This isn't just an alternative theory based on ice cores or tree rings. This is about people's reputations and a whole lot of money."

As Atkinson spoke, Olivia's entire face and body changed. Her eyes showed a ferocity I'd never seen before and her mouth became just a slash across her face. Half rising out of her chair and leaning forward toward the phone, her shoulders shook violently as she attempted to contain her anger. "You mean my brother was killed for discrediting existing climate models? That by proving that everyone on the planet could burn a ton of coal a day and it wouldn't make any difference he became such a threat that someone killed him. Is that what you're saying?" She spat the words out with equal parts disdain and disbelief.

I heard Atkinson's chair squeaking over the line. Based on the cadence, it sounded like he was rocking back and forth. It's not every day that you may have proved that someone was murdered. His voice was shaky as he spoke again. "I'm not saying, I mean I don't know, Jesus, I'm not saying that," he said. "You asked me to look at Tim's work and that's what I did."

In my mind, I could picture him sitting in his chair with his legs drawn up to his chin. "Relax, Steve", I said. I knew I was talking to both he and Olivia. "What you've discovered gives us an alternative theory about Tim's death. The police will need to determine if that's true or not. You said that there was a lot more of Tim's work to go through. If you're up to it, we'd appreciate it if you could continue looking at it to see just how far he got. Although it doesn't seem likely, maybe he did hit a dead end like Professor Knowles said. We need to know if that was true, and only you can tell us that."

Atkinson must have regained some of his composure as his voice was steadier when he replied, "I can do that. In fact, that's what I planned on doing when I called you. It's late and I'm hungry. I'm going to get something to eat and start back on this. I'll call you again with what I find."

I thanked him and said "Good-bye" before I hung up the phone. I looked at my watch and saw it was after 11:00. "It's late, let's get out of here. I'll call Ward on the way home."

Steve Atkinson hung up the phone and rested his head in his hands. His forehead was soaked. He hadn't realized he'd been sweating when he was talking to McKay. He rubbed his left shirtsleeve across his brow, leaving a damp streak from the elbow to the cuff. He turned back to his laptop and then a voice from behind him said, "Late night?"

His whole body convulsed and then he turned toward the doorway and a familiar face. "You startled me. Yeah, I was just about to take a break to get some food. You know how it is when you get into something. Looks like a late one for you, too. Were you there long?"

"Not long, a couple of minutes or so. I didn't want to interrupt you while you were on the phone. I was leaving and I saw your light."

Atkinson gave out a small sigh of relief mainly. He couldn't feel his heart pounding inside his chest anymore, so that was good. What he'd heard over the past 30 minutes was a lot to process, but just seeing someone else gave him a chance to push it out of his mind for a few minutes at least. He began to stand up and looked back at the doorway. It was only then that he saw the gun.

Chapter 21

The temperature had dropped since we'd been in Olivia's office and I gave her my jacket as we walked to the car. Clouds had allowed the moon to go into hiding, but our path to the parking lot was illuminated to a brightness level just short of a super nova by the streetlights lining the sidewalk. It was after 11:00 p.m., so student traffic was virtually nonexistent. We passed by a couple out on a streetlight-lit stroll, three guys returning from some type of academic endeavor—they each had a backpack—discussing how "wasted" they were going to get when they got back to the dorm, and two others who apparently had already established their level of inebriation for the evening judging by their use of every available inch of sidewalk on their journey

As we walked to Olivia's car, I took out my phone and called Ward. He picked up on the first ring. "Just sitting around waiting for me to call?" I kidded.

"Very funny," he rasped in reply. "Kid's got an ear infection and he's been crying all night. My wife called in a prescription, but so far it hasn't kicked in. Someday, you'll know. What's up?"

As I reached for the passenger-door handle on Olivia's silver Audi, I made sure not to bury the lead. "I think we've got an alternative theory on Tim's murder. In fact, I'm sure it's why he was killed."

He was silent for a moment, but the sound of his son's crying filled the void. "Okay, you've peaked my curiosity. What is it, and where are you?"

"We just left Olivia's office and we're going—" I looked over at her as I continued, "back to her house." Her nod confirmed it. "As for Tim's murder, it's a little involved," I said as Olivia turned the key and the car came to life. "I'll give you the abridged version. He was working on a proving a theory that there is a long-term cycle of cloud formation and that's the real reason that climate changes over time. It looks like he might have proved it. It was the topic of his dissertation."

Ward cleared his throat, and even though he must have had his hand over the phone, I could hear him yell to his wife, "Can you please sit with him for a minute? I need to go in the other room to take this call." The soft sound of a mother's comforting words and a door closing indicated that he and wife had shifted roles. "If that's true, it sounds like it would be a pretty major discovery, so why does that put a target on his back? Don't schools live for this shit? Publicity means more applications, more money."

I cut him off with, "Normally you'd be right. But think about it. Everywhere you look someone's talking about how we're all doomed if we don't do this or that about our impact on the climate. It's almost like a religion—no matter what happens, it's because of climate change. If his theory is correct, all that goes away. There's a whole lot of important people who'd be hurt financially and have their reputations discredited, even at MSU."

"Yeah, that makes sense, but do you have any proof?"

"Yes and no. We've got a copy of his dissertation, or as much as he finished. But we found another grad student, kid named Atkinson, who found Tim's files on the school's mainframe, and he looked at all Tim's calculations and models and, so far, he said it looks like he was right. He's probably still there. He said there was still more that he still needed to

159

look at."

"I'm hearing more no than yes", Ward replied.

"It points us in a direction. We need to identify who'd have the most to lose."

"Yeah, but that could be a pretty big pool. You've got professors, other students, hell, even members of the administration. The 'U' could take a fundraising hit."

Olivia stopped at a red light on the edge of campus where we were treated to the sight of boys and girls concussively vomiting on a section of grass on the university side of Grand River Avenue. It looked like more than one person wasn't going to be making it to their eight o'clock class in the morning.

"I don't think it would be a student," I replied as the light turned green and we left the victims of the night's festivities behind. "Tim wasn't terribly social, so I don't think he discussed what he was working on with any other grad students. And I can't see anyone in administration being able to find out what an individual student's dissertation was about and in this case, understand what it meant even if they did. It's got to be someone higher up, a professor or someone else in the department."

Ward pondered my theory for a moment and then replied, "Yeah, that makes sense, at least as a place to start. And the first guy we need to talk to is that advisor he had, Knowles."

"My thought exactly."

"It's almost midnight. 1 don't think anyone's going anywhere. Let's meet at the station at eight. We can fill Harley in and put together a suspect list."

We passed a car with someone sitting in it in front of Olivia's neighbor's house and pulled into her driveway as I hung up with Ward

Chapter 22

Pardington anxiously looked over at the empty Gatorade bottle lying on his passenger seat. He'd been sitting across the street and two houses down from Professor Olivia Price's house for the past seven hours, and although he'd moderated his liquid intake, his bladder was screaming for relief. As he did a seated version of the potty dance, he realized that his first stakeout was suffering from a severe lack of advance planning.

Since his only experience with surreptitious surveillance was watching them in cop shows on TV and they never lasted longer than a commercial break, he didn't figure that his wait would be more than an hour or so. Since it was now after midnight, it was obvious that he'd miscalculated. The first hour had gone alright. He had no problem finding the house, and the volume of trees that bathed the street in shade and lack of children enabled him to watch the house without being reported by a concerned neighbor as some type of pervert. Things hadn't gone so well after that.

As he sat in his darkened car with his back crying out for lumbar support, he occupied himself by making mental notes regarding things to do the next time he felt the need to clandestinely observe a subject. Bringing food topped the list, since the three orange Tic-Tacs he found in the console hadn't proved to be very sustaining. He'd been lucky with the Gatorade. He'd purchased it the night before and left it in his cup holder. The fact that the empty container could also be potentially used as a urinal was an unexpected plus.

Versatility, he realized, was an obvious benefit to any stakeout-related accoutrement.

Some form of entertainment would also help make the ordeal more pleasant. He started out playing music from the library on his iPhone but quickly realized he'd better save his battery. He didn't bother with the car radio for the same reason. He decided that reading material would be a good way to avoid the tedium of sitting for over seven hours in a 2009 Chevy Cruze. Since he'd neglected to bring a textbook, novel, or even an old copy of one of Starnes' *People* magazines, he undertook an exhaustive search for any type of printed material. His search yielded the car's owner's manual. He'd found it wedged deeply between the center console and the passenger seat along with sixteen cents in loose change and what appeared to be a particularly revolting-looking piece of used gum. While it wasn't exactly Raymond Chandler, he had learned how to reset his dashboard clock.

Despite the physical discomfort, and lack of mental stimulation, he didn't entertain any thoughts of abandoning his post. He considered himself to have reasonably good "journalistic instincts." Even though he hadn't uncovered any sensational scandals in the three years he'd been covering Spartan sports, when an ex-quarterback who was kicked out of school but is now a PI comes back to East Lansing and is hanging out with a professor whose brother was just killed, it doesn't take Woodward and Bernstein to figure out there was a story there. Even Starnes could have put those pieces together. Well, maybe not Starnes, but pretty much anyone else. He tried not to let his imagination get the better of him as he contemplated the reasons for McKay's return but seven hours is a long time, and his current scenario involved drugs, organized crime, and a lot of gunplay, all resulting in his becoming the youngest "Sports Center" anchor in ESPN history. His literal vision of grandeur was interrupted by a set of headlights in his rearview mirror. He attempted to duck out of sight but his back was so stiff, his effort to lower his head resulted in his listing slightly to his right. His momentum was impeded by the car's center console. He was pretty sure that since he was close enough to discern that the passing car was an Audi, its passengers had probably seen him. Just as he found himself hoping that maybe they might have mistaken his actions for someone having a stroke, the car put on its left-hand blinker and turned into Olivia Price's driveway.

Chapter 23

It was after midnight when we pulled into the driveway. Olivia hadn't said a word during the ride home. I'd obliged her not so much out of courtesy but because I had no idea what to say. After hearing what Atkinson had found and her initial reaction in her office, I'm not sure how I expected her to act but complete silence would have been low on my list. She believed that her brother had been murdered but despite her conviction, she deeply wanted to be wrong. Now that possibility was gone and "You were right" wouldn't offer much consolation.

The street was dark, with only the occasional porch light illuminated to ward off potential intruders bent on malfeasance. Olivia turned off the car and pressed her head against its gray leather-covered steering wheel.

"Do you want to talk?" I asked.

"I don't think there is really anything to say. Now I—we— know for sure. It won't bring him back." She paused for a second, lifted her head, and turned toward me. As she proceeded to talk, her voice took on a hard edge. "I knew that those kids didn't do it but the police wouldn't listen, especially that asshole Harley. Screw them. They've got no excuse now."

Her outpouring drained the last of her fury. Her body shrank as her shoulders collapsed and the seat seemed to envelop her up as she reclined back into its leather embrace. "I'm tired, Mitch. Let's go in."

I got out of the car and waited for her to come around its

front end. Everything was still, with only the distant sound of a car to break the silence. I put my arm around her and then two things happened almost simultaneously.

A voice from the street called out, "Mitch McKay!", and as we turned toward the source, a bullet slammed deep into the white-wood siding on the front of the house. In one motion, I grabbed Olivia and pulled her down. I twisted to put my body between her and the shooter, and a searing pain radiated from my elbow as we hit the pavement and rolled behind the front of the Audi. Two shots followed the first in rapid succession, kicking up tiny fragments from the cement driveway.

Using the steering wheel for leverage, Pardington winced as he pulled himself up into a sitting position. From his vantage point, he saw two people in the car that he assumed were McKay and Professor Price and they appeared to be just sitting there, although he thought he heard one of them talking. He contemplated walking over to their car but decided against it since unexpectedly knocking on the window would freak them out and make him look some crazed stalker. Neither result would be a constructive prelude to asking McKay for an interview. No, he would just sit there patiently—it had been seven hours, what was a few more minutes?—although his bladder continued to send him messages that his first question should be, "Can I use your bathroom?"

After a few mercifully short moments, he saw the person in the passenger seat turn to open their door and after quickly patting his shirt pocket to double check that his portable tape recorder was still there, he grabbed his phone, got out of his car, and began walking toward the house.

Although it was dark, with only the Audi's dome light dissipating the blackness, as the passenger raised himself to his full height, it was obvious that his vigil had been successful. He saw Dr. Price get out of the driver's side of the car and McKay stop and wait for her. He was about thirty feet from the driveway when they turned back toward the house, and he called out McKay's name. He heard the shot from somewhere behind him, and the two more that quickly followed. He saw McKay grab her and then the two of them were on the ground rolling toward the car. Everything seemed to be moving in slow motion as his mind raced to process what was happening. Someone had a gun and was using it to try and kill people and he was standing in plain sight on someone's front lawn. Despite them currently shooting at McKay and the professor, he quickly concluded that there was safety in numbers and began running toward the car.

Numbness began to replace the pain in my elbow, but a quick inventory said I was otherwise alright. I looked over at Olivia and asked if she was okay. Hitting the driveway must have knocked the wind out of her as she sat gasping for air. It didn't appear that she'd been hit, and when her lungs began functioning again, she coughed out a rough equivalent of "I'm okay."

I pulled my gun just as someone joined us in front of the Audi. His attempt at a slide was pre-empted by the cement driveway and he barrel-rolled in next to Olivia, hitting his head on the bumper in the process.

Before I could shoot him, and despite the bleeding from a cut on his head and a knee that looked like hamburger through his torn jeans, he rattled off, "OWW. WHAT THE FUCK? HEY, MITCH McKAY. GREG PARDINGTON. *STATE NEWS*".

We'd been lucky so far. Turning in response to Pardington's call had probably saved us from the sniper's first shot, but our position in front of the car provided temporary safety at best. Based on the angle of his shots, the shooter was directly across from us, probably in a position between the two houses on the other side of the street. From there, he had a clear sightline to the front of the house, and the narrow space between the homes provided a natural baffle to reduce the sound.

Although his initial efforts hadn't succeeded, the shooter would probably quickly move from his current location to get a better angle or even rush our position. Returning his fire wasn't a viable option. I had only a general idea of his location, and there was no way for me to get a better view of his position without my head becoming a mushroom cloud of pink mist. From where I was, I could see that no lights had come on in any of the surrounding houses. My only option was to take away his main advantage— anonymity. Since killing people is usually an activity best performed in private, I needed to quickly incite the curiosity of Olivia's neighbors.

Another bullet whispered by the front bumper on my side. He was moving. I yelled to Olivia and Pardington to move to the other side of the car and to call 9-1-1. As I did, I began rapidly firing shots into the air to make as much noise as possible. The rounds thundered from my Berreta and once again, we were between the car and the shooter. The formerly darkened windows of the surrounding houses were quickly lighting up the area like a prison yard in a 1940s' gangster movie, and I heard Olivia finish shouting her address into her phone. I moved slightly to my right in time to see our would-be assassin's dark form disappear between the houses from where he'd launched his attack.

"He's gone," I said.

My notice was answered by the welcome sound of police sirens and Greg Pardington asking Olivia if he could use her bathroom.

Chapter 24

Blue and red flashes appeared like strobe lights across the front windows of the homes surrounding Olivia's. Her entire front yard was bordered with yellow crime-scene tape that held back enough curious neighbors to resemble the throngs behind the ropes watching stars walk down the red carpet at the Academy Awards, albeit wearing more bathrobes, T-shirts, and sweatpants then you'd normally see on television. A swarm of blue-clad officers had dispersed to take statements from eager nearby residents and a couple of local reporters were jockeying to get the best position to do their "on-the-scene" reports from in front of the house.

Ward arrived about two minutes after the first squad car had arrived and said, "I only live about a mile away," He looked slightly less dapper in his "evening attire" of an old MSU sweatshirt with matching sweatpants and a pair of multicolored high-top Nikes.

"What the hell happened?" Ward asked incredulously. Apparently, we were dispensing with the usual greeting formalities. "I just talked to you a half hour ago. Is Olivia okay?"

I reached into the sling the paramedics had given me to lessen the strain on my elbow and readjusted the ice pack they'd taped in place and responded, "Olivia's still shaken up. It's not every day someone tries to gun you down in your own driveway, but physically she's okay.

As we were talking, Harley arrived, bringing his winning disposition with him. After issuing a terse command to two young officers compelling both to run off in separate directions, he walked over to where Ward and I were standing. He also dispensed with the formalities, but was considerably less concerned with everyone's welfare than Ward.

"Goddamn it, McKay. I don't know what you've done, but this is an absolute shit storm. The chief called me on my way over. Did I mention that he wasn't enthused about some fucking PI who's meddling in an open investigation, along with the victim's sister and almost getting shot in her front yard?"

"Don't worry Harley," I said. "Everybody's okay. Thanks for asking."

He was about to reply in his own inimitable fashion when Ward stepped in and said, "Look everybody, just step back for a minute. Mitch was just about to tell us what happened. Let him talk."

Harley gave me a look he probably only uses when he's torturing small animals, then pulled out a small leather notebook and said, "Okay, McKay. Let's get started. The anticipation's killing me."

I was just beginning to provide my narrative of the day's events to Ward and Harley when we heard Olivia's panicked voice call out from behind us, "Mitch, all Tim's stuff is gone."
We heard a toilet flush as we walked in the door followed by the appearance of a visibly relieved Pardington in the living room. Ward, Harley, and I had just joined Olivia in surrounding a now-vacant chest-turned coffee table when Pardington asked, "Hey, did you guys know your back door was open?"

Olivia spoke first. "This is where we left all of my brother's stuff. His laptop, a copy of his dissertation, everything.

Whoever killed him must have broken in through the back door and stolen it. I can't believe this–"

I walked over and wrapped her in my arms. "He took everything, Mitch."

"Before we start jumping to conclusions," said Harley brusquely, "maybe we should look through the rest of the house to see if anything else was taken. This could have been just a burglary and whoever did it might have grabbed everything they could, planning to sort it out later."

"Really, Harley?" I said. "You think that by some coincidence someone just happened to break into this house and steal all of the potential evidence pointing to the motive for killing Tim? That's some first-class detective work."

He stepped toward me and yelled, "Fuck you, McKay."

We were about to go at it in the middle of the living room when cooler heads prevailed.

Olivia stepped in front of me and said, "Mitch, stop," and Ward, who had planted his hand squarely in the middle of Harley's chest, shouted, "Knock it off, both of you guys."

"Mitch," he continued, "Harley's right. Even though it looks like Tim's stuff was all they wanted, there is still a chance that this was a random break-in. We need to check the rest of the house to eliminate that possibility. You know that."

It sucks when someone spoils your indignation with common sense.

A quick check of the house confirmed what we all expected, except for maybe Harley. We reconvened in the living room, and everyone went to their respective corners. For the second time, I started to explain everything that had happened that day.

I had only just begun to tell them about what Tim had discovered, when a "Holy shit!" punctuated the room. Pardington had grabbed a chair from the dining room and joined the group. Apparently, Harley prefers his witness statements without editorial commentary as he gestured toward Pardington and said, "Who is this guy? And why the hell is he here?"

Pardington stood up and extended his hand to him, "Greg Pardington, *State News*, sir."

"What? Some kid from the school newspaper? Get him the hell out of here," he bellowed toward one of the officers who had taken a place by the door.

"You might as well let him stay, Harley", I said. "He's a witness to everything that's happened here, and it's all going to come out eventually. Might as well have someone give the real version. Things are already looking bad as it is."

I was sure that this hadn't been standard procedure back in Chicago. "Jesus Christ," emitted Harley who looked like he was just this side of a stroke. "Okay. But you don't publish anything until after this is all over. If I read even one word of this before then, I'll have you locked in a place where they'll be passing you around for a carton of cigarettes." That Harley. What a charmer.

After Pardington agreed that patience was a more prudent course than becoming "Miss Cell Block D," I continued. It took me about an hour, with Olivia jumping in to provide additional details, to finish explaining what had happened and my theory as to why a geophysics dissertation had led to a murder, maybe two, and the need for her to call her insurance agent in the morning. Over Harley's objections, we reconfirmed that we'd meet at the station at 8:00 a.m., but only after he had pointed to Pardington and said, "But not him."

After Ward and Harley left, I told Pardington that there was nothing more to see and that he should go home. Maybe because he thought he had to prove his dogged pursuit of the truth or some other journalistic cliché, he puffed himself up, and with all the enthusiasm and bravado you can muster after someone has tried to put you at the top of the list at the local morgue, he offered up, "And let those TV guys or the *Lansing State Journal* have this? No way. This isn't just about some athlete getting busted for performance-enhancing drugs. This is CNN worthy. I already uploaded a video from my phone to my blog, Facebook page, and Twitter. Who knows what's going to happen? I've got to stay."

I could only imagine how Harley and Ward and the rest of the East Lansing PD would respond when they saw their crime scene getting a few thousands likes and re-tweets.

"Greg, look at all these cops. You don't really think anything more is going to happen tonight do you? Think of all those tweets and likes that are probably pouring in, and don't you want to update your blog? Plus, that knee's not looking so good, my friend."

Attempting to demonstrate he was impervious to the pain, Pardington flexed his leg back and forth. He uttered, "I'm fine, see" but the grimace occupying his face belied his stoicism. "You know, you're right. All these cops—nothing's going to happen now. I think I will go home. I've got a lot of work to do." He held up his phone, "My Twitter is blowing up."

"I think that's the right move," I said as I watched him limp to his car.

As I surveyed the scene that had unfolded on Olivia's front yard, I couldn't help but wonder whether in a perverse way the events that had taken place over the past few days didn't provide a degree of respite for the East Lansing constabulary from the monotony of protecting the citizenry from drunk college students, excessive noise, and parking violators. They certainly weren't holding anything back. The entire front yard was ringed with yellow crime-scene tape and the orange industrial light stands that dotted the lawn had turned night into day. Two officers stood guard over the crime-scene personnel who seemed like they were combing every blade of grass for evidence that might lead to the apprehension of our assailant, while others were busy determining the trajectory of the shots with their partners located on the other side of the street. The house itself now featured an exposed strip of ancient tar paper as evidence of the decision to remove the entire piece of siding that had become one of the bullets' final resting place.

I felt Olivia's fingers intertwine with mine as she joined me in surveying the hive of activity in what had been just a few hours before her front yard. She looked forlornly at the crushed remains of the colorful begonias and impatiens that she had painted her flowerbeds in vivid reds, whites, and pinks. A police investigation has many facets; botanical preservation is not one of them.

"Have they finished inside?" I inquired.

"I think they're just about done. There's fingerprint powder everywhere, but I overheard one of them say that he was sure they wouldn't find anything since it looks like a professional job."

"Talk about stating the obvious. They picked the lock on the back door and only took the stuff related to, or what they thought was related to Tim's work. Of course, we made it easy for them by leaving it all in one place. I should have seen that coming."

She rubbed my back and attempted to offer some consolation, "You couldn't have known this would happen. Who could have anticipated all this?"

I stepped back to let the officers leaving the house pass by. They'd send what they had to the state police crime lab a few miles away in Lansing, but they wouldn't find anything. Even the one shell casing that they found, probably from the shot the shooter had taken when they'd changed position and didn't have time to pick up, wouldn't offer much other than identifying the type of rifle used. Tim's death now appeared to be more of a crime of opportunity. Crushing someone to death with bookshelves is not the same as trying to take out the people investigating his death in the middle of the night with a rifle. Neither is stealing information related to the crime. Whoever was responsible for attempting to kill us, and the theft, knew what they were doing.

Chapter 25

Fingerprint powder clashes with any décor and Olivia's living room was no different. Black residue seemed to have taken up residence on every available surface. Having someone try to kill you in your driveway is bad enough, but to find your house looking like the inside of an Etch-A-Sketch can be filed under the heading "Piling On."

As she slumped into a chair, Olivia noted, "They even got it on my couch."

"Yeah, I think you're going to have to call in one of those services," I said as I dropped into the chair opposite her.

It was two o'clock in the morning and we were both exhausted. My vision was starting to blur, although she still looked great, when I heard her whisper almost to herself, "How can this be happening for a dissertation?" and her voice trailed off.

"It's too big," I heard myself say. "Tim was definitely killed for what he'd found out, but I don't think whoever did it went to the library that night planning to kill him. Maybe they went to try and persuade him to give it up somehow. Then everything just came together, the protest, the vandalism on the third floor, and they took the opportunity. But now, either he or she had help originally or other people who could be affected found out somehow, but they're worried what he discovered will leak out. They're trying to contain it. We're a threat, and so is your brother's work and anything connected to it. That's why someone stole his laptop and everything else and then tried to kill us."

"What are we going to do? We don't know who they are and Mitch, they know where I live."

Sitting in the big overstuffed chair, she looked small and frightened. Even though she's maybe the strongest and toughest woman I've ever met this side of Nikki, what had happened today was overwhelming. In the movies, the hero knows just what to say, because someone has taken hours to write it for him. This wasn't a movie, and I'm no hero, so I just walked over and kissed her softly on the lips. She reached up and put her arms around my shoulders. I picked her up and carried her to the bedroom. We made love slowly while tenderly looking into each other's eyes.

Since I'd only fallen to sleep about an hour before, I decided to ignore my biological alarm clock to get as much rest as I could before it was time to meet Ward and Harley. The sound of my phone ringing halted that plan. The light from its screen helped guide me to where it was vibrating on the nightstand. Discovering the location of my pants in the darkened room took a little bit longer. I wrapped my jeans around the phone to stifle the sound and moved toward the door as noiselessly as I could. I needn't have bothered. When I looked back to check, Olivia lay asleep on her pillow with her head bathed in soft auburn curls.

Standing naked in the living room, I struggled to put on my pants and answer the phone simultaneously. As I attempted to steady myself to align my leg to the proper entry angle, my hello was greeted with an exasperated, "What's going on up there? I just saw you on TV."

I asked Nikki to hold on for a second while I lost my balance and fell sideways onto the couch. I finished buttoning my jeans from there and continued the conversation. "I was on TV?"

I could hear Fang barking in the background. She must

have put her hand over the phone, but I still heard her attempting to calm my pooch down with "Shhh, Fang. You want a treat? Here you go. Good dog."

With Fang satiated, she returned to our conversation, saying, "Yeah, and it's true what they say about the camera adding ten pounds. I've got to tell you. You looked a little jowly."

"Jowly? I weigh the same as I did when I was in school. You used to be on camera all the time. Did you look jowly?"

"Of course not. It's all in the lighting. Those were professional productions. Plus, I'm naturally lean."

I walked across the room and looked at my face in the mirror. No way I looked jowly.

"Okay, how did you see me on TV?"

"I had it on while I was in the bathroom getting ready and, all of a sudden, Fang starts freaking out, barking and doing that thing where she runs around in a circle. Anyway, I walked out, and that gal on Channel 7 was talking about a shooting in East Lansing while they were showing the video, and there you were. Actually, you were in the background with Olivia. She looked good. She must be naturally lean, too."

"I'll pass along the compliment," I responded. "You do realize someone tried to kill us last night, don't you?"

"Hazard of the job. The important thing is you made it *and* it was on TV. You just can't buy exposure like that. Has anybody interviewed you yet? Make sure to mention the web address." Her concern was overwhelming. "But seriously, what is going on?"

I spent the next half hour filling her in on what we'd found. Her red tooth-and-claw capitalism aside, I like to bounce ideas off her. Her questions are always insightful and her gut instincts are usually right. I guess based on where she's come from that makes sense. I reviewed the suspect pool with her, and she immediately ruled out anyone on the board of regents.

"I looked at all of them, especially the ones who would be hurt the most if they did vote to divest. They all live out of town, and I checked the flight manifests from where each of them live into Detroit and Lansing, and none of them have arrived yet. I also checked all the surrounding hotels, not one of them has checked in."

We glossed over the fact that hacking into flight logs is a federal offense, and a government agency would probably have something to say about her perusal of guest statuses of the local lodging establishments, and agreed that Knowles was the key. Either he was directly involved or knew who was. I thanked her for her help and she reminded me again about the web address.

Chapter 26

Fortified by a bowl of Cap'n Crunch, and whatever Olivia had chosen to mix up in the blender for herself—nothing good judging by its deep-green color, we were on our way to meet Ward and Harley when we found the driveway blocked by Pardington and his Cruze.

"All right, I appreciate the whole intrepid reporter thing, but this isn't happening," I grouched.

"C'mon McKay," he opined, "you have to take me with you. You said it yourself last night. The true story needs to be told, and plus, I almost got killed."

I glanced at my watch. We were going to be late. "You heard what Harley said. You're persona non grata. This isn't about Greg Pardington, cub reporter. We all could have been killed last night. Why don't you go home and watch 'All the President's Men' on Netflix."

Judging by the look on his face, I think I hurt his feelings, but we were getting closer to finding Tim's killer and I couldn't think of a good reason to have Harley hate my guts any more than he already did. I was just about to help him move his car when Olivia said, "Mitch, he's going to follow us anyway. Wouldn't it be better if he came along so we could keep an eye on him? Besides, he's only trying to do his job."

"His job? Olivia, he's a kid who works for the *State News*. It's for his own good."

"His own good? You sound like someone's dad. We'll make him promise to stay out of the way. I think after last night, he'll be okay with that."

She had a point. Anybody who gets shot at with a high-powered rifle and shows up the next day for more probably deserves some slack. I put on my stern face and said, "Alright, you can come, but don't bug me and stay in the car. Now move that thing—we're already running late."

He signaled his agreement with a fist pump and a "Yesss," then backed up his car and parked it in front of the house.

Pardington's interpretation of "Don't bug me" was more liberal than mine as he began assaulting me with questions before I could start the car.

"How do you know Dr. Price? Is it strange being back here? Does it bother you that you lost your chance to play in the NFL?"

Olivia turned and silenced him with a knowing look. A meek "Sorry" came from the back seat.

Fortunately, the police station's proximity to Olivia's house eliminated his opportunity to further violate our agreement. We pulled in and after we instructed him to "stay," we walked toward the building's front doors. Two blue-clad officers raced past us as we climbed the front steps and entered the lobby. We were immediately met by Ward and Harley, who were also in an obvious hurry. Harley brushed past me and hit the door with a stiff arm that would make a running back proud.

Before his partner could repeat the process, I stepped to my right and cut him off. "Ward, what's going on? Where are you guys going?"

"We just got a call. That kid you talked to last night— Atkinson. He's dead."

No one spoke for a minute. Olivia in a barely audible voice asked, "How?"

Ward moved toward the door and said, "Let's talk while we walk. He was shot. Some professor found him. She was coming in to pick up some tests that Atkinson was grading for her class."

Smartphones are amazing things. Anyone anywhere can find out about anything virtually instantaneously. I assumed that was the reason for the mass of students being held back by an infinitely smaller number of campus and East Lansing police we saw as we arrived at the Natural Science Building. I've never understood the macabre fascination that draws people to a crime site, particularly one of a murder. The crowd was so thick that most people couldn't see the front of the building no matter how much jumping around they did. A few girls were perched on the shoulders of boyfriends or other well-meaning male students to get an elevated perspective. Who says chivalry is dead? All this in the hope of seeing a dead body so you could ask your friends, "Guess what I saw today?" Maybe I've seen too many in my life to appreciate the novelty.

I parked the car and we hurried to catch up to Ward and Harley. We were going to need some official clout to get through the throng. I told Pardington to give us a few minutes before he could get out of the car. We'd text him when we were on the way out. Harley greeted our arrival less than enthusiastically with "This is a crime scene, McKay. You and the professor have got no reason to be here."

"That would be true, Harley," I responded, "if we hadn't talked to the victim last night and what he told us about Tim's theory hadn't given us a potential motive for his murder. Let's face it, at this point we know as much or more about this case than you do."

Ward continuing in his unwanted role of mediator and said, "He's got a point. He was a cop. He knows his way around a crime scene and he'll keep his mouth shut."

Harley grunted something that was as close as we were going to get to his agreement.

Then Ward turned to me, "But I don't think Ms. Price needs to see this, Mitch. She can wait for us downstairs, okay?"

I looked at Olivia and she nodded in agreement. We followed the two detectives through the crowd and into the building.

The police had cleared everyone out by the time we walked into the lobby, and cops stood at every entrance to make sure it stayed that way. Olivia took a seat on a wooden bench near the main entrance and another uniformed officer led Ward, Harley, and me upstairs.

The scene outside Steve Atkinson's fourth-floor office was one of controlled chaos as police, crime-scene, and coroner's-office personnel jockeyed for position in the narrow hallway. Standing near them was Dean Mallory attempting to comfort a visibly distraught woman, the professor who had discovered the body I presumed. I don't know what he was saying to her, but it didn't appear to be working. Finding someone shot to death in their office is the last thing she expected to start her day. Harley and Ward flashed their badges and the group parted with some of them giving me looks of faint recognition as I passed by.

Atkinson's body was sitting in his chair and his brains covered the beige wall behind him. He'd been shot twice in the chest and once in the head, a sequence that essentially eliminated the possibility that it was an act of random violence. From what I remembered, the room looked like it had last night with one exception—Atkinson's laptop and the copy of Tim's dissertation that we'd left with him were gone.

"Son of a bitch!" I blurted out.

"What is it Mitch?" asked Ward.

"His laptop and the copy of the dissertation that we gave him are gone. Nothing else seems to have been moved. It's the same as at Olivia's last night. Whoever did this is gathering everything that could point to them and eliminate the possibility that Tim's research could become public."

"What are you talking about, McKay? Are you saying this guy was killed over a laptop and an unfinished dissertation that only five people would ever read?" interjected Harley.

"Yeah, Harley, that's exactly what I'm saying. It's like Ward told you—based on what Atkinson told us last night, what Tim found could have huge ramifications. But now whoever it is has his laptop and both copies of the dissertation. We can't get another copy because to print it, we need the laptop, and we don't know what else was on there."

"But why take *this* guy's laptop?" asked Ward as he examined the entry wounds on Atkinson's chest.

"He was using it to access the school's mainframe. The amount of data required for calculations and modeling is too much for a laptop, so Olivia hacked in to figure out his password so Atkinson could get access to his work."

Then it hit me. "If Atkinson was still working on the mainframe, whoever killed him could have gotten rid of all of Tim's work. If he did, we're screwed. There's no motive."

I pulled out my phone and began to text Olivia. Ever suspicious, Harley reached for my phone and said, "What do you think you're doing, McKay? Put that thing away."

"Take it easy, Harley. I'm calling Olivia. We have to know if the files are still there."

She answered immediately. Before she could say anything, I told her the dissertation and the laptop were gone. "Mitch, what about Tim's work? If Atkinson was still connected to the mainframe, they could have deleted all his files."

"I know. You need to try and access them. They've got the dissertation, and if the files are gone, we've got nothing."

"I don't have my laptop. I'll have to find one in an office. I'll call you as soon as I can."

By the time I finished with Olivia, Ward and Harley were both standing in front of the body and nodded to each other in agreement. "Nine millimeter. Coroner will pull the slugs," noted Harley. "Crime-scene guys will go through the place, but if you're right, McKay and this is the same guy or one of the guys responsible for what happened at your girlfriend's house, then I doubt they'll find anything."

Ward concurred, "The shot pattern alone says it's someone who has some sort of professional training. Military, police, whatever. I doubt anyone like that is going to be careless enough to leave their fingerprints as a calling card."

Ward and I stepped into the hall, while Harley kept a menacing watch over the coroner's people who were in the process of bagging and removing the body.

"Aren't there any cameras or security guards that would be able to show us or know who was here last night?" I asked.

"No. That was the first thing we checked," replied Ward. "You said you first talked to him yesterday afternoon. Did you tell anyone else about what he was doing?"

"No one. We went directly to the Computer Science Building and Olivia's office when we left here."

"Then how the hell did they find out what he was doing?"

"I'm not sure. The only thing that makes sense is that they were in the building and overheard our call with Atkinson. But we've got no way to check who might have been here at that time."

"We've pulled a list of all the professors and staff who work in the building, and we've put in a request for a list of all of the students taking classes in the department this term. We'll check all of their alibis but that's going to take a while," Ward told me.

"That could take all day," I replied. "I'm going to talk to Knowles."

Ward shook his head, "Mitch, now you're stepping into our investigation. I know I can't stop you, but when Harley finds out, he'll go right to the chief and nothing good is going to come of that. I'm just giving you a heads-up."

"I appreciate it, Brian, but he's involved somehow. If he's not spooked already, he will be when he hears about this. That can be good for us, but we need to talk to him now before he has a chance to talk with whoever else is involved and start coordinating their stories. I'll tell you everything I find out."

Ward went back into the office as I started towards the stairs. I had just gotten to the stairway when my phone vibrated with an incoming text. "They're gone" was all it said.

Chapter 27

Margaret Sanborn pushed a well-manicured, red-nailed finger down on the green illuminated speakerphone button to end her conference call and walked to her office window. From her vantage point, she counted six television vans representing all the local and Detroit stations, as well as one from CNN. Feeds from their local affiliates would ensure that the national viewers of CBS, ABC, NBC, and Fox wouldn't miss their opportunity to watch "on-the-scene" reporters providing breaking news updates atop chyrons featuring sensational phrases like "Carnage on Campus." She could only guess at the number of newspaper and radio people hidden amongst the crowd of bystanders amassed in front of the Natural Science Building. As she stood there, members of the school's communications team were three floors below turning the building's largest conference room into a makeshift press room big enough to accommodate all the expected attendees for her noon press conference.

The communications team debated whether they could simply issue a press release as they had three days ago, but Sanborn had quickly discarded the suggestion. "It will look like we're hiding. Parents and students, not to mention the regents and our major donors need reassurance that we are doing all we can, and they don't want to hear about crisis hotlines and grief counselors. I've already talked to the governor this morning. He thought we should think about shutting down the campus until the killer or killers are caught. I told him I didn't think that was a good idea since we're in the middle of the semester. He said okay, but I'm sure he's getting the same calls as we are from parents, and if he calls again, he won't be asking," she stated. She insisted that the chiefs of the campus and East Lansing police join her at the podium to provide a uniform front, and because she expected that most of the questions, at least the hard ones, would focus on the status of the investigations. The latest draft of her statement was sitting on her desk waiting for her to read it over.

As she began reading the draft of what she'd say in a little over an hour, she knew she was losing control of the situation. After that little shit Tyler had given up the three Planet Action members, she thought that things would begin to die down. The media had their villains and the fact that they were three young students who looked like they came right out of central casting as examples of All-American youth provided them with any number of engaging storylines. Their readers and viewers were already being served up the first of many in-depth stories centered around variations of the "What makes good kids do bad things?" theme. Just last night, she'd seen two of the parents exposing their souls to some blonde on Fox. The father had looked stoic while the well-dressed woman, who had given her life to her child as the mom who made every birthday special, toted them to all their activities, and served on the PTA and assisted at bake sales, had sat next to him blubbering uncontrollably. All of it was very heart breaking and sure to hold the public's attention for a few days until something better came along to distract them.

Just like a CEO in business, becoming a college president and staying one required a range of skills with the ability to be an effective politician being the most important. Sanborn felt she had mastered that attribute. The students' arrests presented her with an opportunity. She had wasted no time in reaching out to the regents who favored divesture to discuss how they may want to consider the "optics" of their vote. A student, and maybe a professor, had been killed by a campus environmental group. Everyone understands that there are contrasting points of view on the issue of climate change, and the degree that fossil-fuel use contributes to it. Reasonable minds can disagree. But now peaceful protests had morphed into a violent confrontation on the part of someone or some group that was heavily invested in the divest initiative.

Who were the extremists now? Did they want the university seen as endorsing or worse caving to the uncontrollable behavior of a group of violent zealots? Although she hadn't been able to extract firm commitments, she felt that her efforts had been effective with two of the "yes" voters sounding less than steadfast in their position. The events of this morning had changed that. On her conference call with the full board, she'd vainly attempted to stall for time by arguing that due to this most recent tragedy, the prudent thing to do was to delay the vote.

On the call, she had found no allies. The discussion had immediately degenerated into an uproar of raised voices and pointed invectives. Her "waverers" had returned to the fold, and each side felt that delaying the vote would only increase the potential of more violence, with the only difference between them being who would be the aggressors and who would be the victims.

Despite the regents' entrenchment of their positions, what Sanborn had found most disconcerting was that she detected an underlying sense of agreement among some of the call's participants that the ultimate resolution of the issues currently confronting the school might require a change in leadership. Although nothing was said specifically, references to "protecting the school's image" and "a clean slate" elicited very little dissent. The people on the call weren't in their positions to meet a few times a year for some reminiscing and backslapping. They were responsible for the integrity and continued success of the school. Each was successful in their own field of endeavor and, like her, understood what it took to achieve that success and maintain it. It didn't matter that the need for a new president hadn't been explicitly stated — with people of this level of stature and importance, a private conversation with the wrong person could anonymously make their position public. The dynamic had shifted; Saturday's vote might not only be about the contents of the school's investment portfolio, but a referendum on her as well.

She realized there was nothing more she could do. The situation had escalated too quickly and, although the additional perpetrator or perpetrators of the killings might be caught, and with the three students in custody possibly being convicted and imprisoned, a sacrifice on the school's part would have to be made. Saturday would determine if it were her. She finished making a few minor changes to her statement, gave it to her admin to prepare, and picked up the phone to call Steve Atkinson's parents.

It had been a busy morning for Greyson Tyler. Bolstered by a quick hit from his housemate's bong, he was about to leave for his 9:10 class when he heard a news reader on CNN utter something that from his upstairs room sounded like it included "murder" and "Michigan State University." In response, he exhaled the smoke from his lungs, producing a cloud big enough to qualify as a weather system, thrust the bong back in the direction of his roommate with a "Here," and ran headlong down the stairs. He arrived in the living room in time to see a reporter standing in front of the Nat Sci building providing a "Here's what we know right now" to a female anchor who had a look on her face of concern and compassion so intense that it might qualify her for sainthood.

CNN provided just the right level of graphic urgency by flashing a "Breaking News" banner with enough frequency to cause a seizure, while the reporter's hair overcame a losing battle with the wind. Tyler made a mental note to grab a jacket before he left while the reporter continued sonorously informing his deskbound counterpart that the victim was a male doctoral student in geophysics who'd been found shot to death in his office by one of the department's professors. Tyler didn't bother to watch the interviews with the sundry of grieving students.

In Tyler's mind, politics was a zero-sum game. Someone won, someone lost, and there were no moral victories. While it was sad that another student had been killed, he'd be just another fleeting tragedy if the public didn't understand that he was a real-life victim of the zealousness of climate-change deniers. The fact that the report had not included any mention of a possible motive was inconsequential. Atkinson's area of research alone ensured that he was a brother who had just been martyred for his belief that the planet was on an inexorable path toward a cataclysmic future if dramatic action to arrest the impact of fossil fuels was not taken immediately. Not that Tyler felt all that personally invested in the unfortunate death of the guy, but he could only imagine the impact *that* interpretation of the crime would have on people's sympathies. He wasn't sure how much he'd learned from his four years of classes, but somewhere along the line, he'd come to understand that for most people the facts of a story didn't generate anywhere near the level of interest and empathetic outpourings as one that tugged on the heartstrings, and this one would pull hard enough to rip them out of people's chests. The key to political success was to make events work for you and not against you. And that's what he told himself as he dialed the number for Congressman Perkins' communications director.

Since it took slightly less than a minute to convince Communications Director Angela Morrelli of the value of a press release from the congressman condemning the reason for another "senseless death" on "one of our most prestigious college campuses," Tyler was certain he and she shared the same vision regarding effective political messaging. Heck, he'd practically dictated the thing to her. After eliciting her promise, "To make sure the congressman knew where the idea came from," he hung up and began the machinations necessary to ensure that all politics was local.

He called Stewart's apartment. His green-haired bitch of a girlfriend answered the phone with a "Yeah?" He could never figure out the attraction. The green hair he could almost understand; she wasn't the only girl in East Lansing who favored the "Hey, look at me" family of hair care products. Normally, this mode of flaunting convention lasts until the first job interview, but he wasn't so sure in her case. He thought she would even be kind of pretty if she got rid of all the metal on her face. He never got the whole facial-piercing thing. What was the point of having something that looks like a mini-barbell in your eyebrow, and from a practical perspective, isn't it a little messy and difficult to blow your nose if you have a ring through it? Although he didn't understand the desire for the addition of the odd facial adornment, he could even overlook that but all over her face? With a campus population of almost 50,000, and more than half of them girls, why choose someone you wouldn't want to be standing next to at the first sign of lightning?

"What do you want?" she asked in a tone that indicated that she didn't care what he wanted. He knew she thought he was a phony and that she didn't mind sharing that opinion with her boyfriend. He wasn't sure how sure how effective her negative publicity campaign was until recently when Randy began to question more and more of his decisions. He and Randy Stewart had started Planet Action almost two years ago and until the arrival of Emma Williams, things had gone great. Stewart was smart, organized, and most importantly, a bit of a wimp whose passion to serve a cause—Tyler always thought that if he'd suggested starting a puppy mill, Stewart's response would have been "Okay"—perfectly qualified him to be the group's detail man and chief sycophant.

Her influence had changed everything. He knew they were both pissed about his decision to move last Saturday's demonstration inside the library, and that they probably blamed him for Tim Price's death, but they just didn't get it. They were content to stay small, with a few marches now and then on campus. That was never Tyler's plan. He created Planet Action with the idea of creating a *movement*, a nationwide organization that could exercise real political power, enough to be courted by politicians and parties, to have real input on platforms and legislation. He'd studied the radical organizations of the '60s and their leaders like Tom Hayden, Abbie Hoffman, and even Eldridge Cleaver. You couldn't do that with a couple hundred people carrying signs in front of the Student Union. Each event had to be bigger than the one before, with more participants and media coverage. If you weren't on camera, you were just background noise. The library demonstration was part of that plan. The visibility they'd gained would give them an even higher profile at tomorrow's Divest Demonstration. He didn't understand why Randy and Emma couldn't understand that.

"I wanted to talk to Randy about tomorrow", he explained. That elicited a lackadaisical "Uh-huh" from the other end of the line. She didn't make things easy.

"Tomorrow is going to be big for us. With everything that's happened the last few days, there's going to be media all over the place. We need to release a statement about our participation and why we support divestment today."

"I thought this was supposed to be a big unity thing," Emma replied.

"It is. It is. But we need to position ourselves in a leadership role. We can't let some other group steal the spotlight. So what if the African-American Students' Collective and the LBGT Coalition are going to be there. No one gives a crap about what they think about climate change. I need Randy to write something up, that's his thing, and get it distributed. Do you even know where he is or when he'll be back?"

"Nope."

He resisted the urge to tell her to he'd love to help her rearrange her collection of metallic objects with a pair of pliers but said, "I'll just text him" instead.

After he texted Randy, he sent a group text to the entire Planet Action organization to remind them of the meeting they were having this evening. By the time he'd finished, he realized that he'd missed his class. He wasn't concerned. Listening to his professor drone on about public opinion and political behavior was one thing—putting those lessons into practice was something else.

Chapter 28

In starts and stops, we filled Pardington in on what we'd found out about Atkinson's murder as we drove to Knowles' house.

"How come the cops were so sure it was those three kids in the library?"

While I had no love for Harley, I believed he and Ward were good cops and had worked the case as the evidence presented itself. "Everything at the crime scene pointed in that direction. When Professor Price first asked me to look at what happened, I told her I would have handled things the same way they had. All the pieces seemed to fit. The Planet Action people had knocked over rows of bookshelves on the third floor. It wasn't a leap in judgment to see them as Tim's killers, even if it was a tragic accident. Nothing they found pointed to his research as the reason for his death. It wasn't until we found out that the idea for his dissertation might have come from an old friend of Knowles that we had even the beginning of an alternative theory for why he was killed."

"Okay, that makes sense. Let me make sure I've got the rest of this right" he said as he began his summary from the back seat. "This Atkinson guy was killed because he confirmed that Professor Price's brother's theory about clouds and climate change was correct. And the person that killed him might be the same one who tried to kill us last night, or is connected to him. But now, since they stole Tim Price's laptop and the only copy of the dissertation and deleted all the files containing his computations and models, there's no proof of motive. Is that everything?"

"That's the working theory," I answered.

It was Olivia who asked the important question: "How do we prove anything without Tim's data, or at least a copy of what he wrote? If Professor Knowles won't talk to us or isn't involved, we don't have anything that supports the reason he was killed."

Her inquiry was seconded by Pardington's "Yeah, what about that?"

No one ever wants to lose, and prosecuting attorneys tend to be some of the most risk-adverse people you'll ever meet. They might be able to arrest someone with probable cause, but their willingness to pursue a conviction is usually based on a direct relationship between the amount of evidence and the level of public awareness regarding the case.

In other words, based on the circumstances surrounding everything that had happened in the past week on the Michigan State campus, the city prosecutor would be wary of taking on anything that didn't include a full confession and pictures of the perpetrators caught in the act. In legal parlance, this is called a slam dunk. Winning cases like this can be the ticket to maintaining or gaining a political office or becoming a member of a prestigious private law firm. Losing them typically means a lifetime of eating your lunch at a gunmetal gray desk. Even with a copy of the dissertation, they would be a long way from the launching pad for a congressional seat or a corner office; without it, even a first-year law student would tell us to "get lost."

"I won't lie," I said. "Without Tim's data, things are a lot more difficult. We need to get another copy of the dissertation. Whoever killed Atkinson and broke into the house has probably destroyed his laptop and the copy we gave to him already. Hopefully, Knowles still has his. He told us he'd read it. If he's involved like we think he is, it's possible but unlikely. The only other thing I can think of is if Tim emailed it to him, it might still be in his email. The odds of that are still pretty low." Not the best way to rally the troops, but it was all I had.

Arthur Knowles sat at his desk. The sun streaming through the windows felt warm on his face. He hadn't bothered to turn on his laptop or look through the stack of papers and journals that had laid claim to the right side of his workspace. What was the point? Whether the world ever learned of what Tim Price had discovered, he knew and moreover, he knew that he'd been right. Ninety-seven percent of scientists, including him, may have agreed, but they were wrong. And because what he'd found would have destroyed the edifice that had been built over time, they would have fought him bitterly. His doctoral defense would have resulted in him being more like Galileo facing the Inquisition than participating in a scholarly debate, and that would have been nothing compared to the wrath he would have faced from the larger scientific community. But in the end, they would have had to admit defeat. The evidence was incontrovertible. For a moment, he imagined himself standing beside his pupil as they combated the assaults both personal and professional together. He quickly banished the thought. He had his chance to be an advocate for a pure empirical discovery but despite his years of devotion to the idea of the sanctity of science, he was no different than the countless others whose fears had led them to shun what was new and radical in the end. His crime was much greater than his disbelief.

Knowles heard shuffling footsteps and a stifled cough and he turned to see that his father had entered the room and taken his usual seat by the fireplace. He was dressed in a blue suit and a shirt featuring a pattern of blue and red checks. A precise Windsor knot stood atop his red tie. "He's having a good day," Knowles thought to himself. Since his father had been diagnosed, his behavior had evolved into a pattern that provided an accurate predictor of his lucidity for the day. On most days, and these were becoming increasingly frequent, his sartorial selections tended to consist of one of the many track suits that they'd purchased for him and some Velcro tennis shoes. Even though the nurse who came in every morning to help him get dressed, every day that he appeared in an outfit that included elastic waist pants and a zippered jacket provided a visual reminder of his surrender to his disease's inexorable advancement. But on the rare days he maintained a tenuous grasp on his receding faculties, he wore the uniform that distinguished him for over 30 years as a serious man whose occupation was devoted to revealing previously undiscovered truths. He had loved the preciseness and unambiguity of science. Justification and proof weren't subject to outside influence, but rather were determined by the replicability of the results. Knowles could only imagine the disappointment the father would have had with the son. Fortunately, his father's condition would spare him that.

With a "Good morning, Arthur," the senior Knowles greeted his son. "What's so interesting out there? I don't see anything."

"Nothing, Dad. I'm working on my remarks for tomorrow and I seem to have a case of writer's block," he said as he turned his desk chair toward his father. "Looking for inspiration I guess. This divestment vote is important. You probably couldn't even have imagined something like this when you first began your research. You should be proud."

His father dispatched the compliment with a wave of his

hand and said, "I wasn't alone. There were plenty of others whose work contributed to what we know of our own impact on the climate, and your work has helped us understand its magnitude. I'm proud of that, but I can't say I'm happy about this divestment business."

Despite what he knew, Knowles was still surprised at his father's statement. "I would have thought this initiative was would have your full support. Are you saying you don't want to attend the protest?"

The old man unbuttoned his jacket and crossed one leg over the other. "I'll go because you're my son, but that doesn't mean I think this action is warranted. Advocacy isn't science. Based on proven facts we can and should advise, but now so many in their myopia resort to demagoguery and demands."

The stiffness and dull ache in his back told Knowles he'd been sitting in the desk chair too long. He got up and took a seat in the deeply padded chair adjacent to his father. "What do you mean by myopia?"

"If there is anything we should understand from our various scientific endeavors, it's that so much of what we observe is only a small element within a, for lack of a better word, system of great complexity. But now, we insist that our findings are unassailable and we must take draconian action to prevent something that to some degree might happen one hundred years from now. These types of actions could have dramatic consequences economically, socially, and politically and are based on the premise that nothing will change during that time. Man adapts—that's the historical lesson that seems to have been forgotten in all this and research won't stop. What we think we know today may prove to be wrong in that time."

"I don't think that will happen. But what if it did? If everything you've worked for and believed in for thirty years was proven wrong tomorrow, you wouldn't be upset or try to disprove it?"

"Arthur," the old man began, "isn't it our purpose to determine the truth? Of course, I would be upset. What man wouldn't when seeing their entire life's work turn out to be false? But has that effort truly been wasted or is its value now being that it served as the foundation that inspired others to challenge it? Did Newton become less of a great mind when Einstein discovered general relativity? This is the nature of what you and I chose to pursue. Much of what's happening now isn't science," he continued. "Hubris and politics are constraining our ability to question and challenge what we think we know and the freedom to pursue alternative theories. Decrying anyone with different point of view as a 'denier' to discredit them and ridicule their work is wrong. Are we so sure in what we think we know that we refuse to believe that we could be wrong, or are we that afraid? I fear that so many in our field, Arthur, have spurned the intellectual pursuit of empiricism and now serve as a collection of Torquemadas."

Up until a few days ago, Knowles would have argued vehemently against his father's assertions. Now through his actions, he had become the chief inquisitor.

Chapter 29

As we got closer to Knowles' house, I once again informed Pardington that his involvement would be limited to however he chose to pass the time while he waited in the car.

"You know, McKay, it would be a lot easier to report on things if I was, you know, able to see and hear them first-hand."

"I hear you, Greg," I responded, "but imagine how much easier it would be for me to be doing my job without having to worry about the health and safety of my own personal scribe."

"Hey, what about last night? I can handle myself. Besides, you're going to let Professor Price come with you."

"Well, Greg, let's think about this. First, stumbling into a gunfight with no weapon isn't the best way to demonstrate that you can handle yourself. Second, Professor Price is intimately involved in this investigation and has information that you don't. And finally, she's much better looking than you."

Olivia smiled.

I could feel him pouting in the back seat before he said, "I just want to say that sucks. If I can't go in, can we at least stop some place so I can get something to read?"

A stop at a 7-11 later, we pulled up in front of Knowles' house. If it was possible, it looked uglier than the last time we'd been there. We left Pardington in the car to occupy himself with a copy of *Sports Illustrated* and began the trek up to the abode. Confronted once again with a door whose previous employer was a missile silo, I opted to announce our arrival by ringing the doorbell.

Sara Knowles greeted us with all the graciousness and enthusiasm that someone usually reserves for those unexpected visitors who ask if you'd like a free copy of the *Watchtower*. "What do you want now? Arthur isn't here."

"Do you know where he went?" I asked.

"I have no idea. He got a phone call and said he had a meeting that he needed to attend. I assumed he was meeting with Devin, Dean Mallory. They've been talking back and forth since he was here yesterday."

"Doctor Mallory was here yesterday? What time was that?" Maybe my questions seemed a little too urgent but for whatever reason, she shrank back inside the doorway. I'm sure that if the door didn't weigh as much as a trash dumpster, she would have slammed it in our faces.

I moved to speak, but it was Olivia's voice I heard before I could open my mouth. "Sara, could we please come in for a moment? Your husband was very helpful yesterday. It's very important that we speak to him. Maybe you might have an idea where he was going to meet Dr. Mallory."

Mrs. Knowles chewed on her lower lip as she contemplated what Olivia had said. You could almost see her trying to weigh the privacy of her husband versus Olivia's plea for compassion in her mind. I was hoping that like most people she'd find it hard to refuse someone standing right in front of her. I thought our being *Watchtower* free was also a point in our favor. At last, she opened the door and ushered us inside.

The place wasn't so much a home as a bunker. As we walked in, I took notice of the artwork that adorned the walls. Each picture was huge—probably to hide as much cement as possible—and featured a mélange of colors with no discernible pattern. I didn't recognize any of the artists, but I was sure that each one cost as much as an SUV.

She guided us to the living room where Olivia and I took a seat on a flat white-leather couch that was like sitting on a plank, while she realigned her posture in a chrome-and-leather strapped chair that could have doubled as a torture device.

"I don't know what you talked about the other day, but he was very upset when you left. Arthur has always been a social drinker, a scotch or two at a party or some wine, but he sat up all night in his office drinking. He wouldn't talk to me. I finally called Devin."Since it appeared that my mode of inquiry made Mrs. Knowles somewhat reticent, Olivia took the lead in the conversation, asking, "Why did you call Professor Malloy?"

Sara was struggling hard to keep her composure, but the tone of her response suggested a growing sense of incomprehension and fear. She admitted, "I didn't know what else to do. He and Devin have been friends for years and I've never seen Arthur like this" followed by the question that she didn't want to ask but had to—"Is he in some kind of trouble?"

Since telling her we were pretty sure that he'd dropped about a thousand pounds of reading material on his best student didn't appear to be the right answer. Olivia elected to go with a more indirect approach. Leaning forward, she said, "We don't know, Sara. We think the reason Tim was killed had something to do with the dissertation he was working on. What we don't know is who killed him. Your husband could be in danger, so it's important that we talk to him".

"A dissertation?" she repeated, almost to herself, trying to make sense of what Olivia had just told her. "I don't understand."

"My brother found something in his research. Whatever it

202

was, it could have a major effect on climate models. Your husband told us that he had a copy of what Tim had written so far. We think that maybe he might have made some notations on it that might help us determine if his death was deliberate and who might have done it."

She shook her head in angry defiance. "No. No. I can't believe that you think Arthur may be involved in this. He's a brilliant man. He thought so much of your brother. I think you need to leave." Her suggestion was equal parts command and shout.

We had come to talk to Knowles and get his copy of the dissertation and now we were on the verge of neither.

Sara Knowles had stood up and was about to lead us to the door when Olivia crossed the room and took hold of her shoulders and turned her so their faces were inches from each other. Softly but firmly, she looked the wife of the man we believed to be her brother's killer in the eye and said, "Think about it, Sara. If your husband wasn't involved in my brother's death, he is now. Whoever killed Tim knows that he knows everything about Tim's work. That makes him a target. Two, possibly three, people have died over this. Do you want your husband to be next?"

The magnitude of the situation finally overwhelmed her and Sara Knowles collapsed into Olivia's arms.

Chapter 30

Sara Knowles held onto Olivia like a drowning man to a lifeline. Olivia guided her back to the couch. Tears traversed her face as she began recounting the recent changes in the Knowles' home.

"Arthur was your brother's advisor for the last two years. In the beginning, he was excited. Even before we were married, I could tell he was restless about his work. I think he felt that his obligations, all the speaking engagements, conferences, and summits, had made him into some type of figurehead. Maybe it wouldn't have been so bad if Dad's health..." she said, her voice trailing off to some distant place.

I was about to speak when she continued, "I think he felt that he had no one to talk to anymore. Arthur is a very private man and he and his father are very close. He said he hadn't done any real work in years and that working with your brother gave him a chance to be a scientist again.".

Olivia moved close to her and put her hand on her arm. "When did things change, Sara?"

Despite Olivia sitting in front of her, Sara Knowles stared blankly at something over her shoulder. She was hugging herself so tight I was waiting to hear the crack of a rib.

She answered, "About two months ago. He was moody and agitated, and when I'd ask him what was wrong, all he would say was 'Nothing.' He spent more and more time in his office. Finally, one night about a week ago, I asked him how your brother's dissertation was coming. He reached for a manuscript on his desk. I assumed it was your brother's. Most of the pages were dog-eared and I could see that he'd written notes on it."

"Could you read any of them?" I asked.

"Arthur's handwriting is almost indecipherable. There was one thing that did stand out though. Right in the middle of the cover page, it said 'No' and it was underlined multiple times. It didn't even look like it was written. It was more like he'd slashed it onto the page."

No witnesses had commented on seeing Knowles at the library last Saturday night. My theory he had killed Tim that night was built on circumstantial evidence and supposition. I didn't want to push her too far or she'd shut down. She was supported by a thin membrane of denial that was getting thinner. Denial gives us hope. When it gives way, all we have is reality.

I decided to bluff, "Mrs. Knowles, do you know where your husband went last Saturday around eight?" Either a yes or a no would prove my point, but the elliptical approach was subtler than asking her if she knew that he went to library to kill his best student.

It was if she was a precious piece of glass and I'd just hit her with a hammer. Hope had left the building. She melded into Olivia and in between sobs, I heard her say, "No."

"Sara", said Olivia, "I think it would be helpful if we looked in your husband's office. Tim's dissertation may still be there."

My eyes did a preliminary sweep of the room as we walked in. Even with the lights on, the room was dark, and the wall of windows provided a perfect view of a line of swollen black clouds moving in from the west. Sara Knowles clung to Olivia like a frightened child to its mother. Her strength had dissipated in direct proportion to the realization that her husband was a killer. Olivia struggled to move into the room due to the weight of her new appendage.

They hadn't redecorated since we'd last been there, and everything seemed to be as I remembered it: stark, cold, and inhospitable. The man defines the room I thought as I moved toward his desk with an echo following every step. I didn't have to go far to see that wherever he went, he'd taken his laptop. A pile of journals and papers were neatly stacked on the glass desktop, but I knew I wouldn't find what I was looking for. I rifled through the pile anyway. I was right.

In a room with a minimalist design, you don't find too many hiding places. Glass-top desks and coffee tables, along with chairs and couches with no cushions to look under meant it didn't take us long to determine that Tim's monograph wasn't here. I heard a shuffling sound behind me and turned to see Knowles' father dressed in an ancient black-velour sweatsuit, an MSU T-shirt, and some Velcro-topped shoes take his customary seat by the fireplace.

I looked at Sara and gestured with my head toward Knowles Sr. She glanced at her father-in-law with uncertainty. She and Knowles had only been married a short time, and I wondered if she'd ever known him in any other capacity or had his dementia made it impossible for him to recognize his son's wife.

"Does Dr. Knowles spend a lot of time in here?" I asked, "He might have seen where your husband put the dissertation."

Her mascara was a delta of black rivulets and her eyes were angry and swollen. It looked like she'd aged 10 years in just a few minutes. Still holding onto Olivia, and in a voice that had to fight to escape, she said, "He does. He likes to sit with Arthur. Today is a bad day, but we could try."

We walked over to the old man. I knew he was in his sixties

but he looked ten years younger. He was neatly shaved with his gray hair combed straight back and his patrician features had obviously been passed down to his son. He looked like he could have been going out to jog.

Sara softly laid her hand on his shoulder. "Dad, these nice people would like to talk to you. Would you like that?"

Olivia and I introduced ourselves. His gaze lingered long enough that I thought there might have been a hint of recognition in his rheumy eyes.

Before either of us could speak, he said, "What a lovely day. Are you in one of my classes? I appreciate you coming but as you know, my office hours are from three to five on Tuesdays and Thursdays."

When my grandmother was diagnosed with Alzheimer's disease, my Mom and Dad and I had met with a social worker who told us how her condition would evolve, what to expect, and even how to talk to her. The best way to avoid agitating her she said was to "play along" and help her do what she needed to do within that context. I think Olivia was surprised when I said, "Yes, professor. We're in your geophysics graduate seminar. Do you have a moment to answer a few questions for us? We'd appreciate it very much."

"Well, you'll have to make it fast. I've got a class in ten minutes," he replied.

"We understand, sir. What we're interested in is if you are aware of any recent research on a potential link between solar activity and long-term cloud-formation cycles? Ms. Price and I have been talking about pursuing this line of inquiry for a paper."

Maybe it was because I'd asked him about something that had been such an integral component of his life or he coincidentally had a moment of lucidity but in either case, his face became a portrait of concentration.

"Interesting you should ask about that," he began. "I've always thought that line of inquiry has never been given the level of attention that it should. What little that has been published, has been largely speculative and shunted off to more obscure journals with less-demanding peer review standards. However, I did read a very interesting article draft on the subject the other day."

I looked at Olivia. Could he be talking about Tim's dissertation? Knowles had said that he had good days and bad days. Maybe he found it on the desk and started reading it, or knew where it was.

"That's one of the reasons for our interest. So far, we've found almost no publications on the subject. If you wouldn't mind, I'd love to make a copy of that paper."

"I don't know," said the elder Knowles. His face began to recede from a confident visage to its original undecipherable state. I was losing him.

"Did you say you were a student?" He looked toward his daughter-in-law in the same way that a child looks at its mother. "I'm tired."

"It's okay, Dad", she said as she and Olivia helped him from the chair and led him to his room in the rear of the house.

I heard them walking back up the hall. Sara collapsed into a chair and sat looking unblinkingly at the storm front moving in.

Olivia pulled me aside. "I don't think she should be left alone. I should stay with her." The tone of her voice told me that my best course of action was to agree. After making sure that she had her phone, I told her I would keep her updated and to call Ward to let him know what we'd found—the prime suspect in Tim's murder was missing. As I watched her walk over to the chair where Sara was sitting, I could only wonder what kind of person could set all her feelings of anger aside to comfort the wife of the man who had killed her brother. I loved her for that, because I knew if I were in her position, I couldn't have done it.

Chapter 31

Arthur Knowles was drunk. Not "tipsy" or "buzzed" or any other polite euphemism for the state where one has ingested enough alcohol to anesthetize themselves. He laid his head down on the patterned red Formica tabletop, hoping it might make him feel better. The cool surface felt good against his unshaven cheek. He thought he might have even fallen asleep, but he wasn't sure. He tried to lift his head. A puddle of spittle marked where it had been. The room spun and somewhere a light so harsh that it felt like looking at the surface of the sun assaulted his eyes. He slowly moved his head to maintain the delicate balance between his brain and a stomach that threatened to revolt at the slightest provocation.

To steady himself, he took a deep breath. The room carried the faint smell of mothballs combined with mildew and ancient vestiges of Lysol. He wretched and forced himself to sit up. He was seated at what must have been, judging from the looks of it, a '50s-era dinner table. It stood on heavy steel legs and its red top was bounded on all sides by a steel rim. He was sitting in one of the four matching vinyl-covered chairs, one per side. The floor was covered with cracked brick-colored linoleum featuring black fleur de lis.

An old pink stove was housed amongst a line of bruised and scuffed cabinets featuring copper-colored pulls that must have been the height of suburban style when the home was first built. He lifted his hand and shaded his eyes as his gaze moved to the window over the kitchen's sink. Time had taken its toll on the sheer lace curtains that hung from the rod.

Though they'd been crisp and white when the owner first hung them, there was now a pair of moth-eaten yellowed facsimiles in their place.

He tried to stand and immediately sat back down. He closed his eyes and tried to remember the events that had led him here. At first, only random images seemed to flash through the minefield that had replaced his brain. The very act of thinking, or trying to, set off an explosion that reverberated through his head. His mouth was dry and he briefly contemplated attempting to navigate his way to the sink. Remembering his first attempt at mobility, he decided against it. He wasn't sure if the room was warm or cold, but his stomach felt like he'd eaten burning embers and he'd sweated completely through his custom-made shirt. A rank sweet-sour smell was beginning to grow in the room and he knew that it came from him. He laid his head back down.

After a few moments, and a sheer force of will, he pushed up on the table to reach a full sitting position. He spit up some acidic bile into his mouth, but was otherwise able to quell the growing rebellion in his stomach. Slowly pushing back from the table, he put his right hand onto the corresponding knee and pushed as he straightened from the chair. He stumbled but caught himself on one of the cabinets. Using them as a rail, he inched his way to the sink. He'd just turned on the faucet when he heard footsteps behind him.

"Arthur, you're up. Good."

Knowles turned from the sink and saw Mallory and another man he didn't know.

"Devin, how long have I been here? I need to call Sara."

"It's okay, Arthur. I called her. Said we'd all had a little too much to drink, so she's fine."

Mallory looked like he was ready to step in front of a class. He was wearing a blue suit with a light-blue oxford underneath punctuated by a yellow-striped tie. The other man was leaning against the doorframe with his arms crossed. He wore jeans, an old full-sleeved T-shirt, and a pair of running shoes. Mallory guided him back to his seat and then sat in the one adjacent to him.

"Devin, what is this place and why are we here?"

"This," he began as he moved his arm through the air like a flight attendant directing someone to the exit aisle, "is a place I bought a few years ago. It's right off the lake, and I thought it would make a perfect fishing cabin. I guess like a lot of the things that we always mean to get around to, for one reason or another, I never did. But I still enjoy the quiet, and come up here every so often to just to be alone and relax. The lake is beautiful this time of year. There's always a gentle breeze, and in the morning, it seems like it gives birth to the sun. I can sit beside it for hours listening to the roll of the tiny waves and the sounds of the birds and insects. Words don't do it justice. Maybe a poet's would."

He moved a little too quickly and had to close his eyes for a moment. "But why am I—we—here?"

One blue cloth-clad leg went over the other as Mallory turned to face him. "Arthur, you called me" in a voice in which Knowles thought he heard a touch of derision.

"Called you. Why did I call you?"

"You said you wanted to talk more about what we discussed the other day, and based on the nature of that, I thought it made sense to speak in private."

"Yeah, yeah. That makes sense. What did we talk about exactly?"

"You don't remember a word of what we agreed on?"

"Devin, please. I've already said I don't recall anything we discussed. What exactly did we agree on?"

Mallory motioned to the other man who went over to one of

cabinets beside the sink and returned with a glass and a bottle of Grey Goose. He poured until the glass was half full and then set both the glass and the bottle down in front of him.

"I think I've had enough," objected Knowles as he pushed both away from him.

Mallory leaned over, pushed them back into their original positions, and said, "Take the drink, Arthur. What we agreed to last evening was that you would turn yourself in for the murder of Tim Price. I've already contacted a lawyer I know in Chicago. He should be here in a few hours. He's the best I know. He'll meet you at the house."

By the time Mallory had finished, Knowles' head was already in his hands and his shoulders were heaving. "Devin, I'll go to prison. I can't—Sara."

Mallory pushed the drink closer to Knowles and put his arm around his friend's shoulder. As though speaking to a child, he slowly said, "You have the opportunity to take a plea. There is just no other alternative. If you went to trial, I'd have to testify as to what you told me. We've been friends too long for either of us to have to go through that. Take the drink, Arthur."

There was nothing left that he could say. He'd done it. He reached for the glass and drank it down, and looked at his old friend.

"Go home, Arthur. Get some rest. Your attorney will meet you there in a few hours."

"My friend," he said pointing to the man who had retaken his position in the doorway, "will take you."

Chapter 32

Over 200 enthusiastic black hoodie-clad students occupied the seats in one of Wells Hall's amphitheater-sized classrooms to receive their last instructions regarding the tactics they would employ at tomorrow's anti-fossil fuels demonstration. Greyson Tyler stood in front of the black-topped wooden desk that sat on the beige linoleum floor at the front of the room. Every eye riveted on the man who in just over a year had masterminded the group's ascension to a powerful force on campus and enjoyed growing nationwide visibility. As he surveyed the room, Tyler caught himself wondering if he would have to sever his ties to group when he moved on to work for Congressman and potentially Senator Perkins' staff. Lately, he'd been weighing his options on the subject on an increasingly frequent basis.

He'd never imagined that when he and Randy Stewart had come up with the idea to start Planet Action that it would become so intertwined with his immediate—and maybe long-term—future. Sure, at the time he'd thought it would be a nice addition to his resume, but Stewart had been more of the true believer.

Things had escalated quickly. In the beginning, it had just been the two of them and a few others standing on the bridge on Farm Lane Road trying to talk, more like evangelize he thought in retrospect, to passing students about the catastrophic consequences that awaited them if they didn't repent and commit themselves to reducing their carbon footprint. Their ratio of being flipped off to acquiring new converts to the cause would have sent them to the deep minors, if they'd been playing baseball.

It had been Tyler who came to the realization that if they were to be anything other than a small group of dilettantes who had dabbled in the whole climate-change protest thing before they left college for the "real" world, they needed to project an image that dramatically eclipsed their size. Googling "How to promote your interest group organization" had led him to a bunch of seriously boring articles and reading *Rules for Radicals* may have worked for Obama, but isolating the opposition and demonizing them didn't seem like a strategy that was going to turn "Fuck you's" into "Tell me more" with any degree of alacrity.

It wasn't until one of his roommates—between bong hits—mentioned that he should try guerilla marketing that he was able to determine his strategy. The roommate explained how one of those groups that was always quoted in those no-shit articles like "Mexican Food is Fattening" started out as two guys and a fax machine who sent their self-written press releases to hundreds of TV and radio stations with the belief that one or two of them would use the information as fill in on a slow news day. He woke up the next day with two thoughts: One, that anyone who doubted the positive effect of weed on the creative process had never tried it, and two, that a single massive group list eliminated the need for a fax machine—did companies even have those anymore?—was his solution for garnering media attention.

It took him a week to compile the email addresses of the news contacts for all the major cable and network news organizations and 200 or so newspapers, and television and radio stations within the U.S. and Canada, and after that, it had been easy. With his very first release about shrinking ice sheets in the Arctic that he'd put together based on something

215

he'd read in *Time Magazine,* he'd had over fifty requests for interviews and quotes, thereby proving that people were more interested in the climate than in burrito consumption. The television requests began to come in after the third email blast and included one from CNN. In just a short time, he'd become the face of Planet Action and Stewart and his green-haired girlfriend began to bitch about "losing touch with the group's original mission." As the group and its profile continued to grow, so did their resistance to anything that wasn't ten or fifteen people marching around with signs.

Tyler had noticed the divisions within Planet Action over the past few weeks. A small number of the original members had become more vocal in their agreement with Stewart regarding the organization's direction. Although he doubted they would be able to sow the seeds of discontent much further since the new recruits to the cause viewed the prospect of being on television or having their pictures in the paper a privilege of membership, the library protest had brought matters to a head.

Naturally, the Stewart-led faction viewed what happened as evidence of the need to return to their founding principles, but their lack of media savvy blinded them to the opportunity that the events of that night presented. What had happened to Tim Price was a tragedy, but his death was the result of Planet Action members acting out due to their frustration with the university's reluctance to take decisive action to demonstrate their commitment to providing an example for other schools to follow. It was a simple question of perspective. If they didn't build on their current level of visibility, Planet Action would become just another group of tree huggers. Tomorrow was their first chance to capitalize on the opportunity that had been presented to them.

His emergence as a "leading spokesman for the climate

change movement"—the news media's description not his— had recently caused him to re-evaluate his post-graduation plans. The goal of becoming either an elected or behind-the-scenes leader in Democratic politics remained in place, but he had begun to wonder if becoming a low-paid staffer for a congressman or even a senator was the most-efficient route to get there. Producing policy papers wasn't the same as standing in front of a camera projecting his words and face to a nationwide audience. His vision for Planet Action had proven to be successful, and in his mind, the next steps were abundantly clear.

He'd have to get rid of Stewart, of course, but calling him out in front of the group's growing membership would take care of that. Most importantly, however, was the need to establish a funding source to underwrite the ongoing activities of the organization. Naturally, a salary commensurate with his position as its founder and spokesman would fall within those operational expenses. They were already a 527 organization, so the next step was a targeted social-media campaign to sell Planet Action memberships to a target audience whose awareness and engagement with the organization was growing daily. He'd even had calls from a couple of New York- and California-based PR agencies regarding their interest in helping him "define and disseminate" the group's message on a global basis. Increasingly, he felt drawn to a larger social mission than to becoming some low-level political cube monkey.

Like a general marshalling his forces, Tyler laid out his plan to ensure the maximum level of visibility for Planet Action. He'd be on the main speaking platform of course. Volunteering to chauffeur Knowles' dad and his hot young wife to the event had ensured he'd be in every camera shot tomorrow. Getting to the event well before it's 11:00 a.m. starting time was the key objective for the remainder of his uniformly clad followers.

"The people watching need to see a sea of black in front of the stage," he instructed them, "and don't put your hoods up. We want them to see a group of student advocates, not a bunch of thugs. We'll meet in front of the Computer Science Building at eight o'clock where you'll be assigned to your group leader. They'll be responsible for watching for cameras and coordinating your chants. Beth is passing out a list of the best sign slogans that we've used in the past, but feel free to come up with your own."

He walked toward his seated charges, spread his arms as if trying to embrace them all, and spoke in a tone that made each one feel he was speaking to them alone.

"Tomorrow is the biggest and most important event that has happened on this campus since the antiwar protests in the '60s. It's been your dedication and conviction that has played a major role in making it a reality. You've compelled an entire university, not Penn State, not Cal-Berkeley, not Harvard, but Michigan State, to demonstrate that fossil fuels are not our future."

His audience was entranced. He didn't waste the moment. He continued with, "Each of you needs to make sure that everyone watching sees what even a small group of people dedicated to a principle can achieve and inspire them to join us. Tomorrow is about more than a divestment vote. It's your moment. This is what change feels like. Take hold and revel in it."

After he'd dismissed them, he decided he was going to have to have another talk with the congressman.

Chapter 33

The Knowles' lawn was accumulating an impressive collection of increasingly larger portions of the surrounding trees when I stepped out of the front door. The angry-looking clouds that I'd seen were being ushered in by winds whose speed and ferocity was literally making the surrounding maples and oaks bend to their will. An ominous green-tinged sky was retreating quickly in the face of cloud-swept darkness, and the first drops of rain landed hard enough to sting my face. My car was a fading silhouette against the gathering blackness. A soft glow from its interior told me that Pardington had resorted to the dome light to continue his in-depth study of the *Sports Illustrated* that we'd bought him.

Someone's lawn furniture tumbled across the street as I prepared to pit my formerly 4.5 forty-yard dash speed against the mass of thunderheads preparing to unleash their full fury on the surrounding area. A crooked scar of lightning erupted in the distance, leaving the smell of burnt ozone in its wake as I raised my jacket to cover the side of my face and sprinted toward the car. I've been hit by 300-pound linemen bent on causing me extreme bodily injury, but the force of the wind was turning a variety of objects like branches, bikes, and even a garden gnome, into projectiles that could have easily done the same job. Circumnavigating the latticed brick path might have offered firmer footing, but the front lawn offered a more direct path to the car, so I hurdled a short boxwood hedge and ran. I reached the car just as the clouds decided that they could hold their burden no longer.

I pulled my already water-saturated leg inside just as the wind slammed my door shut.

"Jesus Christ!" exclaimed Pardington in response to seeing two bolts of lightning lay waste to a pine tree about twenty feet from us. "Did you see that? Man. I was sitting here reading my magazine—did you know the Chargers were playing in a soccer stadium this year, and all of a sudden, it was black. I had to turn on the dome light to see. I couldn't even see *you* until you opened the door."

I pulled out my phone and felt for my keys in my jacket pocket as the rain pounded out "The Anvil Chorus" on every available metal surface of the Infiniti.

"Where did this come from?" Pardington asked. "The rain's almost horizontal; I just saw a big-ass tree branch fly by."

"It's a derecho," I said.

"What the hell is a derecho?"

"Technically, it's straight-line wind storm associated with fast-moving thunderstorms. Lansing lies within an area that gets an average of one a year."

"Where'd you learn that? Sounds like you know a lot about the weather."

"I heard it somewhere, I can't remember. My brain is a repository for tiny bits of useless information."

"I don't know. Sounds like it would come in handy with your job."

"Not really. I can answer more questions on 'Jeopardy' than the average person. For instance, I can tell you that there was a fourth Marx brother named Gummo, but I can't remember the combination to my office safe. Not a lot of bang for the buck."

"So, how do you get into the safe?"

"Nikki," I replied.

Apparently, he was losing interest in this line of questioning since he didn't bother to follow up by asking who Nikki was. He'd have to develop better instincts in this area since the answer to that question was the most interesting part of the entire discussion.

"Isn't the professor coming with us? And where are we going anyway?"

"No, she's staying with Mrs. Knowles. We strongly implied what we think her husband did. She's not taking it well," I said before dialing the number for Devin Mallory's office.

His assistant answered, leaving Pardington hanging in mid-question. She informed me that the dean had finished packing up his office and had left for the day, presumably to go home to help his wife finish up with their final preparations for their move to D.C.

Sara Knowles had said that Mallory only lived about a mile away. A second call to Olivia provided me with his home address.

I started the car and put the windshield wipers on the highest setting, thereby producing a small tidal wave with each sweep. The night had embraced the storm and the porch lights of Knowles' neighbors looked like flickering candles in the distance as we drove off.

Chapter 34

"So, where are we going?" inquired Pardington.

"Dean Mallory's house. Knowles told his wife that he was going to a meeting and she assumed that that's who he was meeting with. His wife told us he was in the library that night and that something about Tim's dissertation upset him, giving him opportunity and motive. I don't know if he went there intending to kill Tim, but he did it. But she also gave him an alibi for Atkinson, so someone else killed him. I think he can give us the answer to the question of who did."

If it was possible, the storm seemed to worsen on our way to Mallory's. I could say that the wind made it difficult to stay in our own lane, but that would mean I could see the lines on the road. Pardington had a death grip on the passenger handle over his door and I was squeezing the steering wheel hard enough to leave indentations as each car that passed us going the other way was just a brief flash of light. The sewers must have given up the fight as the water volume the storm was generating eclipsed their ability to dispose of it, which explained the wakes we left in our path before we finally reached our destination.

Pardington made a half-hearted move towards his door with a pleading look in his eye, but I sentenced him to another term within my car's tan-leather confines with a quick shake of my head. Resigned to his fate, he reached around and grabbed his *Sports Illustrated* from the back seat and tried to engross himself in a story asking the eternal question, "Can Aaron Rodgers Take the Packers Back to the Super Bowl?"

My phone rang as I was about to get out of the car. It was Ward.

"Hey, what happened to you guys?", I asked. "I thought you were going to come to Knowles' house after you finished at the crime scene. He wasn't there. His wife said he left for a meeting but she wasn't sure with who."

Ward's response was succinct and direct—"He's dead, Mitch."

Based on everything that had happened, Ward's information didn't surprise me as much as it might have. Someone—I was coming to believe I was sitting in front of his house—was taking care of loose ends, and by default, he looked like the obvious winner of the who-has-the most-to lose sweepstakes.

"When?"

"Today. Couple of kids found him in his car. The coroner thinks he can only have been dead for a couple hours at most. Blew his brains out, or at least it looks that way. Body smelled like he'd taken a bath in alcohol. Half a bottle of vodka was on the seat next to him. He left a note. Said he killed Price out of jealousy. A student surpassing the teacher kind of thing and he couldn't deal with it. He'd met him at the library a few times, so knew he'd be there. He didn't say why he went there, but he did say that he didn't go intending the kill him. Said it was an impulsive act."

"Do you think he killed himself?"

"Can't be sure. He was shot in the temple. There were powder burns around the wound, and that's consistent with someone shooting themselves at close range."

As I held up my hand in response to Pardington who mouthed "Who died?" I asked Ward to tell me about the note. "Did he write it, or was it typed? Was it folded or wrinkled at all?"

223

"Typed. Printed off on a regular piece of paper. He signed it. The paper wasn't folded. Why? Is that important?"

"Think about it", I answered. "First, he didn't handwrite it. I've seen it happen once or twice, but ninety-nine percent of the time, if someone leaves a note, they've written it themselves. Second, he obviously doesn't have a printer in his car, so he had to print the note off and take it with him. Seems odd that he didn't fold it to put in his pocket.

It's not a lot I know, but it's not consistent with the suicides I saw when I was a cop either."

"Your saying you think someone offed him because he killed Price?"

"No, I'm saying someone wants us to think he killed himself because of *why* he killed Tim."

I asked him where he was and he said that he and Harley were on their way to Knowles' house to break the news to his wife. I didn't envy them that task, and was glad that Olivia had decided to stay behind. After telling him where we were, I told him I'd call as soon as I finished to update him on what I'd learned.

The Mallory home resembled an English manor—I guess the academic world paid better than I thought. Ivy adorned its cut stone walls and a trio of large stained glass windows punctuated the area above the recessed arched doorway with a heavy wooden door that looked like it had been imported from an ancient castle located at its apex. A driveway bordered on both sides by a series of equally spaced oak trees led up to a massive stone-and-mortar portico that served as a way station to a carriage house that judging by the number of wooden garage doors could house at least four cars. The unrelenting rain and the continuous assault of lightning that briefly illuminated the house like a spotlight made it look like the kind of place you saw in the movies where evil scientific experiments were conducted or the wolf man called home in-between his lunar-fueled rampages.

Through a series of contortions, I separated myself from my jacket, which I threw over my head as I opened my door and prepared to sprint to the Mallorys' front door. I've never been sprayed with a fire hose, but I've got to believe it feels like what hit me as soon as I stepped from the car. The wind left me clutching my jacket with one hand as I covered my eyes with the other and my rain-soaked clothes were clinging to me before I'd even reached the front of the car. I made it to the sanctuary of the porch without losing any important articles of clothing and rang the doorbell. Chimes resonated from deep within and by the completion of my second ring, the porch light came on and the door opened.

A woman cautiously peered out from behind the door, which made sense since unless she'd ordered a pizza the weather made it unlikely that someone who was just in the neighborhood would be stopping by. My resemblance to drowned vermin must have made me harmless looking enough for her to open the door further and ask, "Can I help you?"

I introduced myself, and presuming that she was Mrs. Mallory, explained that I was helping the police in their investigation of Tim Price's death—which, using a broad definition of helping, I was. I told her I was looking for her husband and Arthur Knowles.

"I'm Jean Mallory. I'm afraid they're not here. Would you like to come in for a moment? I can get you a towel to dry off." That sounded like a fair exchange, so I stepped inside.

Jean Mallory was pretty, about 5' 5" and looked to be in her late 40s or early 50s. Her brown hair was pulled back into a ponytail and a pair of tortoise-shell glasses hung from a chain around her neck. She was dressed in old sweatshirt with "U.S

.Army" on its front and jeans. The foyer was lined with polished wood and moving boxes in various stages of being packed were spread across the black-and-white marble-tiled floor.

"You'll have to forgive the mess. We're moving to Washington and I'm afraid my husband has abdicated all responsibility for our preparation to me. Here, let me get you a towel. I'm sure there are some in one of these boxes over here."

"Yes, I heard about his new position. You must be excited."

She responded as she rummaged through a box perched atop a stack of three others, "I suppose. We've lived there before when Devin was at the Pentagon. It may be the nation's capital, but it can be smothering. Petty gossip tends to be the lingua franca and it doesn't take long to recognize the same faces at the same parties and gatherings."

"I wouldn't characterize that response as unbridled enthusiasm."

She found her towel stash, grabbed one, and offered it to me as she continued, "I'm sure that sounded ungrateful. Certainly, it's good for Devin and provides recognition for his work. It's just that I like it here. I thought this would be our last stop. It's also been a long day of packing. Not a great combination. You said you were looking for Devin and Arthur. What made you think they were here?"

I used the towel to dry myself off as best as I could, although it was more of an exercise in futility since neither the wind or rain were demonstrating any signs of stopping. Based on her question, she hadn't heard the news about Knowles' death.

"Arthur told his wife he was leaving for a meeting and she thought it was with your husband. I called his office and his admin said that she thought he'd come home to help you pack," I replied.

"Bad assumption. He told me he'd be in meetings all day. I didn't bother to ask where. I tried to call him about an hour ago, but he didn't pick up."

I thanked her for her time and was about to leave when I remembered what she'd said about the Pentagon. I handed her back the towel and said, "I didn't know that Dr. Mallory was in the military. Judging by your shirt, I'm guessing the Army?"

"It was a long time ago. He was Special Forces. I knew less about his whereabouts then than I do now. He could never tell me where he was going or where he'd been. There's a picture here somewhere. I just finished packing up his office."

She walked over to an open box nearby. "Here it is," she said as she handed it to me. Major Mallory stood in the center of a group of men who, judging by the condition of their camouflage uniforms, must have just completed a mission. The picture was at least fifteen years old, but there was no mistaking the Green Beret at the far right of the picture. Kevin Harley was smiling back at me.

Chapter 35

I handed the picture back to Mrs. Harley, said good-bye and ran back to the car. Pardington gave me a confused look as I slammed my door and said, "It's Mallory and Harley."

My pants squeaked as I slid across the leather seat and hit the start button. I turned up the heat. "They were in the Army together. One or the other of them killed Knowles and Atkinson."

After I grabbed my phone, I punched in Ward's number. He didn't answer and my call rolled to voice mail. "Ward, Harley, and Mallory were in Special Forces together. They're the ones who killed Knowles and Atkinson, and tried to kill Olivia and me. You've got to stop Harley and get Olivia and Sara out of there."

Pardington was only able to blurt out, "What's going—" before I cut him off with, "I'll explain on the way" and dialed Olivia. She answered on the first ring.

"Mitch, where are you? The power is out here—"

Before she could continue, I said, "Olivia, I need you to listen to me. Are Sara and Knowles' dad with you?"

"Sara is. I think his dad is in his room."

"Are Harley and Ward there?"

"Yes. They got here right after the power went out, and then there was a crash in the back of the house. Ward went to check it out, and Harley told us to get into the bedroom and lock the door."

"Okay. I need you to stay calm. Knowles is dead." An audible gasp was her response. I heard Sara Knowles ask,

"What is it?" in the background. I hurried on, "Mallory and Harley are in this together. One of them, I'm not sure which one—maybe both—killed Knowles and Atkinson. Stay where you are. I should be there in a few minutes. Make sure the door is locked and don't come out until I tell you to."

My car began to hydroplane as I took a curve on the way back to Knowles' house. Oncoming headlights glared across the windshield as I eased off the gas, steered into the slide, and then spun the wheel back toward my side of the road. Out of the corner of my eye, I saw Pardington brace himself for impact.

The set of red taillights that appeared in my rearview mirror confirmed that we'd averted catastrophe, and he eased back into his seat gulping down air while repeating a mantra of "Oh, my God. Oh, my God." Having given sufficient thanks to his lord and savior, he began his inquest, "Knowles is dead? And that cop and the Dean are in on it? What the hell is going on?"

"Some kids found Knowles' car. He'd been shot in the head. It looks like someone tried to make it look like he killed himself."

"He killed the professor's brother. Maybe he couldn't live with it and really did kill himself."

"That would make sense, except Knowles' wife said he so upset yesterday that she called Mallory and had him come over to see if he could calm him down. Now, Knowles is dead, and Mallory's wife just showed me a picture of him and Harley when they were Green Berets together. I think Knowles told Mallory what he'd done, and Mallory was worried that the findings in Tim's dissertation would come out if Knowles were arrested. I don't think they would cost him the EPA job, but they'd throw a lot of things into question. Atkinson confirmed Tim's findings, so they both had to go. Mallory must have reached out to Harley to help him contain the situation. Harley and Ward are at the house now, and if he and Harley are working together, Mallory's either on his way or there already."

The power outage and storm had turned the area surrounding Knowles' home into a black hole where no light was able to penetrate. I slowed to a crawl as the rain made the effective range of my headlights measurable in inches and parked cars arose like icebergs around the *Titanic*. I had Pardington grab the heavy police flashlight I keep in the glove compartment and call out the obstacles and street signs that we passed on his side of the road. We almost passed the street before he yelled out, "Turn here!" and we slid around the corner.

I stopped at what I guessed was midway down the street and cut the lights. It was doubtful that anyone in the house could have seen me coming, but I didn't want to take the chance of trying to drive up any closer. I was sure there would be no cops other than Ward and Harley there since they would have had no reason to call for backup. If Mallory wasn't there, he soon would be, as he still needed to find the missing copy of Tim's dissertation to remove the last bit of evidence that could point towards Atkinson's and after the ME's examination, Knowles' murders back to him. I wondered if the crash that Olivia had mentioned hadn't been the diversion needed to isolate the house's occupants while he got inside. I could only hope that Ward had gotten my message; otherwise, I'd be going into a dark house with two government-trained killers waiting for me inside.

Even though it was unlikely, I couldn't take the chance that Harley didn't have one or more partners in the East Lansing PD so I told Pardington to call the state police and tell them where we were and that I was going in after two suspects in the Atkinson murder and that one of them was a cop. On a good day, they would be here in five minutes or so. Obviously, this wasn't a good day but with Olivia, Sara, and Knowles' father inside, I couldn't wait.

I grabbed my gun, took the flashlight, and got out of the car. I started walking in an arc toward the left side of the house. If they were looking for the dissertation, they'd start in the study, which was on the right and I'd be easy to see through its window wall despite the darkness and rain. As I got closer, I saw the unmarked blue Charger that Harley and Ward had arrived in and a dark SUV that looked like it could be an Escalade. Mallory was here. From where I was, I didn't see any beam from a flashlight, but that could mean that they hadn't looked in the study yet or had moved on from there. Based on their training and experience, either Harley or Mallory would have a substantial advantage on me without the weather conditions and the power outage. With them, my odds of getting into the house undetected, neutralizing them, and getting everyone out were better—not by much, but it helps to be optimistic.

Staying near the tree line, I made my way around to the back of the house. I approached it from an angle until I came to the rear wall. I moved slowly along the smooth concrete looking for a way in. The rain slammed into my face. The windows I saw were too high to get through easily. Even though the wind would probably cover the sound of my breaking the glass and climbing through, I preferred not to take that chance. A door that opened from the house onto the backyard's patio and pool provided me the opportunity I needed. It was locked, but the window was divided into twelve individual panes. I wrapped my gun in my jacket, and just to make sure, I broke the window nearest the door handle in concert with a huge blast of thunder. After clearing the stray glass from the frame's interior, I reached down and turned both the dead bolt and lock on the handle, slowly opened the door, and stepped inside.

I tried to let my eyes adjust to the darkness. The house was so still I could hear each drop that fell from every part of me hit the room's tile floor. I shivered violently as the dampness seemed to bore deep into my marrow. My visual reconnaissance of the room enabled me to discern what must have been a large washer and dryer to my left, and what appeared to be a bench on my right. I stuffed the flashlight into my back pocket to keep my hand free to help me navigate by feel to avoid stumbling into something and announcing my presence. I began moving in a half shuffle toward the door. I'd only taken a couple of steps when my foot struck something solid.

The object moved slightly and I knew I'd found Ward. I bent down and my fingers touched his arm. As hard as I tried to listen, I heard no breathing. I moved my hand up until I reached his neck and found a weak, but steady pulse. Pulling the flashlight from my pocket and using my jacket to hood the light, I surveyed for injuries. No blood had pooled around the body itself, so it didn't appear that he'd been shot or stabbed. As the light reached his head, my suspicions were confirmed. A deep cut curled around the area behind his ear. The blood had largely dried, so he'd been here for a while.

I crawled over to the washer and dryer and felt around the areas next to both. My search uncovered a basket of laundry, and I felt through it until I found a couple of towels. I covered Ward with one and folded the other and placed it under his head. There wasn't anything else I could do for him. Carefully moving around his body, I felt along the wall until I my hand hit the doorknob. Gently pushing his legs away with my foot, I cleared enough room to open the door and stepped into what I thought was the main hallway that ran through the center of the house.

Based on my understanding of the layout gained through my two previous visits, the study, living room, and whatever else I hadn't seen were to my left, and I assumed since I was in the rear of the house that any doorways to my right would be bedrooms or bathrooms. I moved slowly towards the front of the house, concentrating on placing one foot completely down before moving the other forward to ensure I was as quiet as possible.

Using my left hand to probe what was on that side, I tried to stay in the path's center to limit the chances of an unfortunate encounter with any unseen pieces of décor. No sounds punctuated the silence. If I was being optimistic, this might have meant that Harley and Mallory were so unnerved by the prospect of my arrival that they had fled the premises. Since being realistic tends to increase the odds of surviving situations like this however, they either knew I was here or were expecting me. In either case, they had three advantages: One, they knew where each other were; two, I had to come to them; and three, based on their backgrounds, they had probably done this at least a couple of times in the past. As a cop, I'd had to go into buildings and houses after suspects and that was always a dangerous proposition, but none of them had been trained in how to ambush and kill someone.

In the police academy, you spend a lot of time learning how to clear a building. The first thing you learn is not to walk past a doorway since whether it's open or closed, an attacker may be waiting within to take you from behind. Of course, either I was absent that day or they didn't cover what to do when you can't see any doors. Based on what had been done to Ward, they didn't see him as a direct threat. It was reasonable to assume he didn't know that Harley and Mallory were working together, and that he wouldn't expect his attacker to be his own partner.

Unlike Ward, they were certain of what I knew and I was sure they planned on a more permanent method of dealing with me. The one thing in my favor was that since Knowles' father, Olivia, and Sara were hidden away, they wouldn't want to risk having to shoot me before they found what they were looking for. That way, Mallory could leave, and Harley could say he shot me by accident as Ward and I mistakenly fought with each other in the dark. It would be considered just an unfortunate accident, leaving no physical proof regarding Tim's murder and the subsequent efforts to cover it up.

Even though I couldn't use it for its intended purpose, I figured it wouldn't hurt to have another weapon at my disposal, so I grabbed the flashlight from my back pocket and continued to move up the concrete tunnel that ran through the Knowles' home. I'd made it about a third of the way toward the front of the house when what felt like a baseball bat hit me between the shoulders and drove me face first into the wall. The blood cascaded down into my left eye as a fist slammed into my kidney with the force of a sledgehammer. An intense pain exploded through my body, and like a distant echo, I heard my gun hit the floor and bounce away. The attacker brought his right forearm up around my neck and his left reached up from under my arm to grasp it and apply additional leverage to my windpipe.

I rotated to my right and brought my heel down on the inside of his ankle, but my position against the wall didn't provide the room I needed to generate enough force to break it. My lungs were screaming, and I was becoming light-headed from the crushing force of his forearm on my throat. My arms were pinned against the wall and I knew I had only a few seconds before I lost consciousness. His breath was hot against me as I quickly moved my head forward and then snapped it back. I heard a loud crack as the back of my head collided with his mouth.

In response, his grip lessened just long enough for me to rotate my neck to provide me a clear angle on his right wrist. My teeth bit down hard on his arm, and I angrily shook my head back and forth like a dog trying to break the neck of its prey. Instantly, my mouth was filled with the copper taste of blood and his scream of pain echoed off the concrete walls. His arm flew away from me, and I heard a metallic sound hitting concrete as I let the flashlight slide down my hand until I was gripping it by its end while pivoting violently toward my target. My arm accelerated through its rotation and the crunching sound of metal meeting bone told me I'd hit my mark.

His body landed behind me with a loud exhalation of air as he hit the floor. My eye stung from the blood that continued to seep into it, and I held my arm against the cut to staunch the bleeding. I coughed and struggled for air as I fell back against the wall and bent over to catch my breath. The sound of the struggle ensured that my assailant's partner knew where we were and wouldn't wait to find out the outcome.

The importance of concealing my position now gave way to the need to find my gun as fast as possible, so I clicked on the flashlight and swept the hallway. I heard the frantic sound of my attacker searching for his own weapon behind me and then saw my Berreta on the rug five feet ahead of me to my right. A paroxysm of pain surged through me as I leapt toward the gun. I grabbed it and as I rolled into a sitting position, I shone the light toward the source of the sounds behind me. Its beam landed on Kevin Harley. His jaw was covered with black blood and his eyes blazed directly into mine as he raised his gun. I shot him in the face.

Chapter 36

I shone the light up and down the hallway to find some cover, but as with the rest of the house's furnishings, a couple of leather-and-chrome chairs or oversized paintings didn't offer up any particularly robust defensive possibilities. The sound of heavy footsteps sounded like they were coming from the study, which meant I didn't have much time. I grabbed Harley's now-faceless body and pulled it in front of me to use as a shield. My options were limited. Other than my breathing, I detected no other sounds, so the cops still weren't here. I didn't know what rooms Olivia and Sara and Dr. Knowles were in, so I had to assume they were somewhere between Mallory and me. Since he knew their location, he could get to them before I could, eliminating the possibility of trying to wait him out. My only choice was to keep moving forward.

The footsteps I'd heard stopped. I realized that Mallory was facing a dilemma of his own. Still being in the house meant that he hadn't found the copy of the dissertation, and worse, that he'd heard the gunshot but didn't know who had been on the receiving end. Without being sure if Harley had been successful in removing me from the equation, he had to wait to see who the victor had been. If it was Harley, his search for the manuscript could continue and Harley's "tragic-accident" story would explain the two dead bodies; if it was me, then he'd have to finish both jobs himself. The only sounds I heard were the wind and the rain. Then Mallory yelled out Harley's name. I didn't bother to respond. He had his answer.

I called out to Olivia and told them to run, but the thunder had reached a crescendo and I could only hope that they'd heard me. I tore a piece from Harley's shirt long enough to tie around my head as a makeshift bandage and turned off the flashlight. Leaving it on might make it easier to locate Mallory, but it would also enable him to see me.

The door to the study loomed just ahead of me. I crouched low as I approached it. If Mallory was armed and I assumed he was, he would be positioned away from the door to give him the best possible view and the most time to determine who entered the room. In the unlikely event that he didn't have a gun, I was sure he'd be located along the wall on either side of the door, probably the left since most people are right-handed and tend to enter a room in a position that doesn't require them to immediately turn and shoot. Of course, although I understood the strategy, that didn't mean that's what he'd do, so what might seem like a 50/50 decision on my part was probably less than that.

The wall of windows opposite the door did nothing to lighten the veil of blackness cloaking the room. I'd carried Harley's body on my back to this point. Upon reaching the edge of the doorframe, I pushed up with my legs standing it erect as I rose. I've done more than my share of squats while weightlifting but this was the first time I've done it with a dead man. I twisted the faceless Harley in front of me and moved through the door. As I pushed the corpse of his former collaborator into the room, I ducked and moved to my left.

Mallory said nothing as I slid in behind the fireplace chair nearest the door, and two bullets pounded into the wall behind me. From my position I blocked a door near the fireplace that led to the back of the house. Although I hadn't seen exactly where the shots had come from, their general direction told me that Mallory was across the room from me.

Since nothing provided effective cover, the only option available to each of us was to outflank the other. This meant either moving for the hallway door or the windows. For him, the windows offered only the possibility of escape, but with no obstacles to inhibit my pursuit. The door led to the hallway where he could either get to Olivia or Sara or keep me pinned down while he chose either the front or the back of the house for his escape. He would go for the door. I had to get to there first.

Rapidly, I fired three shots in the general direction of where I thought he was to pin him down and ran back towards the door. Neither of us could see the other in the blackness, but we could hear that we each had made the same decision. His gun belched a ribbon of flame as he fired in my anticipated direction. I hit the floor and slid along its slick concrete toward our mutual objective. A black blur of motion told me he'd been closer than I thought and was going to get there first. He lunged through the frame just as my bullets threw off sparks against the metal doorframe. I was on my feet now, and his boot hammered into my leg as I turned into the hall.

The pain was intense as I twisted in the direction of Mallory's kick and landed on top of him, pinning his gun hand in the process. He rolled towards me and pounded his left fist into my jaw. I could feel his nose explode as I drove the butt of my gun down into his face and tried to get my feet under me. Like a linebacker, he drove his shoulder in under my ribs and lifted me up before pile-driving me back into the floor of the study. My gun was jarred away and a sharp crack emanating from my rib cage pierced the room. He grunted, and his blood rained down on me from the pulp that had been his nose, while he pushed down on my chest with his left hand and moved his right into position to shoot. I caught his wrist with one hand and pushed to deflect his shot and jammed the fingers of my other hand into his eye. The sound of his gunshot drowned out his scream when my fingers found their mark and pressed into the socket.

He fell back as I punched him in the throat. As he brought his hands up in response, I grabbed his wrist and pulled his arm forward while delivering a hammer blow to it with my other hand. His gun flew toward the wall and came to rest under a liquor cart. Despite my attempt to bandage it, blood began to flow down my face from the cut above my eye, obscuring my vision. I tried to stand but Mallory again lashed out with a heavy kick that caught me in the chest and staggered me backwards into the desk that collapsed under my weight. I pushed back against one of its metal legs to keep my balance while I struggled for breath. Seeing his chance, he lowered his head and raced toward me. Shards of glass burst around me when our collision propelled us through the window.

I landed face down. Before I could move, Mallory leapt on me and begin to pummel me from behind, forcing my face into the mud and grass. Desperately, I thrashed my head back and forth to come up for air as his fists landed with the ferocity of a man whose only thing left to achieve in life was taking mine. Suddenly, it felt like he was hurled off me and then that sensation was followed by two shots.

A barrage of images awaited me when I looked up. The scene was bathed in blue and red flashing lights accompanied by a plethora of state police, a rain-soaked and mud-covered Greg Pardington sitting next to me, and Devin Mallory holding his chest while Patrick Knowles stood over him holding a gun. In a staccato delivery, Pardington filled me in on what I missed, "Man, I couldn't sit in that car any more so I got out and was walking toward the house when you and Mallory came flying out of the window. He was beating the shit out of you, so I ran up and grabbed him and pulled him off. The next thing I know, that old guy over there in the sweat suit just kind of appears and shoots him."

Dismissing a paramedic's command to "Stay down," I stood up. At that point, my legs decided that they'd had enough and only the intervention of Pardington and a nearby state trooper kept me from becoming reacquainted with the sod. Olivia and Sara emerged from the house escorted by two umbrella-carrying troopers, as I took my seat in the rear of the ambulance. The paramedic's efforts to address my injuries were escalated in their degree of difficulty by Olivia's embrace and non-AMA recommended attempts to kiss my wounds away.

"Mitch, I was so scared. Sara and I heard all the shooting, but we locked ourselves in the bathroom and waited to hear your voice. You look horrible."

"Yeah, but did you get a look at the other guys?"

I winced as her embrace moved into anaconda territory but was spared from further bodily harm when my attending medical professional advised her that, "We need to take him to the hospital so they can take a closer look at him. He's got some broken ribs and that eye doesn't look too good, and that's only what we can see here. You can ride with him if you like."

Agreeing with that diagnosis, she hopped in and they closed the doors.

Though the ride to Sparrow Hospital was uneventful, they did turn on the lights and sirens just for me. I asked Olivia about Ward.

"It looks like he's got a fractured skull, but he was conscious when they found him. They'll need to do a CT to see how bad it is, but he'll be in for at least a week."

A flurry of X-rays, a lot of poking and prodding and a CT scan followed my arrival, and proving that there really is no rest for the weary, Michigan State Police Detective Jack Butler was waiting for me when they brought me up to my room.

He introduced himself and dispensing with the perfunctory "How are you?" asked me to describe the "events of the evening." I recounted how we figured out that Knowles had killed Tim, and Mallory's and Harley's interest in making sure that his dissertation findings never came to light.

"Your girlfriend told us about that. We searched the place and found it and the roommate's article in the old man's room. It was hidden in a stack of books."

"Why did he shoot Mallory?"

"He says Mallory killed his son. As best we can tell, he read the papers and understood why his son was so upset, and when he heard that he was dead, he figured it had to be Mallory who killed him. He said he heard the fighting and the gunshots, found a gun in the study—since it wasn't yours it must have been Mallory's—followed you outside and shot him. He's still alive. Took two to the chest, but they say he'll make it. We're testing the ballistics to see if it's a match to either the Knowles or Atkinson killings."

"It'll match on Atkinson. Harley killed Knowles. You'll probably find that gun was used in a crime a long time ago, maybe in Chicago. If he didn't get rid of it, I think you'll find the rifle he used to try and kill us at Professor Price's house when you search his things."

"Interesting theory. What makes you think it works that way?"

I tried to shift my position in the bed but the pain emanating from my ribs signaled their disapproval.

"First, Atkinson was killed late at night in the Nat Sci

Building. That's where Mallory's office is, and it makes sense that he was the one who overheard him talking to us. Atkinson could validate everything. Second, Harley served under him in the Army. He had no vested interest in what Tim had found other than protecting his buddy. Plus, he'd be the one with the best background in faking a suicide."

With his chair legs screeching against the floor, Butler closed his notebook and prepared to leave. "Can't say that it doesn't make sense. We'll know more in the next couple of days."

As he sauntered to the door, I figured I'd take a chance, even though I knew the answer. "I don't suppose I could get a copy of the dissertation and the Adams article."

Butler chuckled, "Nice try. They're already in evidence. Ms. Price already asked. You'll get them back after the trial, although I have a feeling the press might give you a hand with that one. I think you have a visitor."

Olivia passed him on his way out the door.

Chapter 37

They'd taped up my ribs and stitched up my eye, and although my entire body felt like it had been worked over with a tire iron, I was deemed worthy of being discharged. I didn't want to leave without checking in on Ward. An orderly wheeled me down to his room. He was sitting up in bed watching the demonstration on TV as I came through the door. His head was swathed in white gauze and an IV was imbedded in his right arm. Other than that, I thought he looked pretty good.

"Not too many guys can pull off the half-turban thing," I teased, "but on you, it looks good."

He smiled or winced in return—giving myself the benefit of the doubt, I'm betting on smile. "You're not looking too shabby yourself. That bandage really brings out the black and purple around your face," he returned.

We talked for a few minutes about our respective conditions. He did have a fractured skull, and though it wasn't as bad as they originally thought, they still wanted to keep him another two or three days for observation.

"I thought I'd get a chance to meet Mrs. and junior Ward"

"They'll be here later. She was here all night. In fact, she just left. I told her to go home and get some sleep. I talked to the little guy on the phone this morning. He's at my in-laws. He was really concerned about his daddy for about thirty seconds, but something big was going on with Daniel Otter."

"A kid's got to have priorities."

"Yeah, he's a piece of work."

The dancing period of the morning's events ended when he said, "So you got that prick Harley."

Since the statement was rhetorical, I parried with, "I tried to call. What happened at the house?"

"Well, the first part you know. We got there and broke the news to Knowles' wife. That went pretty much as you'd expect. Then the power went out. I looked out one of the front windows and the street was totally dark. I'd just gotten back to Harley and Mrs. Knowles and Professor Price when it sounded like a window in the back of the house busted. I said I'd check it out, and Harley said he'd watch the two women. I guess he took them to one of the bedrooms and told them they'd be safe there. Anyway, I'd just gotten to the laundry room when he clocked me."

"Did you see him?"

"No. When I first came to, I thought someone had broken in and been the one who did it. Taken out by my own partner, un-fucking believable."

"Well, you said he was a dick. He and Mallory served together for ten years. Unless, you've heard something, Mallory isn't talking, so I don't know how he convinced him to help him."

"Probably, promised him some kind of job in Washington. In case you don't remember, Harley wasn't exactly a Boy Scout before he got here. Guess getting back to the big time was all the motivation he needed."

He asked me if I could pass him the cup of water on the bedside table. I wheeled over and handed it to him. He was taking a long pull on the straw when I said, "I think you're right, but we'll probably never know. He's dead, so Mallory will try and convince the jury he was the one calling the shots. He better have one hell of a lawyer if he's going to try and pull that one off. Have you heard anything more on the

245

investigation?"

"Not much. The Staties are running the show. I talked to some of the guys earlier, and they said they did find a rifle that had been fired recently when they searched Harley's place. Looks like it's the one that was used to try and take you out at the professor's house. Sounds like ballistics will seal the deal. On Mallory, too."

A nurse came in to check his vitals and brought some pills with her. I backed out of her way and was just about to say good-bye when I happened to look up at the TV screen. I pointed to it and said, "I'm surprised they're still doing this, especially since they're light a couple of speakers."

The camera panned in on the crowd, a black mass of hoodie-wearing spectators near the front of the stage told me that Planet Action was out in force. As it moved across the stage, I saw Tyler sitting toward the center. He was wearing another checked flannel shirt. I was wondering if he had a closet full of them when I remembered he was wearing the same thing in the mug shot that Nikki had found. Not a hoodie like the other group members arrested that night or standing in front of him on the television.

I waited until Ward had taken the pills that had been in the tiny paper cup the nurse handed to him before I said, "Brian, you need to call your guys and tell them to arrest young Mr. Tyler there for the murder of Dr. Walker."

"What? Why? I think the kid's an asshole, too, but what makes you think he killed Walker?"

I wheeled up closer to the bed and laid out my case. "He's not wearing his Planet Action hoodie. He wasn't in his mug shot the night he was arrested either, but according to the other members, they all had them on before they went into the library. When I talked to Stewart and his girlfriend, they told me they were all in Walker's class together and that Tyler was failing but he got a 96 on his mid-term. Didn't you say that when you searched Walker's office, there was a test up on the screen?"

He sat up a little, or as much as he could. I could tell he knew where I was going. "Yeah. It was the mid-term for his geology class."

"The same one that the three of them were in, and Tyler goes from failing to a 96 on the same test. And when I met him, he had a bandage in the middle of his hand. He said he'd poked himself with a meat thermometer helping a friend move. I think you'll find that he has the same blood type as what you found on that paperweight."

I excused myself after I handed Ward the phone.

Epilogue

Nikki opened the door for me since I was holding the wooden cane I was using in my right hand, and after a few minutes, followed me into my office. It was the first hot day of the spring. The temperature was expected to reach the high 80s, and she had selected her outfit accordingly. A sheer red blouse accentuated by the red bra underneath, a black skirt short enough to ensure a healthy degree of air movement around her legs, and red pumps made me think that we wouldn't need to turn up the air on her account.

"Thanks for getting the door for me, Nick."

"What? Oh, The Fed Ex guy was right behind you, and he was carrying a package. It looked heavy."

"I'll just pretend I didn't hear that and chalk it up on the ledger as a goodwill gesture. Thanks for watching Fang, by the way. She was so excited to see me that she jumped down from her chair and waddled right up."

"That's her favorite chair. She can see the TV better from there. I don't know about the waddling—she looked emaciated when I got there. She needed to put on a couple pounds."

Sarcasm and contrition didn't seem to be on intersecting paths, so I decided to change the subject to finding out how things had gone while I was in East Lansing.

"First, don't forget that guy from ESPN is calling you at 10:00 for a reference on that Pardington kid."

With notable enthusiasm, she proceeded to describe the impact that case had on the fortunes of McKay Investigations.

"You wouldn't believe the calls we've gotten. Like I told you, you can't pay for advertising like this. I posted some pictures of you on the website. Your face is so swollen no one would even know that you look jowly."

"I don't look jowly".

"Not now you don't 'cuz your face is all swollen, but the important thing is we can use this in our brand positioning."

"Brand positioning?"

"I'm taking a class in marketing this semester. I even thought of a tagline, 'We put our lives on the line for *you*.'"

"Catchy. You know, Nick, people died over this, and others could have. We might want to rethink how much 'brand positioning' we do. What I'm saying is, why don't we let thinks settle down a little first?"

She sat down in one of the chairs across from my desk, ran her hand through her Ravishing Raspberry hair, and said, "I'm joking with you, Mitch. I couldn't believe it when I saw what they'd done to you. I can't imagine how scared you and Olivia must have been. Those guys wanted to kill you, what am I saying—they almost did. What happens now?"

"The ballistics test proved Mallory's gun was the one used to kill Steve Atkinson, and Harley's rifle was the one used to try and kill me and Olivia. Since the .45 used to kill Knowles was tied to an old Chicago homicide, it looks like that was Harley as well. They've already charged Mallory with murder and conspiracy."

"I saw that Tyler kid doing the perp walk on TV last night. He'll have fun in prison."

"Yeah, I don't think I'd want to be him. It didn't take long for Congressman Perkins to distance himself. I don't think Tyler had even been in handcuffs for five minutes before he put out a statement denouncing violent extremism. I suppose he had to. Between Tyler's arrest and the university's voting not to divest, his green position took a hit. At least this way, he can blame one for the other when the time comes."

Haltingly, as if she wasn't totally sure she wanted to, but finally decided she had to know, she asked, "Are you going to see Olivia again?"

"We've talked about it. I think we'll try. She'll be back on Friday. Her parents are having a memorial for Tim."

"What about his paper? If he proved that this whole climate change thing is a pile of crap, shouldn't people know?"

"Most of it will come out during Mallory's trial I'm sure. Unfortunately, all his calculations and models are gone, so all that's left is the hundred or so pages that he wrote. Olivia's decided that after the trial is over, she'll post the dissertation online so anyone who wants access to it can. Maybe they'll be able to recreate what he found. Of course, there are still a bunch of people, schools, and even businesses with a vested interest in proving he was wrong. I wouldn't get my hopes up about that debate ending any time soon. The worst thing is that a kid who didn't have any agenda and only wanted to find out the why behind it all, and maybe was on his way to finding at least part of the answer was killed because some other people were so afraid of what he found." I shook my head. "Science," I said softly to myself.

Nikki got up and walked over to my little refrigerator and pulled out a Diet Vernors. She brought it over, opened it, and set it on my desk in front of me. Then she did the most "un-Nikki" thing I could imagine. She bent over and kissed the top of my head.

"You're a good man, Mitch McKay."

93046209R00143

Made in the USA
Lexington, KY
12 July 2018